GHOST
on the Path

Gail A. Webber

ARCHWAY
PUBLISHING

Archway Publishing books may be ordered
through booksellers or by contacting:

Archway Publishing
1663 Liberty Drive
Bloomington, IN 47403
www.archwaypublishing.com
1 (888) 242-5904

Because of the dynamic nature of the Internet, any web
addresses or links contained in this book may have changed
since publication and may no longer be valid. The views
expressed in this work are solely those of the author and do
not necessarily reflect the views of the publisher, and the
publisher hereby disclaims any responsibility for them.

Any people depicted in stock imagery provided by Thinkstock are
models, and such images are being used for illustrative purposes only.
Certain stock imagery © Thinkstock.

ISBN: 978-1-4808-3931-1 (sc)
ISBN: 978-1-4808-3932-8 (e)

Library of Congress Control Number: 2016918148

Print information available on the last page.

Archway Publishing rev. date: 11/14/2016

CONTENTS

Chapter I

Before the Attack: Sarah—1675

SARAH LEFT HER BASKET OF beach plums above the high-tide mark and walked down to the water. This was her favorite spot on the island, and her wanderings often brought her to this very place. But despite that, she couldn't look at the ocean without remembering where they came from, what they had suffered to get here. They'd left behind the squalid crush of humanity, trying to build lives in the rubble a few thousand years of civilization had produced and traded it for even more horrific shipboard conditions. But except for the nightmares, that ordeal was over. This island was almost an Eden, a clean and open world shared only by those who arrived on her ship.

Almost an Eden. Life could be harsh here, but all who stayed on were willing to pay that price, and those who wanted an easier life had already retreated to mainland towns. For her, the positive aspects of island life far outweighed the negative. They governed themselves, and there were no agents of the Crown to harass and imprison them. What Sarah most appreciated was how everyone worked together, helped each other, and looked out for everyone else. She'd been doubtful about their emigration at first, but now Sarah knew that Tom was right to bring them here. The hardships were worth the rewards.

The pang in her chest was still there. "Hardships," she murmured. Was that how she was supposed to regard losing her son? Simon was only ten years old when he died aboard ship from what the captain called "the common illness." Many others got sick, including her husband, Tom, and people panicked thinking they would all die, but only Simon failed to recover. He was buried at sea. *No, not buried,* Sarah thought, and tried not to imagine what happened to him in that deep water teeming with giants.

A squeal of laughter from down the beach chased her painful thoughts and announced seven-year-old Daniel. "Mama!"

When she turned, her smile changed to a look of fear. A huge dog was chasing her son! She hated dogs, had been afraid of them since a childhood attack had left her physically and emotionally scarred. Still, she ran toward them.

"Daniel, come to me!" she cried.

"Look!" he called, running so fast that sand flew in all directions. "Look what me and Traveler found!" Daniel held one end of a heavy rope festooned with bits of

Chilliwack Health Unit

Chilliwack Mental Health & Substance Use Services
2nd Floor - 45470 Menholm Road
Chilliwack BC V2P 1M2 Canada

Tel **(604) 702-4860**
Fax **(604) 702-4861**
www.fraserhealth.ca

fraserhealth

Better health.
Best in health care.

Your appointment is:

With: _Lesley Mc Phenson_

Date: _March 31/17_

Time: _P/U 9:45am_

Please advise office if you cannot attend this appointment.

Crisis Line: 1-877-820-7444
Suicide Line: 1-800-784-2433

7 appt
1030

seaweed, and the other end was in the dog's mouth. "From a ship, Mama, I know it! From some ship!"

"I see it," she said, watching the dog. "Come over here, Daniel. Now."

Realization dawned on the boy's face. He stopped short, and the dog sat beside him, its whip tail thumping the sand. "It's just Traveler, Mama. You know him. He never hurt nobody."

Sarah sighed and composed herself. What an example to set for her son, that he should see her afraid of something as harmless as this dog. That wasn't the kind of thing she wanted to teach him.

"Of course he hasn't," she said and strode over to them with a stiff smile. "I was just startled. You were running so fast!"

"I know! So, do you think it's from a ship that sank?" Everything excited this boy, one of the many qualities she loved in him.

"I don't know, but it could be. Where did you find it?"

"Out on the point. I was digging quahogs like Emma told me, and I saw it sticking out of the sand," he said. "So I pulled it!"

Emma was their second child and eldest daughter, an organizer at heart, and so good with the younger children. She made chores into games for them. Sarah nodded and smiled again. "I see. And did you get many?"

Daniel's face blanked. "Many what?" Then dismay washed over him. "Oh, no! I left the basket, and the tide's coming in!" He raced back the way he came, bare feet drumming the sand and Traveler following hard behind.

After a final glance seaward, Sarah trudged up the rocky beach to retrieve her own basket. Tomorrow she and Emma would make beach plum jam so they'd have fruit after winter set in. Thankfully, they still had enough sugar. It would be their second winter here, and God willing, it wouldn't be as hard as the first one. They hadn't known what to expect then, but this year they would be better prepared.

There was a path up through the dunes toward a little cluster of cabins on the ridge, the heart of their settlement. Another path led to the dock they built in a protected bay on the north side of the island. Both paths were already here when they arrived, though the island had been uninhabited. What made those paths was a mystery. The company that arranged their passage told them to expect Indians on most of the islands in the area, and when they reached this one, they were prepared to negotiate, to trade or pay for land, even to share if they had to. They wanted to live in peace. But instead of living people, the settlers found only artifacts in a burial site that looked ancient. The paths couldn't be animal trails either, because until they brought their own livestock, there were no animals on the island large enough to make such trails. Maybe it wasn't animals or Indians, but simply where the rain ran downhill.

Indians, Sarah thought. Before she and Tom left England, they heard so many stories about those primitive people of these new lands, and some of the stories were frightening. But the only Indians she'd actually seen were at the monthly trade markets on the mainland, and they seemed friendly enough, if distant. Sarah was surprised how many of them spoke English and French as well as their own language.

Despite stories, the truth was that most encounters between European colonists and Indians had been peaceful—until recently, that is. There were rumors of conflict on the mainland, and Sarah was glad they lived on an island. About a fortnight before, a trio of canoes arrived at their little dock. She hadn't seen the visitors herself, but those who did said that one of the natives was a man who held himself like royalty despite his advanced age. They met with the settlement leader, Pastor Stayman, and a few other men but didn't stay long. After they left, none of the men said anything about what the natives wanted, so it must not have been important.

The path up to the settlement was steep, and the dry sand sliding under her feet made walking difficult, so halfway up Sarah stopped to rest next to a tumble of huge boulders that looked like castle ruins. The whole island was rocky, but these rocks were immense, and each time Sarah passed them she wondered what great force could have stacked them here. She leaned back against the warm stone while her breathing slowed, and then she continued on her way, planning the rest of the day as she walked.

What would she and Emma make for supper? They were low on meat, so normally Tom would have taken their eldest, Elias, and gone hunting. But both of them were helping the pastor with an outbuilding instead. Sarah smiled at the thought of another sturdy building added to their settlement. At first, families had huddled together in makeshift huts and shacks, but now each family had its own cabin, and the community was hard at work adding permanent chicken houses and barns.

So, chicken tonight, she decided. Too many cockerels had hatched in the past six months, and that wasn't good for a flock. They ran the hens ragged. So killing one young rooster for dinner would mean getting two birds with one stone, both flock-thinning and supper. *Two birds with one stone*, she mused. Little Prudence would have giggled at that, and Ruth would have wanted to see the two birds. They were a year apart, five and four, but people thought they looked like twins.

We thought Ruth would be the last, Sarah thought. Her birth had been a very hard one, and the midwife back home told Sarah she wouldn't have any more children. But then baby Elizabeth, conceived on the voyage over, had been the first child born on the island.

Six living children. Not many families could say that all but one of the children born to them were still alive. What a blessing, Sarah knew, and yet there was pain. *All but one*, she thought. When she prayed, she thanked God for his providence, cried for Simon, and vowed she would keep the rest of her children safe, whatever the cost.

CHAPTER 2

The Attack: Sarah—1675

As SARAH FINISHED NURSING LITTLE Elizabeth, she watched Emma making breakfast for the other children and reminded her to save some for her father and brother. Tom and Elias had left the cabin a little before dawn that morning, intending to get a turkey or two as they dropped from their roosting places at first light. They'd be hungry when they got back.

When Elizabeth started to fall asleep at her breast, Sarah refastened her bodice and put the infant in her cradle by the fire, hoping she would go back to sleep for a while. She was always in better spirits if she took a nap after feeding, and she was used to sleeping while the other children chattered, laughed, and teased each other. It was a normal morning.

Until it wasn't. What began with one dog barking quickly escalated into frenzy as every dog in the settlement took up the alarm. Even before the first gunshots, Sarah and Emma exchanged one fearful look, and then Sarah rushed to slam and bar the shutters as Emma barred the door. Neither of them needed to say a word. Though they prayed this would never happen, they had practiced for it.

Through a shutter loophole, Sarah saw horses and men running, all in war paint. There had always been the possibility of an Indian attack, especially with recent events on the mainland. But after so long with no trouble, the settlers had assumed they were safe. Sarah wondered how so many men got to the island unseen and with all those horses. Screams filled the air—horses and people, invaders and friends. The din was deafening.

"Fetch the muskets!" she shouted while she tried to see where the closest of the Indians was, and she knew Daniel and Emma would obey. She and Tom always assumed that if this happened they would be together. But Tom wasn't home.

"I can only find one, Mama. I loaded it!" Daniel said at her side.

"Look again!" Sarah answered as she grabbed the musket from him and rested the muzzle on the window sash. *No,* she realized, *of course the other two muskets are missing. Tom and Elias have them.* They would be back, though. Wherever they were, they would hear this hellish noise, and they would come. Meanwhile, one musket was what she had.

Both Daniel and Emma stood frozen on either side of her while the two littlest girls peered out from behind Emma's skirts, all big eyes in pale faces. Baby Elizabeth was shrieking from her cradle. Sarah breathed a quick prayer and struggled to keep her voice calm, though she had to shout to be heard. "Don't worry. We'll fight, and God will protect us. Daniel, go make sure the bedroom window is barred, and then hold the baby. Emma, build up that fire as big as you can." Sarah didn't think anyone could climb down that way, but it was better to be safe. "Then come feed me powder and ball," she said to her daughter.

To the two little girls she spoke as gently as she could. "Prudence and Ruth, you stay with Daniel. You'll be all right." *God willing*, she added to herself. *Please, God, I vowed to protect my children. Help me do that.*

Musket balls rattled against the sides of the house, and arrows thwacked into the shutters behind which Sarah hid as she continued to load and shoot, reload and shoot for what seemed hours. Returning fire from the settlers grew more sporadic, and she watched small groups of attackers begin to move from cabin to cabin. She aimed carefully, trying not to think what was happening inside those cabins. "I need more shot!" she shouted to Emma.

"It's all gone, Mama," was her daughter's quiet response.

"There must be more! Look in the cedar chest." All at once there was pounding at the door. They were right outside! "Everyone get something!" she shouted. They would understand what she meant—a poker, a skinning knife, anything, but she knew only Daniel and Emma had any chance of defending themselves. Then from the bedroom came a crash. As Sarah reached for the axe with one hand and shoved Emma toward the younger children with the other, she was shot from behind. The room whirled; time stopped, and for a moment Sarah's world went silent. She staggered forward a few more steps but remained upright, conscious only of an unbearable burning. The axe fell at her feet.

Then sound came rushing back. "Mama, you're hurt!" her son wailed, staring at her bloody shoulder. She had only a moment to wonder what happened before her vision tunneled and she fell. She never saw them.

When she awakened, Sarah was on her back in the sand, and it took her a few disoriented moments to figure out where she was—beside that pile of rocks where she'd stopped to rest the day before. It was very quiet. Normal sounds seemed muted after the pandemonium of the battle.

The battle! The children! She lurched to a sitting position but immediately fell back, all her attention on the searing pain in her shoulder, her chest, and her back. Looking down, she saw her dress was bloody to the waist. *My blood?* Bracing against the boulders, Sarah pushed with her legs until she was standing, and then all she could do was stare.

Carnage. Bodies lay strewn about like dirty clothes, many stripped and disemboweled. Her stomach roiled, but she didn't retch. These were people she knew. Who would think there could be so much blood in a person, but the ground around each body was red with it. Indians walked among the fallen, many of them wounded. Some cradled stolen ducks or chickens, and others carried items taken from the settlement or stripped from the bodies. Still others herded captured horses and other livestock toward the beach. The horses avoided stepping on the dead, but most of the other animals didn't. Sarah tried not to dwell on what some of the pigs were doing.

Her eyes searched desperately for a familiar face, but there wasn't a single one. Where were the other survivors, the prisoners? Where were her children?

"You, woman," said a gruff male voice behind her in English with a British accent.

She whirled toward the sound, gasping at the pain her movement caused. Sarah's vision blurred, but she forced herself to focus on the man who'd spoken. She thought she recognized him from the trade market but wasn't sure. He would have looked quite different then, with no war paint and no headdress, and he wouldn't have been carrying this knob-headed club covered with gore.

The Indian touched his own face in the places where her scars were the worst. "Among the Mi'kmaq is a legend, a woman whose face was scarred. She could see spirits and what is to come." Sarah shook her head in confusion.

"Are you gifted, woman? Can you see the unseen? We have need for such a one, so you live." He waited for only a moment. "Or are your scars from carelessness? Or disobedience?"

She didn't know what to say, and before she could decide how to answer, he shook his head. "Only scars," he said and grabbed her by her good shoulder. With his other hand he poked her wound. Sarah cried out and tried to pull away, but he held her with one strong hand, prodding and squeezing the wound until her blood flowed freely. Turning her around to examine a corresponding hole in her back, he stuck two fingers into the wound, and she nearly fainted. Finally he released her and stepped back. "The ball is out, Scarred Face, but the bone is broken. A strong woman could heal."

Sarah fought to settle her racing mind. *Scarred Face, was that a name? He said I could heal if I'm strong, and that wouldn't matter if they intend to kill me. Does that mean I'm a captive? Then there must be other captives.*

Putting aside her pain and fear, she faced him and raised her chin. "Please, where are all the little ones, the children?" She was worried about Emma, almost a woman, and hoped no one would misuse her. If she was safe, Sarah knew she would guard the younger ones.

Instead of answering, the Indian only asked her, "Will you come, or will you die?"

What? With a shock, Sarah realized he was giving her a choice. She could be their captive, or they would kill her here.

For as long as she could remember, Sarah had played a "what if" game with herself, considering all sorts of life scenarios, running them through her mind like plays, and deciding what she would do in each situation. In those mental plays, she had always chosen to die rather than be taken captive—by anyone. There were awful stories about how female captives were sometimes treated by their captors, and though she didn't know if they were true, they could be. A clean death seemed the better choice. But never had she considered she would have children to worry about, children to protect. Choosing death now would mean leaving her children alone to face whatever came next.

Death or captivity? Her mind whirled while this man stared at her. There had to be another choice. *Yes*, she thought. She knew that some tribes held captives safely for ransom. If this was one of them, then all she had to do was gather the children and then do whatever was necessary to keep all of them alive. *Please, God*, she prayed again, and then said, "My husband will ransom me."

He scowled. "Which fate, Scarred Face?"

"Please," she begged. "Do you understand ransom? Redeeming?"

He stared at her for the space of three heartbeats, and then he raised his club.

Sarah staggered backward, holding one hand palm out in front of her and fighting not to pass out from the pain. "I'll go with you," she gasped. Slave or not, at least with life there was hope, and there would be time to talk of ransom. Meanwhile she had to find the children. He lowered his club and called to another Indian, who walked toward them leading two horses. One of them was a gray decorated with war paint, and the other was Pastor Stayman's bay.

Was one of these horses for her to ride? If she was to be a slave, then why this kindness? Maybe they thought her injury would worsen if she walked or that she might die. So captives must be worth something to them. Ransom. Anyway, she would only be riding a little way—to the boats or rafts or whatever they used to get to the island.

For the first time she wondered where they lived because it was where she was going.

Looking around her again, the brutal truth of what had happened that day on their piece-of-heaven island hit her. Her knees buckled, and she went down on one knee. *All these people*, she thought. *What if I can't find the children? What if Tom never finds me?* Tears threatened, but she swallowed them. "Not now," she whispered to herself and struggled to stand back up. To keep the panic at bay, she filled her mind with questions. Why would they attack now, after all this time? They hadn't done anything different, hadn't offended anyone. Did this have something to do with the Indians who came to speak with Pastor Stayman a few weeks ago? There were rumors that the organized Indian attacks farther north on the mainland were in retribution for the hanging of three Wampanoag braves. Was that what caused this? Surely all these people hadn't been killed because others they didn't even know had wronged these natives. Surely she wasn't going to lose everyone she loved because of what others had done.

When the Indian with the two horses got to where they were standing, Sarah ignored him and faced the man in charge. Indians were supposed to value courage, but she didn't know whether accepting a captive status meant she couldn't speak. Still, she had to try and make him understand. "There were five children in the cabin with me, including a baby." She couldn't see their cabin from where she stood, but the heavy black smoke filling the sky in that direction told her all she needed to know. Sarah held her arms as if she were cradling a baby. "A baby," she repeated. Even if he didn't know that word, certainly he would understand the pantomime.

He shook his head, and shoved her impatiently toward the horses. "We go," was all he said before he leapt onto the gray and cantered toward the beach, sand flying.

"Please!" she called after him, but he didn't turn back. She wondered again about being given a horse and thought, *Aren't they afraid I'll escape?* While she was thinking about escape, the Indian who held the bay horse slapped her. The horse whickered and danced, but the Indian quieted him and motioned for her to mount. Sarah knew what he expected, but there was no saddle, and Pastor Stayman's gelding was over sixteen hands. She tried twice, but with only one good arm and nothing to hold on to, she couldn't manage it. When he finally he lifted her up, Sarah registered his look of disdain.

Hunched over the horse's neck, each jarring step a torture, Sarah tried to sit tall. If she could step back from the pain, then she could use this higher vantage point to find her children. She grabbed a bit of flesh on the inside of her arm and pinched as hard as she could. Her mother had long ago taught her how to distract herself from pain or crying by pinching herself, though not in circumstances as dire as these, and she hardly felt the pinch at all. As they approached the water's edge, Sarah craned her neck to look for what had to be a large group of survivors, but the only living people she saw were the Indians. The children and the rest of the captives had to be somewhere else.

Somewhere else, yes, they had to be somewhere else.

Sarah smiled for the first time since the attack began. She reasoned that if she couldn't find them, then that meant they were in hiding, all of them. That was it! They were holed up somewhere safe, waiting until the invaders left before they came out. There was hope after all.

Still smiling, she watched an older Indian approach them, his arms full of something wrapped in a soot-blackened blanket. He spoke to the brave leading her horse, and when the horse stopped, the old man held the bundle up to her. Sarah recognized the blanket and couldn't believe the blessing. It was baby Elizabeth! She was so quiet, apparently sleeping through all this chaos as only very young babies could.

Gently, Sarah pulled back a corner of the blanket to reveal the little face, peaceful in repose. Murmuring a prayer of thanks as she cuddled her daughter, Sarah was sure this was a sign from the Almighty that she would find the others soon enough. She was still smiling when she turned to the old man to thank him. He was talking to the other Indian as they examined the musket the young Indian held. Her smile faded. It was Tom's, his carved initials clear in the stock that was covered with dried blood. He would never have given it up while he lived.

Sarah swallowed hard. So then, he was probably dead, and Elias as well, since they would have been together. But no, she wouldn't give up hope. Surely she hadn't seen them for the last time. Maybe they were only wounded and in hiding somewhere, just like all the others.

At least she knew Elizabeth was safe. Sarah turned her attention back to the baby, crooning to her as she tried to wake her. She needed to see the baby's eyes. But Elizabeth didn't wake, and though she was breathing, she never moved. Carefully, Sarah pulled the blanket back farther only to find more and more blood. This wasn't sleep. Elizabeth had been wounded in her little belly, and she was unconscious.

Awkwardly, Sarah slid down off the horse, ignoring her own pain. She sank down on the sand, trying to get a better look at her daughter's wound. It must be a bad sign that she wasn't crying, though a blessing she wasn't awake to feel the pain.

Sarah's heart sank when she saw how bad the wound was. This was too serious an injury for her crude medical skills. But perhaps the Indians had someone who could help. A medicine man would surely know how to treat this kind of wound. Sarah stood and looked around for the leader, the one who spoke English, but he was nowhere to be seen.

That was when Elizabeth felt suddenly different, heavier. Afraid to check, but desperately needing to do that, Sarah laid the precious bundle across her lap. Even before she put her hand on the baby's chest to feel for breath, she knew. Elizabeth was gone.

With the realization of this tiny death, Sarah allowed another possibility to crash in on her. What if none of them were hiding, not even Tom? That could be why she couldn't find them; they were all dead. If that were so, then she'd broken the vow she made when Simon died, when she promised God she would protect the rest of her children, no matter what the cost.

Sarah looked down at the little body in her lap. Added to the horrors of that day, this tiny death was too much. Every bit of hope and much of Sarah's mind left her in one long cry of anguish. She huddled over the baby and rocked her as she sang a lullaby in thick and wavering tones. The Indian holding the pastor's horse shouted at her, and when she ignored him, he dragged her to her feet by her throat. He slapped her then and pulled at the bundle she held in her one good arm, but she shrieked at him and held on with strength she didn't know she had. When he threw her to the ground, she laid Elizabeth beside her and reached for a rock. Baring her teeth at him, she brandished the rock over her head. When he retreated one step, she threw the rock as hard as she could at him and then reached for another and threw it as well. He scowled and shouted something she didn't understand, appearing annoyed instead of afraid, maybe even amused. As Sarah was searching for another rock to throw, the Indian with the British accent, the leader, cantered up and motioned for the brave to leave. The old man went with him.

The leader was talking to her, she knew, but he sounded so far away. They were leaving, he told her, and if she wanted to live, she had to come with them. He said he couldn't kill her the way she was now. But Sarah had retreated to a place where she didn't see him, couldn't understand his words, hardly heard them at all. She picked up baby Elizabeth and held her close. For a few moments, he watched her rocking her motionless child, and then he rode away.

She said she wanted to go with them, but that was

no longer true. All that she loved was here, though they were likely all dead. The Indians could have forced her to go with them or they could have killed her, but they did neither. They simply left her there alone.

Chapter 3

The Making of a Ghost: Sarah—1675

O NE DAY FADED INTO TWO, two into three, and three into more as Sarah wandered the island. After the fires died and the ashes cooled, she sifted through the remains of her friends' homes, looking for food. There wasn't much left. Water was the hardest thing to find because the central well and all the cisterns had carcasses in them. That couldn't be an accident. Even puddle water with mosquito larvae was better than what was in the well and the cisterns.

Once she took the path to the dock on the other side of the island, but the dock was burned to cinders, bodies rising and falling with the waves, bumping against the charred timbers. There were crabs on those bodies. Along the way, she found a spring, but she never went back to it because there was a dead child there. At first she thought about going into the woods, but she was afraid she might miss whoever landed on shore to rescue her. Besides, who could tell what was in the woods?

The only place she could find food was on the beach—seaweed and periwinkles, sand crabs and cockles, sometimes a clam or a dead fish that washed ashore. Before the attack she considered these fit only for pig food or fish bait, but now she ate them raw.

Those first nights, Sarah returned to the mound of boulders on the path to the beach, carrying the baby with her, hoping against hope that Elizabeth wasn't really dead. Finally she laid the little body in a hole she dug with her hands at the base of those same boulders. She tried to tumble rocks from the pile onto the grave to keep the scavengers away, but they were too heavy. So one and two at a time, she carried the biggest stones she could lift up from the beach and piled them over Elizabeth.

Before Elizabeth died, Sarah had told herself that some people were still in hiding and had her children and Tom with them, and at some point she returned to that belief. She scanned the ground for their footprints, sometimes following her own in circles for hours. *They must be afraid to show themselves*, she thought, so she called until she was hoarse, "They're all gone! Come out!"

She told herself she only had to survive long enough for the rescuers to come. *People on the mainland heard the shooting, and they're gathering a rescue party in case the attackers are still here. Probably bringing soldiers, too.* When they came, they would help her find her family and anyone else still alive. *I didn't keep the children safe. But I'll find them.*

As night fell each evening, she returned to her perch on the rocks and listened to the night scavengers feeding, grateful that the island had no large predators. It was at night that doubt returned. *What if the mainland was attacked too? What if there's no one left anywhere?* She was hungry and thirsty, and every day the pain was worse. But the loneliness hurt more. Sarah had no one to help her deal with all that happened, no one to cry with or to hold when holding herself wasn't enough. Two people in trouble can reassure each other, keep hope of escape or rescue alive, but Sarah had no one. *I didn't keep them safe, and this is my punishment. But someone will come.* Finally, troubled sleep would take her until she awoke with the next dawn, when she climbed down the rocks and began walking.

Sarah talked to herself constantly, reliving the attack and the days following. She refought the battle in the cabin, mouthed every word she said to each child that morning, remembered every look and every touch. She felt the bullet enter her shoulder, awakened among strangers who massacred her friends and neighbors, experienced her joy believing the baby survived, and fought with rocks when the Indian tried to take Elizabeth from her. After those events played and replayed, the ache of life in lonely silence returned.

Once she saw sails on the horizon and splashed out to where the waves broke, waving her one good arm and screaming to them, but they didn't come. For days after that, Sarah scoured the shoreline for anything that might float, any conveyance to the mainland. She had searched before and found nothing, but seeing the ship renewed her hope. There was still nothing.

As the long days and the longer nights dragged by, events in Sarah's life leapfrogged, and she couldn't keep straight exactly where or when she was. *When this ship finally finds land, Tom and I will build our new life with the children*, she thought, or *Someday I'll get married and have children.* As her wound festered and spread poison throughout her body, the fever made it even harder to remember events in the right order—or at all. *Where has everyone gone, and why did they leave me? Surely they'll come back soon.*

There were flashes of clarity, moments of beauty, like the afternoon she found the wildflowers on the dunes, so impossibly blue that she held her breath and touched them with one finger. She considered picking them to put on Elizabeth's grave but decided to leave them where they were so she could see them again. Another time after a hard rain, she found a puddle of clean water. Reaching down to cup some of it to her lips, she caught sight of her reflection and was appalled. When Tom came to find her, would he recognize her? Would he know his own wife, so grimy and gaunt? Of course he would. But maybe she would bathe in the sea to make sure, and she left the water where it was. Then she forgot about it. Flashes of clarity never lasted long, and as time passed, they became rarer.

Sarah wandered, growing weaker day by day. She watched the grisly process of decay as it affected the bodies of all her friends. Gaunt faces darkened before they swelled and bloated, finally bursting in a mass of writhing maggots. They weren't people anymore, and as Sarah lost the ability to feel sympathy for them, neither the stench nor the maggots bothered her. She simply observed. Their wounds were clues to the mechanisms of their deaths, nothing more, and she kept a catalog in her mind. Sometimes she sang bits of songs as she examined them.

Jonah's skull was cracked, and most of his face was gone. She knew him by the burn scars on his hands from the stable fire last year. Mariah had four arrows in her: one in her arm, two in her thigh, and one in her neck. Sarah hoped that the one in the neck had been first. A man was face down with a spear through his back, scalped. Sarah didn't turn the body over, but she knew from the clothing that it was Pastor Stayman. She hoped the Indian who had Tom's musket was taking good care of Pastor's horse. These corpses weren't people, merely examples of the many ways a person could die. Here was a gunshot to the face, there was a series of knife wounds, over there a gaping thigh wound exposed a splintered femur, and there an axe wound split the chest.

The only bodies Sarah avoided were the little ones. *Why did the children have to die? The Wampanoag always take captives—why not this time?* Once at the edge of the woods, she stumbled on little bodies with clothing she knew well. She'd made those things by hand, washed them a hundred times, and mended them. "They're all there, the children, all together. At least there's that," she murmured to herself. And Emma apparently hadn't been harmed beyond a musket ball to her chest. That was a blessing.

But after she found them, Sarah never went back to where they were. She nodded to herself, thinking she was right to stay out of the woods. If she never saw these little bodies again, then she could convince herself they weren't there.

I didn't keep them safe.

There were dead animals too, only a few horses, but more dogs. Since not all of the dogs were here, some must have gone with the attackers or been taken. Knowing that gave her an odd sort of comfort. She hoped for Daniel's sake that Traveler was alive and that the Indians wouldn't eat him.

A couple of times she saw a living dog, one she wasn't sure she recognized, red and black with floppy ears. She couldn't get near it though, because it ran away whenever she approached. Dogs scared her, but at least it was another living thing, and Sarah thought if she could get it to stay with her, then she wouldn't feel so alone. She followed, afraid to get too close but unwilling to give up until the dog made the decision for both of them. When Sarah crested a dune, she found herself face to face with it, suddenly all bared teeth and tucked tail, and she screamed. As it ran away, Sarah could see that it had wounds of its own. She only saw it once after that, digging where Elizabeth was buried. She killed it with a rock.

Sometimes Sarah lived a different reality, one that didn't include any kind of attack. In that reality, all her cherished memories replayed in her mind, making her smile and bringing happy tears.

She remembered the joy of seeing each of her babies the moment after they were born. All thoughts of birthing pains were gone, and though they were still wet and bloody, that kind of blood wasn't sad. Nothing else mattered when unfocused blue eyes met hers, and she knew she would love that little soul forever.

She remembered Ruth and Prudence, born less than a year apart and looking like twins with their blonde curls and ivory skin. Their favorite game was "all hide," and sometimes she played it with them, making believe she didn't see them sticking out of their hiding places.

Since she was the last, Sarah remembered all of baby Elizabeth's firsts, like when she first held her head up, when she first giggled and scared herself, when she mimicked Tom sticking out his tongue.

Sarah remembered how Elias would tell stories to the little ones at night. How proud he looked, standing at the door, ready to go hunting with his father that first time. He was a good boy, strong and kind, like his father.

She remembered the fun she had teaching Emma to cook and to sew. Emma was so bright, so good with the children, so willing to help. Organizing was her gift, and Sarah could still see her with the three younger ones around her, all of them giggling as Emma played school with them or assigned chores.

Sarah remembered lying in the dark with Tom, laughing when his beard tickled her, and how he held her closer when she told him she was cold. He always teased her about her cold feet.

Sarah also remembered events that never happened. She remembered her children married with children of their own. She remembered them bringing her grandchildren to sit on her lap, and she remembered their first words. Sarah remembered growing old and gray with Tom, the love of her life. On countless winter nights, they sat by the fire together, with him telling stories about the past when their children were young.

But again and again, the truth returned to batter her. Her shoulder and upper arm had blackened, and the stink was sickening. The pain was constant. There was always gnawing hunger, raging thirst, and she was shaken by alternating chills and fever. The most horrible truth that came with time was the piece she tried to deny: no one was coming. To silence that voice, she sang to the children. As the days stretched into weeks, her voice rasped and cracked like the ever-present crows, but still she sang.

More than a few times, Sarah considered ending her own life, walking out into the water to let it cover her and fill her. She had even found herself waist deep a few times before she returned to the shore, wet and shaking, and still miserably alone. But she was unwilling to give up. Someone might still come, she thought, and she resolved to endure. When someone came, they would help her find her family. Someone would come. She just had to wait long enough.

Sarah believed that right up until the moment death took her body, there on the rocks at night, along the path to the beach. But on that moonless night, what the islanders called the night of an underground moon, only her body rested. Her spirit remained on the island, left to wander alone, still waiting for someone to come. Anyone who had known grief and loss, anyone with painful regrets, they would understand all that she suffered, and their pain would call to her. Whoever came, she would awaken and rush to them. She wouldn't be alone then, and maybe there was still hope of finding her family after all. Maybe. However long it took, she would wait for the rescuers among the bounders on the path to the beach. She would wait.

CHAPTER 4

The Ghost Awakens: Sarah—1775

A KEENING WAIL SOUNDED FROM THE highest point on the island, a cry of yearning bereavement that echoed down the path until it reached the ancient pile of bounders. Gradually a figure emerged from the darkness, a young woman running through the razor grass toward the beach.

And Sarah awakened for the first time. Her journey had begun here a century before, but it wasn't over, because she was still waiting.

The woman was sobbing when she reached the place where Sarah stood invisible and passed though her. Both Sarah and the woman gasped at the contact, and with great effort Sarah held on. Someone had finally come! She didn't know where she'd been before this moment and could perceive only shadows, but this woman's sorrow had snapped her back to this familiar place once more. Sarah knew grief, and so did this woman. They could comfort each other. But the wait had been so long!

Though it was hard for her to hold this woman's mind, Sarah clung to her, inserting herself more deeply, wrapping herself in the woman's dark feelings. After all Sarah's waiting, someone would now share her pain. She was no longer alone. She tried to show the woman all that happened: the attack, herself the sole survivor, the bodies of friends, choosing captivity, her family lost, being abandoned.

I didn't keep them safe, Sarah screamed in the woman's mind. The woman didn't seem to hear. She saw what Sarah tried to show her, but she didn't understand.

Sarah didn't know that her own pain and grief amplified dark feelings in others. Her blind grasping, her very presence, intensified whatever negative energy she encountered. The stronger those feelings were in those she contacted, the more tightly Sarah could cling. It was as if they fed on each other, both only growing hungrier.

The woman dropped to her knees, face pale and slack as fragments of Sarah's past played before her mind's eye, a stranger's gruesome memories becoming her own.

Sarah would hold fast to this one as long as she remained here or came again to this path. She had tried reaching out before, but this was the first time she succeeded in touching anyone; it would not be the last. With each successful contact, she would be stronger.

Other people would come, but not all of them would feel her. Of those who could, some would be easier to reach and hold than others. It took so much effort, every scrap of energy that Sarah had, but over time, she would learn to find some of them in their dreams. That was easier.

Always her strongest hold was here by these rocks.

Always she tried to make them stay.

Always they left her.

Alone again, Sarah would return to the nothing place until the turmoil of the next anguished spirit reached her and she woke to try again.

Chapter 5

Amanda Nickerson—1858

S THE SUN SEEMED TO sink into the waves on the horizon, Amanda shivered and pulled her shawl more tightly around her. "Nathan, where are you?" she whispered.

Her roof walk circled the highest turret of the house Nathan had built for her. From it, she could see the rocky shoreline and watch for his ship, but he and fourteen-year-old James had been gone eighteen months with no word. Voyages could last that long, and she knew she shouldn't worry, but there was something different about this time, something wrong.

As captain of his own whaling bark, the *Gull*, Nathan followed whales. Local waters used to teem with them, but no more. Now whalers had to go farther, around the Horn of South America to the Pacific, into the Sea of Japan, or north to the treacherous North Sea. That was where

Nathan was this time. A small fleet from these islands had accompanied him because he always found whales. It was an exciting life, a good living for them, and this was the first time since their marriage that she hadn't sailed with him.

The wind carried harsh cries of herring gulls up the cliff face to her as the sun's last rays reflected peach and purple in heavy clouds. It would be a dark night because of the cloud cover but also because there was a new moon. People here called it an "underground moon," certainly a colorful term, but there were superstitions about those nights too. From the time of the earliest settlements, there were stories of bloodshed, unexplained savagery, and strange disappearances all attributed to the underground moon. Amanda didn't believe any of it. There was a logical reason for anything that happened. Logic and God's will.

The black hound beside her lifted his muzzle to sniff the wind, and when Amanda laid her hand on his head, he met her gaze. She'd never known any dog to look right at people the way Pharaoh always did, and had never seen another dog with gold eyes. When she first saw him, she thought he looked like a black wolf and wanted to call him Lupo, but Nathan said his name was Pharaoh.

Footsteps thundered up the spiral staircase inside the house. "Mama!" Edwin shrieked as he crashed through the doorway, running past her to the railing. She grabbed him away from the edge, trying to hold flailing arms and legs and settle the agitated seven-year-old.

"What is it?" She crouched down, examining him all over for blood, but he seemed physically fine. He was so small for his age that people always took him for younger than he was. At the moment, he was such a combination of distraught and angry that he couldn't catch his breath. When she tried to wipe his tears, he struggled backward, and she only succeeded in making muddy streaks on his face. She let him go then but held out her arms. Still crouching, she coaxed, "Edwin, dear, what's happened?"

He stepped close enough for her to grasp his shoulders, and then his words came tumbling out. "She … killed them … *all* of them!" He was sobbing and shaking, huge blue eyes riveted on hers. "And for no reason!" Then his voiced dropped low, and he threw himself into her arms. "Oh, Mama, my ants. They're the first ones this spring, the first ones! And Marion stomped them! Why did she *do* that?" While Amanda held the little boy, Pharaoh nuzzled him.

Another figure filled the doorway, staring emotionlessly at the scene. With one arm still around Edwin, Amanda got to her feet. "I thought you and Martha were at Mrs. Agnew's learning to quilt, Marion." Amanda couldn't teach her daughter homey skills like that because she never learned herself. Having the children learn those "land" skills was one of the reasons she and Nathan had decided to keep them at home this time instead of the whole family sailing together as they'd always done before. "So why were you down at the beach with Edwin?"

Marion stood ramrod straight while her mother waited. Finally, the girl said, "He wouldn't come home." She knew that didn't answer her mother's question, but it was obviously all she intended to say. When Amanda remained silent, Marion sighed, pursed her lips, and explained. "We were on the path. The sky was coloring up, and I told him we had to go home." There was no note of apology or regret in her voice, only flat explanation. Still Amanda waited. "He's supposed to come in when it starts to get dark. I told him that. When he got to the top of the path, he stopped. I told him twice more to come along, but he kept counting those stupid insects. Besides, he was digging where we planted those bleeding hearts and tulip bulbs. I solved the problem. They were just ants."

"All I was doing was *counting*, Mama, honest! I didn't touch those bloody hearts, honest I didn't!"

"Bleeding hearts, dear," Amanda corrected softly. "You know you're supposed to leave them alone, Edwin, and I believe you did." She took a step toward her daughter. "He should have listened to you, but we don't need aggression to convince others to listen. You *know* we've discussed this before, Marion. Twelve years old is quite old enough to understand."

Amanda waited for a response, but the girl was silent. "It's not so much a matter of ants, Marion. What you did was unnecessary, and it was cruel to your brother." She narrowed her eyes at her daughter before turning back to Edwin. "I'm sure your sister is sorry." She looked back at Marion. "Aren't you, Marion." It wasn't a question.

"Of course, Mother," was all the girl said, her thin face a mask.

"Fine," Amanda breathed, "then that's that. I'm sorry about your ants, dear, but there must be thousands you didn't see, and they're such busy creatures. I'm sure they're rebuilding their hill right now. You'll see that when you check on them tomorrow."

There were still tears standing in his eyes, but he smiled at his mother and then his sister.

"Well then, that lamb stew should be ready by now. Are you hungry?" Edwin nodded with enthusiasm, but Marion didn't respond. "It sounds good to me, too," Amanda told her son. "Marion, please go down and set the table. I'll be there directly." Without a word, Marion wheeled and disappeared inside.

Amanda sighed. Something would need to be done about that girl's behavior. She was bright and could be so engaging, but then without warning she would get sullen and morose or angry and snappish. Even as a young child, she'd been moody, but back then the happy moods had far outnumbered the rest. Lately she treated important things as if they were trivial and raised insignificant problems to monumental challenges. There was no talking with her either. She would withdraw, as if to a tiny room in her mind, and close the door.

Perhaps she and Nathan should look into putting Marion in a good school, where other adults could instruct her. Sometimes a mother wasn't the best teacher for a headstrong girl. Being away at school might help smooth her edges. Amanda hoped they were only rough edges added to the emotions of her years, but sometimes she wasn't sure.

A soft tugging at her skirt brought her back to the present moment. "Now me, Mama, what can *I* do?" her son piped, wiping his eyes and making even more mud.

"Well, let's see. How about checking on the chickens? If they've gone to roost, you can lock the henhouse. After that you could fetch us some wood from the shed."

He flashed a smile and raced inside, footsteps pounding down the stairs. That boy never walked anywhere.

Pharaoh followed Amanda inside, through her bedroom, and down the staircase. As she lit tapers in the parlor, she remembered the day Nathan brought home a puppy and a blue velvet box. He patted her barely-swelling belly and told her that the puppy was his first gift for little John. He was so sure the baby would be a boy. Then he handed her the velvet box and said, "This is my heart for my one true love." In the box was a silver heart locket that he fastened around her neck, the locket she'd been wearing since.

Nathan left for the North Sea the following day, knowing their baby would be born long before he returned. He was right that the baby would be a boy, and when John was born, she sent word. Amanda gulped against the lump in her throat. That little puppy had grown into the wolf-sized dog now at her side, but the baby never thrived. She never wrote Nathan when John died. It hurt too much to put it into words.

Amanda took the tinder box from the mantle. She and Nathan used a new kind of match on the ship, but she liked using the tinder box at home. It was a soothing ritual. After a few practiced tries, she caught a spark. Then she touched a sulfur match to the flame, and with that she lit the first candle.

Circling the parlor as shadows deepened, Amanda lit

more lamps and candles. Since the baby's funeral, it seemed she couldn't bear the dark. There were other changes in her too, like fretting more about Marion and Edwin. She'd never been overprotective before, but now she struggled not to hold them too close, not to smother them. They could never mature into strong and independent adults with that kind of mother; she knew that, but she was afraid something horrible would happen to them.

Her nightmares were a new development too. She'd always been a sound sleeper, but lately she woke multiple times during the night with awful scenes in her head. Sometimes she was suffocating, maybe drowning. Other times she was being chased by a shadow, and her feet wouldn't move. The worst ones were of being completely alone in a desolate world of ashes. Once she awoke in the early light of dawn, on her knees beside John's lonely little grave in the clearing among the pines, not remembering how she got there.

Edwin scurried in and out of the parlor with armloads of wood—he would need a good washing later tonight. She chuckled to herself watching him. He was so eager to please her, so different from his older brother, James, who only wanted his father's attention. From the beginning, James had been Nathan's shadow, imitating his mannerisms and his speech. Sometimes that was cute, but not always. Between Edwin being so obviously hers and James fighting for all of his father's attention, Amanda knew that hadn't left much room for Marion. Once Nathan was back, they should address that issue too.

"Once Nathan comes back," she said aloud, savoring

the words. It had been too long. She should have insisted on going along again; they could have left the children with her brother. Raised in New Bedford in a whaling family, Amanda understood "the life," and in her, Nathan had gotten a true whaling captain's wife, one willing to share both the blessings and the hardships that life brought. She bore their children aboard the *Gull*, and all three of them were more at home on a rolling deck than in a parlor. Their children knew more about whaling than most adults did.

Amanda sighed. That was another reason they had stayed ashore this time. She and Nathan wanted the children to have choices about their lives, something impossible if all of their growing years were lived on a ship. First of all, the children had no friends their own age, and then there was the question of manners and "civilized" ways. What was appropriate aboard your own father's ship, far from land and surrounded by hardened seamen, was quite different from what passed for culture in a mainland home. For them to be able to choose the lives they wanted, the children needed different sorts of experiences and training. Only their oldest son, James, had gone with Nathan on this voyage. But that was because of his future too. He was assigned to the ship's doctor so he could see if medicine was what he wanted to study. They would have to see, Nathan had said, about that and about how they would handle future voyages.

But Amanda had already decided. She reached up onto the mantle and touched the narwhal horn from one of their voyages. Running one finger across its surface, she

thought about the creature it came from, the unicorn of
the sea. With such wonders in the world, no person should
spend their one precious life in a single place.

No, she knew what she would do, and it wouldn't be to
stay home again. Being separated might be fine for some,
but Amanda would never allow it again. This time had
been for the children. Fine, she loved her children, but
they were not her life. Besides, she wasn't sure she was the
one to teach them proper ways. Her brother in Boston was
the gentleman of the family, and he had offered to keep
the children and send them to the same school his own
attended. It would be good for Marion and Edwin to learn
mainland ways, and Amanda thought they would enjoy
the richer variety of sights and activities. The next time
Nathan sailed—and God willing, every voyage after that—
she would go with him. He might be initially surprised at
her decision, but she was confident he would agree.

"Aren't you going to build a fire, Mama? I brought the
wood." It was Edwin, puffing at her side and smiling up
at her with his adorable, grimy face.

"I certainly am," she told him. "And thank you for all
your hard work." She grinned when he plopped down on
the floor next to Pharaoh. Apparently he was going to wait
for her to make good on her promise.

"That's that, then," he said when she had a good fire
going. "Okay, I'll go help Mar now. Bye, Mama!" She
watched him skip off.

Amanda could hear Marion and Edwin talking in the
kitchen. She couldn't make out the words, but Marion's
bossy tone was evident. She was about to investigate when

Pharaoh stared at the door and growled. She couldn't hear anything out of place, and sometimes he seemed to growl and bark at nothing. Then he growled again, putting himself between her and the door, and finally she heard it too.

Footsteps crunched in the sand outside, getting closer. They weren't expecting anyone, and islanders didn't usually drop by. There was a quiet knock, so soft she could almost dismiss the sound as imagination. The second, louder knock startled her.

"Are you there, Mrs. Amanda?" a muffled voice called through the door, a voice she knew. "It's just us, Jamie and Silas."

Amanda unbarred and pulled open the heavy door. Silas and Lydia Greene were their nearest neighbors and closest friends and Jamie was their son. She'd known the family since Nathan first brought her to the island as a bride.

"What a surprise," Amanda said, noticing Marion and Edwin peering at the visitors from the kitchen. Edwin waved, and Silas nodded to him. "Come in and warm yourselves by the fire," Amanda told the two men.

Silas was a powerfully built man who was as comfortable holding babies as hauling in the heavy nets of his fishing trade. It was a good thing, because he and Lydia had nine living children. Jamie stood beside him outside, a tall and narrow young man built more like his mother when she was younger. Neither man moved to come in. Instead, both of them removed their caps and stood holding them, their eyes locked on the threshold.

This is no social call, Amanda thought as she motioned them in again. "Please, come in out of the dark," she said. When they were inside, she came right to the point. "What's happened?" She could hear her own heart drumming in her ears and felt her breath coming faster. She knew.

"It's bad news ..." the younger man began but stopped short when his eyes met hers.

No no no no no, Amanda thought but didn't speak it. She raised her chin and clasped both hands in front of her to stop them from shaking. She knew, but she wouldn't let herself believe it yet.

Turning to the two children, Amanda said, "Go back to the kitchen and wait for me there." When they were out of sight, she looked hard at the older man and whispered, "Silas, tell me now, straight out. Please. But don't let the children hear."

Silas stepped closer to her, offering his hand. "You should sit down, Mrs. Amanda." His voice was quiet and soft, the kindness in it terrifying.

She felt tears threatening and shook her head. "No, I don't need to sit. Say it."

Silas hesitated for only seconds, but to Amanda it seemed much longer. She could see the pain in her old friend's eyes. "It's the *Gull,* Mrs. Amanda. We just got word."

She shook her head, trying not to believe what she knew he was going to say. If she didn't believe what he said, would it still be true? She waited as he struggled to continue, his voice full of emotion when he finally spoke.

"Seven months ago she froze in. They abandoned ship

when she started taking on too much water and tried to cross the ice to find the rest of the fleet. But it was near eighty miles. You've been in the north. You know what those eighty miles were like." There was a long pause. "Only five made it out."

A chill swept through Amanda's body, leaving her sick and light-headed. If she could have brought herself to believe the look on his face, she wouldn't have asked, but hope was not yet dead. "Nathan?" she breathed. Her face blanked at the shake of Jamie's head. "And James?" When Silas also shook his head, she closed her eyes and died inside. The kindly hand on her arm didn't matter.

"Won't you sit down now, Mrs. Amanda?" His voice was gentle, his kindness unbearable. "I know what a sad and awful shock this is. But we'll all stand with you."

Stand with me, Amanda thought. *What does that matter?* She couldn't speak, couldn't even breathe.

"We'll stay with you, or you can come with us to our house. You need your friends around you, and we can help you when you tell the children," he said.

Amanda shook her head again, tears leaking from one eye as she gulped and tried to calm her racing mind. *He couldn't be dead, he simply couldn't be. Nathan! Oh, Nathan*, she thought. When she found her voice, it sounded strained and coarse even to her. "Who got out?"

"That's not for now, dear friend."

"Who?" she repeated.

"Simon Mayhew, Juan Alvando, James Eaton, Mingan the native, and Harold Gardiner," he said.

"Only those few," she whispered, and her shoulders

rounded. "Nathan knew those men his whole life, worked with them and trusted them. I'm glad Mingan will be coming home. He has new twin sons, I'm told." Then she straightened. "Someone is carrying the good news to their families, I trust? Do we know when they're expected back? And is someone informing ... the rest?"

"So like you to think of others. Yes, they're all being told. Runners are carrying the word to islanders, and a boat's going to the mainland. I sent young Seth on the mare to the lighthouse. Clendon Royce was like a second father to Nathan, and we thought he should be special told." He fastened his gaze on the hat he still held with both hands before him before he answered her other question. "The ship bringing the survivors is about a month out." He paused and met her eyes again, "Now about you, Mrs. Amanda—will you come with us? You and the children should stay the night at our place. Or would you rather the women come and stay with you? Jamie can go back to fetch Lydia and Patience if you want. Whatever you need. You just tell me."

She couldn't think. Hope and grief flickered alternately. *They could be wrong. Maybe he was with a different group of survivors.* But she knew in her heart that hope was futile. With forced calm, she raised her chin. "I want," she began, but her voice cracked as she realized she wasn't sure what she wanted except that she wanted Nathan. She cleared her throat. "I'll come to your house, and thank you, I think we might want to spend the night with you all. You're right, it would be good to be with friends. But first I need time alone, Silas." When he didn't move or respond, she picked up the hand he had offered her earlier and looked into his eyes. "Could you take the children with you? They'll wonder why we're visiting so late in the day, but if you take Edwin to see the animals, he'll be fine. Marion will wonder, but she won't ask. I'll join you later, and I'd be grateful for you and Lydia to be there when I tell the children. But not yet, Silas. Please, I need time."

He hesitated, and Amanda could see that he didn't want to leave her, but finally he squeezed her hand, his eyes never leaving her face. "If you're sure."

"I am," she said, withdrawing her hand. "And thank you, Silas. It's never easy to carry such news."

"That's not a concern, but I thank you for your heart. Nathan was my good friend, honest and true. I'll surely miss him, but my heart aches for what you must be feeling." He still looked unsure about going. "You're sure you'll be all right here alone?" When she nodded, he said, "Then we'll take the children and expect that you'll be along in a bit."

She watched the two men pass through the dining room into the kitchen and heard them usher the children out the back door so they didn't need to pass her. Edwin seemed to think it was an adventure.

When the sounds of their footsteps and Edwin's excited chatter faded to silence, Amanda sank to her knees, burying her face in her hands as she rocked. Nathan was gone! From the beginning, they both recognized the inherent risks in this sort of life, even talked about them. But never once had she considered she might be left without him, never thought of facing a future without his touch, without his love. Her throat burned, and a weight in her chest made it hard to breathe. One groaning cry escaped her, and then she was still. This wound was too deep for tears, maybe too grievous for healing. How could she go on without Nathan? Pharaoh stayed beside her, watchful and silent.

Amanda stared into the flames for a long while, remembering small things from their life together. Fourteen years had passed like a lightning flash, but at the same time it felt like they'd been together her whole life. What would she do now?

As if sleepwalking, Amanda rose and climbed the spiral stairs to their bedroom. The wedding-ring quilt his mother had given them the day they were married covered their bed. Their bed. On a low table by the window was a piece of scrimshaw Nathan had carved for her. Next to it was a stone he had found on the beach, one he claimed was the same green as her eyes.

Amanda picked up the stone, felt its cool smoothness in her palm, and then put it back down. Across the room was the armoire with what Nathan called his dry-land clothing inside. She opened the armoire and buried her face in his frock coat, inhaling his scent. He always preferred traditional men's clothes to more modern styles. How long would his scent cling to those clothes, she wondered.

There was a looking glass on the inside of the door, and when she caught sight of herself, she was shocked. She looked like someone else, someone sad, someone lost. But there at her throat she saw the heart locket Nathan gave her, the one she always wore. She touched it, and for just a flash, she thought she could see him. But he wasn't there. He would never be close enough to touch again. Gently, she smoothed the fabric of Nathan's jacket and closed the armoire.

Guilt washed over her. Not since Silas had given her the awful news had she thought of James. He was her son, lost as surely as his father, and she wasn't even thinking of him. They were both in the sea, would be forever in the sea. Then a thought occurred to her. All the seas of the earth were connected. If she stood in the sea that touched this island, then wherever they were, she would be closer to them. She could share the sea with them, at least for the time it took to say good-bye. Then she would go and tell the children.

With that thought, Amanda gathered herself and stumbled down the stairs with Pharaoh at her heels. Outside she ran to the head of the path, swaying in the rising wind before starting down to the beach. She seldom used this path because it always made her uneasy. It was so secluded. But it was the fastest way to the sea, a sea she would share with Nathan and James half a world away. Just to say good-bye. It was chilly outside, but she didn't go back for her cloak.

Pharaoh ran ahead of her, stopping every few yards to look back over his shoulder. The farther she went along the path, the more agitated the dog became, and more than once she had to push him aside to get past. The heavy clouds on this night of an underground moon made it impossible to see even the stars, and she tripped repeatedly. Amanda could hear none of the normal night sounds, no owls, no insects, only the distant rumble of the surf. As she walked, her shoes filled with dry sand, and razor grass whipped around her legs whenever she wandered off the path. The farther she walked, the more desperate she felt. Nathan was gone! Finally she lifted her long skirts and ran as great tears streamed down her face. She nearly crashed into the pile of boulders midway to the beach but saw it at the last moment and slid to a halt with her hands against the cool stone.

And Sarah awakened. It took such effort to wake, such strength to reach out and hold on, but someone had come, someone who could understand.

As Sarah clutched for a hold on this grieving mind, held tightly, and began to weave herself into Amanda's thoughts, Amanda collapsed. The sound of the sea became muffled, as if she was packed in cotton wool, and she felt so heavy it was hard to move. Amanda could think only of her loss, only of the past. Silent, remembering, aching, the aloneness seemed to swallow her, as if she were the only person left alive. Amanda's heartbreak made Sarah stronger.

I didn't keep them safe. Dead, all dead except for me, and I was alone. But finally you came! I didn't keep them safe...

What? Amanda heard the words, but they were in her head instead of her ears. Feeling the grit of sand on her cheek, she was aware of images surfacing in her mind, memories, but they were not her own. She had a vision of a cabin on the hill where her house stood. But her house was huge and stood by itself, while this little cabin was surrounded by others as primitive as it was. It felt long ago—and there was an attack. She forgot about Nathan because now there was no Nathan. There was only Tom.

So many ways to die, but in the end all are the same. If only the children had lived. If only there had been grandchildren to love. But now?

Maybe they're hiding, but where are they, and what's happened to Tom and Elias? We have to find the other children and protect them!

Why was she so frightened, like she was lost in a nightmare that wouldn't stop? "That's it, this must be another nightmare," Amanda said out loud, and the voice in her head faded to the background. The children were safe, Amanda thought. They were with Silas and Lydia. "I have to make myself wake up," she said. But even if this wasn't real, Nathan was gone. Nathan was never coming back. She groaned, giving in to the grief again, and the voice in her head grew louder.

Remember when baby Elizabeth learned to giggle, and how proud Elias was to go hunting with his father? Are they still together? Remember showing Emma how to make trousers for the little ones, how the legs were different lengths? Remember where I last saw those little clothes. I didn't keep the children safe.

Barking, loud barking. *I hate dogs! No, go away!* Amanda shook her head, confused. She didn't hate dogs. And was the barking from Pharaoh or some other dog? Those children she remembered, they weren't hers, and her husband was Nathan, not Tom. How could she remember things that never happened, people she didn't know? Was she losing her mind?

The barking faded as thick, oily smoke surrounded her, forcing her to breathe it in. A strangled wail tore out of her throat that was tight and raw. *The baby!* "Which baby?" she wondered. *Baby John?* She was so thirsty, and her shoulder hurt terribly. Amanda shook her head, trying to separate the real from the rest. It was as if she was someone else. She remembered that she meant to go down to the beach and stand in the sea. She would be closer to Nathan there. Yes, stand in the sea … and then she would walk out until it covered her, dragged her down, and gave her peace. Amanda got up and started toward the beach.

Barking again, this time louder and vicious, broke through the cloudy haze, and Amanda's thoughts cleared when she felt teeth on her arm.

Attacked by a dog! No, not again! Get away from me, get away! Amanda threw her hands up to cover her face as Sarah remembered being attacked by a dog and was terrified by the barking around her now. Sarah struggled to hold on, even though she feared the dog. She couldn't bear to be alone again, not now, not when someone had finally come for her. Someone who could hear her and understand. Someone who could help her.

Amanda felt teeth bite deeper into her wrist, and Sarah screamed in her mind, terrified of the dog. *But I'm not afraid of dogs*, Amanda thought again as Sarah's grip on her loosened and Pharaoh's teeth closed tighter still on her arm, dragging her backward. "No, Pharaoh!" Amanda shouted, completely herself again. She tried to pull away, but Pharaoh held her fast. He wasn't aggressive, had never done anything like this before, but now he looked like a mad dog, and for the first time in her life, Amanda was afraid of him.

"What's wrong with you?" she yelled, hitting him with her free hand and kicking hard at his side. With a grunt, he let go and took two steps back, still staring straight at her with his gold eyes as she stood on wobbly legs. Amanda's head cleared enough to make her wonder again if she was going mad. She felt the shadow of those strange images in her mind. *What on earth?* Then she lurched forward. Pharaoh was pushing her from behind, nudging her inch by inch back toward the house. She took one step and then another, still wondering what had happened.

But Sarah was still there, and a voice that was not a voice said in Amanda's head, *No one will stay. I'm trapped here, and I can't find my children. I can't find anyone. Stay with me!* Pharaoh growled again and jumped in front of her, looking as if he intended to grab her arm again. "No!" Amanda shouted. She glanced back toward the water once but then focused on the great hound, fisted the loose skin at the back of his neck, and allowed him to pull her uphill.

And Sarah slept.

The front door was still open, and they entered without closing it. It was only inside that Amanda let go of Pharaoh. The fire had burned low, and she sank down, staring into the dying embers. Whatever happened to her on the path had nothing to do with losing Nathan, but what it was she had no idea. Tom? Elias? Other children? Had grieving for Nathan and James snapped her mind?

Amanda recalled dark thoughts, remembered that she even considered suicide. It must be her grief, the shock of this horrible loss. There was no other sensible explanation.

Those strange thoughts were gone now, but she believed the pain of losing Nathan and James would be with her forever. They were gone, just like baby John, forever. Could she go on without Nathan? She didn't know. She remembered that on the path she considered walking into the sea. Maybe dying *was* the answer. At least then the pain would be gone. But that would leave Edwin and Marion alone. Tears streamed down Amanda's face again as she struggled with conflicting desires. She honestly didn't know if she had the strength to live, wasn't sure she wanted to live. It was too hard.

"One thing," she said aloud, wiping her tears on her sleeve. Her father used to say, "When tasks are overwhelming and you don't think you can do everything, then do one thing, only one."

One thing. She thought of her children.

Edwin's running, his smile, his ants, how he always wanted to help. What would happen to him if he lost both parents in the space of a few days? And what about Marion? She had such promise, but could she mature into kind and confident womanhood without a mother? God, this hurt. Every breath in this life took effort, and the hard truth was that living itself hurt.

Nathan had never promised her an easy life, but up till now it *had* been easy. Maybe now was when the price for that ease had to be paid. She would need greater strength to live than to die, she was sure. And it would take greater love to honor Nathan by raising their children as best she could alone instead of giving up and abandoning them.

Amanda stood up and straightened her back, then sighed as she took her cloak down from the hook by the door and wrapped it around her shoulders. This wouldn't be easy, this different kind of life, and her heart hurt. But she was strong. Right now she had to go tell the children that their father and brother were gone. She would cry with them, agree how much they would miss them, and then she would make sure they understood she would take care of them. Life would not be as it had been, but their life on the island would go on.

As they stepped outside, Amanda felt the sting of Pharaoh's bite and could see his teeth marks through her ripped sleeve. There was blood too, but not much. It had been strange behavior from the beast, but she knew that strangeness probably saved her. She patted the great head and smiled at him. "Everyone should have such a protector. Now let's go find the children." As for those strange visions on the path and her disconnected thoughts, she would have to think about those in the days and weeks to come. She was sure there was a logical explanation.

CHAPTER 6

Amanda and Marion—1858

THERE WAS SO MUCH BLOOD that Amanda was afraid to look under the canvas hat Edwin was holding down with both hands. Blood didn't unnerve her, not given how many nasty wounds she'd seen aboard the *Gull*, but this was her seven-year-old son. Carefully she toweled the blood from his face but found no wound there.

"Let go of your hat, Edwin," she urged. "I'll be careful, but I need to see." Slowly she peeled away the hat and saw his blond hair matted sticky with red, and with the hat removed, more blood ran down his neck and onto his jacket. It was a good scalp laceration that would need a few stitches, but it didn't look more serious than that. "I'm sorry, dear. I have to put pressure on it," she said. Then she held his head against her chest and pressed down hard with the towel.

He yowled, but she held him close, reassuring him. "It's all right. I know it hurts, but this stops the bleeding." She hoped that was true. "I know all that blood must have scared you, but you're okay."

"Mama?" His voiced was muffled in her dress until he lifted his face to look straight at her. "Am I going to die like Papa and the baby and James?"

Her heart melted. "No, of course you won't. We'll have the doctor take a stitch or two, but don't worry. You'll be fine, truly. Head wounds just bleed, Edwin. Now hold still a few minutes more."

It occurred to her then that she hadn't seen Marion. Could whatever have hurt Edwin have—? "Marion!" she called. "Marion, where are you?" There was no response. "Edwin, where's your sister? What happened?"

"I don't know." He craned his neck to look around the room. "It was like I was asleep. I think she carried me back, and then I went to sleep again. When I woke up, you were here. Didn't she fetch you?"

"No, I heard the door." Amanda looked around again, expecting to see Marion sitting somewhere nearby, watching silently. She wasn't. But if she'd carried Edwin home, she must be safe. Why then had she left him alone in the hallway? What in the world happened out there? As soon as she was sure Edwin's wound had stopped bleeding, Amanda resolved to go looking for the girl and get some answers.

Amanda peeked under the towel and saw that the flow of blood was slowing some and getting thicker. That was a good sign. She pressed down again on the wound, and

Edwin winced. "I'm so sorry. But the pressure's working, so just a little longer." He relaxed into her and sighed, trying to be brave.

"Don't be mad, Mama," he said after a few moments. "She didn't mean it. I wanted to see the beach after we were gone so long, and Marion said I could. I ran ahead, and then Pharaoh starting barking and barking and barking. I kept trying to figure out what he was barking at, so I ran back to look." He paused then and shifted. "I know she wasn't throwing that rock at me, Mama, so I must've got in the way. Don't be mad at her. I know she didn't mean it."

Amanda's heart sank. They'd spent the last three months in Boston with her brother and his family. It was meant to be time away, time to grieve surrounded by family who loved them, and it was a blessing. The surprise was the change in Marion. While they were there and the children were getting to know their aunt and uncle and all their cousins, Marion was a different person. Despite dealing with her own grief at having just lost her father and brother, she was a delight, interested in everything, and smiling more than Amanda remembered her ever doing before. She seemed especially taken with music. Each of her cousins played at least one musical instrument, and Marion was fascinated by the cittern, an English guitar. Her aunt showed her the basics on it, and she learned quickly. She'd so taken to it that when they left to return home, the cittern went with them as a gift.

Amanda thought about how much she enjoyed that time away. The two families got on so well together that her brother and his wife offered them a permanent place in their home. He advised her to sell the island house and leave that life behind forever. Amanda considered it—someone else being in charge was a relief in many ways, and being with family would be a comfort. But she decided that wasn't the right choice for her or the children. The island was their home, and the house was one Nathan planned and had built for them, so she couldn't imagine letting it pass to strangers.

Now she wondered if she'd made the right decision, at least as far as Marion was concerned. Since they'd been back, her good nature had vanished. The day they arrived, she turned all stony and quiet, and then last night she stormed out of the house in a shouting temper. Now this.

"Let go a little, Mama." Edwin was wiggling against her, and despite the blood on his clothes and drying streaks on his face, she could see he had some of his color back. When she loosened her hold on him, he sat up and heaved a deep breath.

"You look better already, sweetheart." She smiled. "Here, if you want to hold the towel right there, you can do it yourself. Keep pressing on it hard as you can. Good. If you think you'll be okay, I need to find your sister."

Edwin nodded, adding, "Please tell her I'm okay? That I know she didn't mean it?"

"I will, dear," Amanda answered and then called for Marion. No response. Thinking that perhaps she was outside, though for the life of her she couldn't imagine why, Amanda went out to the yard. "Marion?" she called again. Silence. Walking around the house, Amanda shaded her eyes and scanned as far as she could see in all directions, into the woods, down the path to the beach, and then out toward the point. "Marion, where *are* you?" She felt herself getting a little frightened, but she was also angry. There was no good reason why the girl should leave an injured boy if not to go for help. But apparently she simply went off somewhere. What was wrong with her?

Around the back of the house, still with no sign of Marion, Amanda heard two sharp barks from inside. Pharaoh! Edwin told her that Pharaoh was on the path with them, but he'd been notably absent while she was tending Edwin. More barking. Amanda rushed in the kitchen door, skidding to a halt at the sight before her.

There was Marion, sitting on the floor with her back against the wall, staring with terrified eyes at the dog in front of her. "Get it away from me!" she shrieked. "Get it away!" Marion had one arm flung up to protect her face while the other hung loose at her side. Blood soaked the front of her dress, and tears were streaming down her cheeks while she stared wild-eyed at Pharaoh. Amanda couldn't help remembering Pharaoh's strange behavior with her that one night and wondered if he'd hurt Marion.

Amanda told the dog to be quiet, took him by the scruff, and settled him on the other side of the room. She told him to stay, and she knew he would. As soon as Pharaoh was out of plain sight, Marion seemed to collapse in upon herself.

Amanda knelt in front of the girl and tried see if the blood was hers. Edwin said she carried him, so it was probably his blood, but she had to be sure. "Are you hurt, Marion?" she asked, trying not to sound as frightened as she felt. "Let me see, dear." Marion lowered the arm that had been protecting her face and wrapped it around her knees. She hugged them tight to her chest and rocked, all the while mumbling a steady stream of unintelligible words.

Amanda tried to get Marion to look at her, but Marion's eyes focused alternately on the floor or the dog peering around her mother. Gradually her mumbling got louder and separated into words that Amanda could understand, but the meaning still escaped her. "They were all dead," Marion said. "I fought them, fought those savages, but all I had was rocks."

Amanda was alarmed. "Was someone there with you and Edwin? Did someone hurt you, Marion?"

Marion sobbed, "And that dog tried … tried to … dig up Elizabeth!" Great tears plopped onto her bloodstained dress.

Now that she could understand what Marion was saying, Amanda was more frightened than before. Mentally, she sorted through all the women named Elizabeth that they knew, but none of them had died. Who was Marion talking about?

"The baby died, and I'm alone," Marion whispered.

What baby? Certainly not baby John. Maybe she was thinking of Edwin as a baby? "No, sweetheart," she said, "Edwin is fine. And you're not alone. I'm right here."

"I can't find a boat, there's no one to help me, and my arm hurts so bad," Marion moaned. Amanda looked but couldn't see any blood on Marion's arm. She had always been a stoic child, so if there was that much pain and no blood, Amanda thought her arm might be broken.

Aboard their ship, Amanda had seen more than a few broken bones and helped treat them, so she knew what she was looking for. She reached out hesitantly, speaking as softly to Marion as when she was a tiny girl. "I'll be careful," she said, thinking it was exactly what she said to Edwin earlier. Running practiced fingers along Marion's limp arm, she felt for telltale signs. But the bone felt intact, and Marion evidenced no discomfort at her prodding.

Only when she heard Pharaoh whine right next to her did Amanda realize that the dog had crawled up beside them. She thought nothing of it until Marion struck out at him and screamed when he tried to sniff her. He sat back then, but he didn't leave her.

If this had happened before her one experience on the path, then Amanda would have been sure Marion was deranged. But some of her daughter's ravings sounded eerily familiar. She could recall only fragments from that night, flashes of images and feelings like a forgotten dream, but she did remember pain like Marion's. Amanda had attributed all of that to imagination, illusions brought on by shock and grief. Now she wondered.

"The baby," Marion moaned.

Not sure what to do but needing to snap Marion out of whatever this was, Amanda took her by the shoulders and brought her own face close to her daughter's. "Marion, look at me." She raised her voice, adding a stern note. "Look at me, girl. Come on, let's get you up. We'll find Edwin so you can see he's fine."

"I'm right here, Mama." There he was in the doorway, still pressing the towel to his head. Before Amanda could help Marion to her feet, Edwin squeezed in and sat next to his sister on the floor. He put one arm around her neck, laid his cheek on her shoulder, and began to hum one of the tunes she'd learned on her cittern. When he was done, he touched her face. "Want me to go get your cittern thing, Mari? You always felt good when you played." She didn't answer, but she seemed at least to hear him.

Amanda watched as Marion slowly came back to herself. She unwound her arm from her knees and stretched her legs out in front of her. Then her eyes focused, and she reached out to stroke Pharaoh while her gaze moved from her mother's concerned face to her brother's head resting on her shoulder.

Recoiling from him, she croaked, "You're bleeding!" She looked at her mother then, near panic in her eyes. "He's hurt, Mama!" Then her expression blanked for a moment before her shoulders dropped and she bowed her head. "I remember," she whispered.

"No, no. I'm okay, Mari. Don't worry," Edwin insisted. "It's only a little bloody, and it doesn't even hurt anymore. It was a stupid accident. See, it's stopped bleeding already," he said and lifted the towel to show her. It hadn't quite stopped. "Please be okay now, Mari?"

Amanda noticed how Edwin was patting his sister's hand, just like he'd done since he was little. Whenever people were hurt or sad, Edwin would pat them. It was sweet to see, and it seemed to calm Marion, but Amanda still wanted to get the girl up and out into the air. She wasn't sure who needed more help, a little boy with an obvious physical injury or Marion. "Come on, you two," she urged, bending down to help both children stand. "We'll all go out back. There's shade and always a breeze. You can rest there, Marion, while I get Edwin cleaned up. Then we can talk."

In the back yard, she settled both children on the long wooden bench under the pines. Marion didn't say anything, but she seemed anxious, glancing back and forth between Edwin and her own bloody hands. Amanda thought her eyes looked old.

There will be time to figure all this out, but not now, Amanda thought and turned back to the tasks at hand. The amount of blood on the two of them was frightening, all from one little boy who seemed to be doing pretty well at the moment. As the blood dried and turned from red to brown, it was easier to think of it as dirt, but Marion still seemed disconcerted by it, so she would clean them both up as best she could. Then they could see about getting the doctor for Edwin.

"I'll be right back," she told them and went inside. The water she'd drawn earlier that morning was still cool despite the growing heat, and it was only moments before she was headed back out with a full basin and clean cloths. Marion was sitting half turned on the bench, staring into the trees behind her, and Edwin was stretched out on the ground at her feet, his eyes closed.

Amanda stopped short and gasped, spilling half the water. Why was Edwin on the ground? But then he opened his eyes and smiled at her. He had one hand on his head, fingers curiously exploring the wound.

"Leave it alone, dear," she said. "Here, let me clean you

up. Don't worry, I'll try to stay away from the cut." She knelt on one knee, put the basin on the ground beside him, and began gently cleaning his face. "Does it hurt much now?"

His answer was a whisper. "My head aches awful bad, Mama. And my neck. But don't tell Mari, okay?"

"I won't, Edwin. I won't." Amanda glanced up at Marion at the same moment Marion turned back toward them. The girl's face was very pale, but at least she wasn't terrified of the dog anymore. He was up on the bench with her, one paw in her lap, and she had one arm around him.

As the water in the basin went from clear to cloudy to a deep brownish red, Amanda was aware that Marion watched them. "There, that will do," she finally told Edwin. "I'm afraid I've started it bleeding again though. Here's a clean cloth to hold on it. Remember now, press as hard as you dare." She threw the bloodied water under the pines, thinking absently that it would be good fertilizer, and went back inside to get more clean water.

When she came out, she held out the basin to Marion. "Wash your hands, dear, unless you want me to do it for you. It'll make you feel better." When Marion sat staring at her bloody hands, Amanda picked up one hand at a time and put it into the cool water, washing until both were clean. Then she dried them on her own dress. There was no help for Marion's clothes at the moment, but that wasn't important. Pharaoh had been notably quiet through the whole process, but now he crowded in closer, whining as he laid his head in Marion's lap. Amanda saw great tears welling up in her daughter's eyes.

"There's something wrong with me, Mama," she said.

"No, sweetheart, you had a bad scare, that's all." It might be more than that, Amanda knew, but this wasn't the time to think about that. Whatever had happened to Marion sounded a bit like what happened to her, but Marion seemed much more traumatized. Maybe talking about it would help both of them. Later.

"No. Sometimes I feel like ... You must think I ... I'm scared and ..."

"Whatever you feel," Amanda interrupted, "it will pass." Gently pushing Marion's hair out of her eyes, Amanda waited until her daughter met her gaze. "Put it all aside for now. We'll get it sorted out and deal with everything together," she said. "As for what I think, I understand it was an accident, and so does your brother."

Marion didn't answer her, but she seemed to be listening, so Amanda tried to soothe her. "It's over now. You're both safe."

Marion closed her eyes, and the tears spilled out. "I don't think so. This happened before, and I didn't want to tell you because I know it means I'm crazy." Now her eyes were wide open, pleading, "Can't we go back to Boston, Mama? Please? I felt good there."

"Of course we'll go back to visit, probably at Christmas. I know you liked it there."

"No, not to visit. I want to go and never come back here." The look of utter despair on Marion's face wrenched at Amanda's heart, but she didn't want to encourage the girl's hysterics Young girls sometimes let themselves get too agitated. "I said we'll talk about all this later, Marion. Right now let's see about a doctor for Edwin."

Marion's chest hollowed and her chin sagged. "Please listen to me, Mama. We can't stay here." Then she straightened, and the expression in her pleading eyes hardened. "I hear you, you know."

"You hear what?" Amanda was confused.

"At night, I hear you crying. And sometimes you scream." Marion turned her head away so that Amanda wasn't positive what she said, but she thought it was, "You're not the only one who has nightmares."

When Marion turned back to regard her mother, her expression was flat, and before Amanda could ask her to repeat what she said, Marion smiled. It was a cold smile that took Amanda so much by surprise that she forgot what she was going to say.

"Never mind, it's really not important. You go ahead, Mother. Take Edwin and get him fixed up. I'll wait for you." She looked down at her skirts. "While you're gone, I'll get some fresh clothes on and soak these."

So now she was back to being Mother instead of Mama, Amanda thought. At least her daughter seemed herself again, but regardless of how reasonable she seemed now, just a few heartbeats ago the girl had been ranting. "No, Marion. I'll need help with Edwin," she said, "so we'll all go."

"Ready, Edwin?" Amanda asked as she helped him stand. They would get Edwin to the Greenes' place, and Silas and Lydia could send one of their boys on horseback to fetch the doctor. That would be much quicker than she could get a doctor for him any other way. Besides, the comfort of friends would be good for all of them.

CHAPTER 7

Amanda and Lydia—1858

USUALLY AMANDA WAS GLAD THEY had no livestock besides chickens to care for, but a horse would have been useful in getting to the Silas and Lydia's house. She considered carrying Edwin, but it was too far for that, so she and Marion piled the boy into a hand wagon and wheeled him. Despite his headache and the rough ride, Edwin was a trooper. Marion helped her mother maneuver the wagon over the ruts and places where the path got steep, her mood seeming to improve the farther they got from their house.

After the worried commotion of their arrival and then everyone's relief that Edwin's wound wasn't as bad as it looked, things happened fast. First, Silas sent Jamie to fetch Dr. Worth. Meanwhile, Lydia gave Edwin some cider and talked to him to take his mind off what was about to happen; he understood what "stitches" meant. Meanwhile,

Lydia's oldest daughter, Patience, took Marion upstairs and lent her a clean overdress to wear while they soaked the bloody one. Lydia put coffee on to boil while they waited for the doctor to arrive.

Before long, Jamie returned with Dr. Worth close behind in his carriage. From the look of the supplies he and Jamie carried in, the doctor came prepared for an injury much worse than Edwin's. The cleaning seemed to hurt Edwin worse than the stitching, but when it was done, the doctor praised him. Then he cautioned Amanda to keep the wound clean and watch for signs of corruption, leaving with a promise to check on Edwin in a few days. All the children filed outside to watch him go.

"Well, I think that's enough of that," Silas told the children outside. He had one arm around Edwin's shoulder. "I know," he said to the little crowd. "How about we leave your mamas in peace and show Edwin and Marion what's in the barn?" The surprise was the latest litter of puppies that Silas suspected Pharaoh had sired. All seven looked exactly like him.

"They'll be a while," Lydia told Amanda with a broad smile, "surely enough time for us to finally get some coffee." After she'd poured a cup for each of them, Lydia sat down at the table to nurse the newest addition to the family while Amanda watched. "I thought I was done with birthing, but then this little one surprised us," Lydia beamed. "I suspect he'll be the last, though."

"He's beautiful," Amanda said. She was having trouble finding the right balance between interest in the baby and fixation. He was so like little John that she was both drawn to him and unnerved by him, so she studied the tiny pink and violet flowers painted on her china cup. "These cups are so delicate. How do you keep from breaking them with…?"

Lydia barked her hearty laugh, but the baby didn't seem to notice. "You mean with this great horde crashing about, including my bear of a husband?"

That was exactly what Amanda had been thinking, at least about the children, but instead of answering she just smiled.

"All our china came from Silas's mother. She brought it with her from England, though I have no idea how she managed it. We've only broken a couple of pieces since the set came down to us." She leaned forward with a mischievous grin. "Silas's mother likely turns over in her grave every time I drink coffee from her teacups!"

"Well, they're beautiful," Amanda said, "a real touch of elegance. And this coffee is just what I needed. Thank you, Lydia."

"A pleasure, my friend." She nodded to Pharaoh, who was making a slow circuit of the room, sniffing the food smells in the air. "Love that dog of yours," she said. Pharaoh looked from one woman to the other and then curled up in front of the iron stove with his head on his paws and closed his eyes.

"He seems perfectly at home here," Amanda said. "I'm grateful he's quiet now. Lately at home, he stands and barks at nothing. He used to be my constant shadow, but since we've been home, he follows Marion around. She can hardly turn without tripping over him."

"No telling what animals are thinking. Likely he just missed you all. Right there by the stove was his place while you were away. Of course there's no need of a fire today, but he settled himself there just the same," Lydia said. "It's a wonder he's content to be inside with us, especially with all the activity outside. Our Star doesn't want to stay in more than a minute except sometimes at night. Of course, that was before the puppies. But your Pharaoh, now there's a dog who likes people."

"I appreciate your keeping him when we were in Boston, Lydia. We couldn't take him along, and I don't know what we would have done if not for you."

"Think nothing of it. I never expected him to be so comfortable with us, as attached as he is to you folks. First he'd follow one of the little ones all about and then another." She kissed the baby's head and smiled at Amanda, "Got along fine with our Star, too. That litter of pups in the barn is the proof."

"Puppies are something special, aren't they? I'm sure Edwin will be begging for one on the way home. I'd like to see them later."

"Well, you know you're welcome to one or more than one, Amanda. The fact is, I've seen other dogs about that favor your Pharaoh. But if they take after his nature as well, there's a blessing."

"He's a good dog," Amanda answered. Her cup rattled slightly in its saucer when she tried to lift it, and it made her realize how much her hands were shaking. Rather than anything else, she thought it was probably because the baby was so close. She hadn't been around any tiny ones like this since losing baby James. It still hurt.

When she looked up, she met Lydia's eyes full of concern. Lydia shook her head, "You gave us quite a scare, Amanda. When you all came into the yard, I had a moment. All that blood on both of them, well you know what I thought. That it was happening again."

As Amanda was about to apologize for frightening them, she stopped. What did Lydia mean? What did she think was happening again? Her confusion must have been evident on her face.

"You haven't heard, then?" When Amanda shook her head, Lydia continued. "I don't know how you've missed all the talk, even though you've only been back a few days."

Amanda waited.

"Well, not long after you all left for the mainland, old Clendon Royce heard some hullaballoo on the beach down by the lighthouse."

"The lighthouse keeper," Amanda said. "Yes, he was a special friend to Nathan. Brought us a bucket of clams yesterday as a welcome home gift and paid his respects."

"He's been kind to us over the years, too. Crusty old geezer, but he's got a good heart. Well, he checked on the noise and found 'Ginia Poole down by the water. You know Virginia, don't you? Abby Poole's eldest? She was alive but beat up bad enough to not know who she was. Couldn't even speak to tell who did that to her, but later on, young Zebulon Crow showed up in that same spot, fists all bloody and out of his head. You recollect him, don't you? The one whose intended went off with that school teacher who was here two months back?"

Amanda shook her head.

For a moment Lydia looked puzzled and then shook her own head, "No, course you don't. What am I thinking? Seems like it's been one thing after another, but I guess all of it happened while you were away. Well, they say the boy was beside himself, threw himself down on the rocks, wailing things nobody could understand, and before anybody could get to him, he stabbed himself in the stomach. With his fish knife, no less. Torturous way to die, and die he did. But if he's the one harmed poor 'Ginia, probably better that than have her father find him. Don't know which was the greater sin, what he did to her or what he did to himself."

Lydia stared out the window for a moment and then gazed down at the little one in her arms. "Such a terrible business. I'll bet you don't know about the Murphy girl drowning either. Susanna would be about Marion's age, and I imagine she knew her. Well, two such deaths, first her drowned and then the business with Zebulon Crow and 'Ginia Poole. Seems like violence and grief follows grief and violence, starting again after all this time. Nothing like this has happened since—" Lydia stopped short and blushed, "Well, not for a long time."

Lydia looked genuinely flustered, and Amanda couldn't remember ever seeing her that way, not in all their years of friendship. "Not since what?" she asked.

After a pause, Lydia swallowed and said, "I hear there's

going to be a town meeting next Tuesday. Do you want to go with us?"

"Don't you dare try to change the subject, Lydia Greene. What were you about to say?"

Lydia's reluctance to explain was clear in her changing expression. Finally, she sighed. "It's just that I was reminded about all those stories people tell, but I know you don't put any stock in all that clishmaclaver. Besides, Silas would skin me for running off at the mouth." There was another long pause while Amanda sipped her coffee without taking her eyes off her friend.

"Tell me," Amanda finally said.

Indecision showed clearly in Lydia's eyes. "At this point, I suppose it's almost worse not saying."

Amanda nodded and waited.

"Okay. How much do you know about Keziah?"

When Amanda asked who that was, Lydia blushed again and looked down at the baby, stroking his head. "With Nathan gone, I feel like I'm telling tales behind his back," Lydia said. "If you don't know her name, then Nathan never told you, and if he didn't tell, then it's not my place. Oh, my goodness, I should have kept quiet."

"But you didn't. Nathan's gone, and you're my friend. Right? You're scaring me, Lydia."

Lydia sighed again, "Okay, but I hope this isn't hurtful." There was another long pause before she said, "It was before Nathan ever knew you, you understand. Way before. He had a sweetheart."

"Oh good gracious, is that all?" Amanda blurted. Did Lydia think she was some silly girl who wanted to know every detail of her husband's life before her, needed to know all that happened when he was away? "He was forty years old when we married. If he'd never had a sweetheart by that time, he likely wouldn't have married at all." She waited for her friend to relax, but Lydia was still looking down at the baby. When she finally looked up, she still didn't speak.

"What are you not saying, Lydia? What do you know?"

After another long pause, Lydia said quietly, "Keziah was Nathan's first wife." Then she opened her mouth as if to say something else but didn't.

Amanda was caught by surprise. She never considered a wife, though it was common enough. Men didn't have to bear children, a risky business even in this day and age. Women did, so men often outlived more than one young wife. But why hadn't he told her? "Go on," Amanda coaxed her friend, wondering if there were children she didn't know about. "I want to know what you know about her. I'm not upset, just curious."

"Well, in for a penny, in for a pound, I suppose. You already know that Nathan learned whaling early, that he'd been to sea and wanted his own ship. His family had money, so they commissioned a ship, the *Gull*. Keziah's father was a shipwright, and that's how he met her. Silas and me were already expecting our eldest, and we met her before they were married. He built her a little cabin right where your house stands now, and they planned a bigger place up on the point." She paused. "Right where you laid your little John to rest."

Amanda thought of Nathan's excitement about

building the house for her, how he hadn't let her see it until it was done. He never told her it was built where he'd built another house for another woman, and she wondered if he'd torn that first house down with his own hands. She'd always thought they told each other everything.

Lydia was still talking. "Her younger brother visited them and was climbing those treacherous cliffs off the point above your place. It seems like all the stories happen on that end of the island. Anyway, he fell and split his head wide open, died right there before anybody found him. Of course, losing a brother is an awful thing, but Nathan said it was more than that. Keziah started acting strange, talking to herself without seeming to know where she was, and disappearing from their bed in the middle of the night. She told him she saw things. He fetched a doctor from the mainland for her, but it didn't help. A few months later, she disappeared. One thing after another, just like what's happened here of late."

"What do you mean she disappeared? Poor Nathan," Amanda said, but that wasn't all she was thinking. Why had Nathan kept this a secret? Was it that he still loved Keziah, or was there some other reason?

"We all searched," Lydia said, "but didn't find a trace of her. Nathan was distraught, and for a time we worried he might do himself injury. He didn't want to believe she was dead, so he convinced himself she'd left him and found a way off island. Nobody else thought that. That girl loved him. Finally, his father helped him pull himself together, told him to gather a crew of whaling men he could trust, take his new ship to sea, and find whales. That's what he did."

Amanda sat quietly, thinking about her husband. It seemed impossible to have lived here on such a small island all these years without anyone once mentioning Keziah. It didn't matter, really, but she couldn't help feeling betrayed. Had Nathan told people not to tell her? If so, why?

The silence made her look up at the face of her old friend. Lydia looked crushed. "I can't tell you how sorry I am," Lydia said. "For me to tell you *now*, to add to your burden at such a time, it's unforgiveable. Lord, what I've done to Nathan's name with him gone and no way to explain his reasons to you. Oh, I'm no friend to either of you."

Amanda reached across the table and patted Lydia's arm. "Nonsense. You didn't do anything wrong telling me. I'm fine, and what you said changes nothing."

"Seems like the older I get, the harder it is to separate what I'm thinking from what comes out of my mouth. Talking about that string of horrid events lately made me think about the island legends. Those catastrophes came in clusters too, and some families had more than their share. Families like Keziah's. First her grandfather, then her brother, and then her. Then once I thought about that, well—"

"It's fine," Amanda said. "I'm sure Nathan had his reasons for keeping silent." Then she glanced down at Pharaoh and changed the subject. "Look at that dog, cleaning himself like a cat. Did you ever see such a fastidious animal?" Lydia didn't answer.

"Really, Lydia, I wouldn't have cared if Nathan told me himself, and I don't care about it now, so please don't be upset. As for the stories, I know about them." Amanda didn't add that she didn't believe them because she wasn't sure anymore. Given her experience on the path the night Nathan died, she was seeing the whole subject from a different perspective. Add to that the visions that haunted her dreams and the desperation in her daughter's eyes as she sat on the floor talking about dead bodies, and she had to wonder. *Some families have more than their share,* Amanda thought. Perhaps the shock of losing Nathan wasn't the only reason she saw things that night. Something else might be going on here, though what it could be, she didn't know. Lydia might know something more.

Families, Amanda thought. "You said something happened to Keziah's grandfather. What was it?"

"Oh, that. I was a child then, but I remember him. He ran the mercantile in town, an old man with a big laugh. But when he lost his wife, he stopped smiling, and he died all of a sudden. It wasn't till I was older that I found out what happened to him." She paused and looked over toward Pharaoh, her eyes flitting back and forth. "He slit his own throat with a scythe. They found him in bed like that, with his nightshirt on. People whispered about it for months. It all came up again when Keziah's brother died, and then again when she disappeared.

"And you say those calamities you're talking about," Amanda prodded, "they run in families?"

"Sometimes, but not always. Nobody remembers any misfortunes of that sort among Zebulon Crowe's kin."

Misfortune, Amanda thought. What a strange word for what he did.

"He was a good boy," Lydia said, "not a mean bone in his body, and for him to attack 'Ginia and then do what he did to himself, it makes no sense. It's like Keziah disappearing when she had every reason to be happy. No sense at all. But I don't know; maybe I'm being foolish to connect everything. It's a long reach."

Amanda didn't think so. If she could bring herself to tell Lydia her own story—or Marion's—what would she say?

But it was Lydia who was talking again. "So you see why my heart about stopped when you got here with Edwin in that wagon, blood all over the three of you. Lord knows I was relieved to know that Edwin's hurting was innocent."

Amanda put her cup down and held one hand with the other while she tried to decide how much more to tell Lydia about Edwin's "accident." All Lydia knew was what she told the doctor, that Edwin had banged his head and passed out, and that Marion carried him back to the house. Now Amanda told it all, first the truth about Marion hitting him with a rock, and then about the strange way Marion acted and what she said sitting on the kitchen floor. "As if she'd seen the aftermath of a battle or been attacked herself." Amanda didn't say a word about her own experience.

Through the telling, Lydia nodded without interrupting, but when Amanda finished by saying she was honestly concerned for Marion's sanity, Lydia shook her head. "No, Amanda. I know it sounds the same as those other things, but when it's children, it's different." She shifted the baby to the other breast and then looked up at her friend. "Children get into all sorts of scrapes. Why, I think seven of our nine have cut their scalps open one time or another, some more than once. Whether it's throwing rocks or falling down, children always get hurt. As for Marion, well, she made a mistake that hurt her brother and likely scared her to death. With what happened to her papa and her brother, she must have been terrified. Sometimes folks talk crazy when they're shocked or scared or feeling guilty." She shifted a bit in her chair and readjusted the baby again.

"Maybe you're right." Amanda leaned back, her hands on the oak tabletop. She noticed for the first time the splotches of dried blood on her sleeves and rolled her cuffs to cover them. This was Edwin's blood, but it reminded her of the night Pharaoh bit her arm and probably saved her. "I'd like to believe I shouldn't worry, but you should have heard her, Lydia, and seen her face." Amanda was talking about Marion, concerned for her, but she was also thinking about herself on the path and remembering more of what happened that night.

"I can only imagine how you felt, and you all by yourself over there. It's always harder alone. Gracious, you must be thinking you can't take anything else." Lydia leaned forward a little, careful not to pinch the baby against the table, and laid her hand on Amanda's arm. "But don't make this more than it is. Trouble is enough on its own without making it bigger, and Lord knows you've had enough of trouble. Let this pass by. You're well situated, so no one will go hungry, and it will all smooth out, you'll see. Edwin will heal, Marion will grow up, and you'll move on with your life."

Amanda could hear delighted squealing from little ones in the yard and wondered absently what Silas had found to amuse them so. Then she focused on Lydia again. "I'd like to forget about it, but I'm afraid of not paying attention to something I should, afraid of missing something important." She remembered Marion talking about a baby dying.

"Understand me, it's not like all this is new with Marion, her strangeness I mean. But I think it's getting worse." Amanda considered for a moment, wondering if what she wanted to say about Marion told too much about herself, but she decided to say it anyway. "At one point today, she told me that she knew I had nightmares, but that wasn't the first time she said that to me. I woke up a few mornings ago to find her on the floor next to my bed. She said it then, 'You're not the only one who has nightmares.' Then she got up and walked out, like she was sleepwalking. I found her out back on the bench with Pharaoh, the two of them all squeezed in together and Marion asleep. I'm telling you, Lydia, I'm frightened for her."

"You've tried talking with her?"

Amanda nodded. "I asked about her nightmares, but she won't tell me anything. I haven't had a chance to address what happened today. I don't know, do you think we need to talk with someone else? A doctor?"

Lydia shook her head. "I doubt it. Time is probably what she needs. She can't be used to the idea yet that her father and brother were dead for more than half a year without her knowing. That sort of thing makes a person feel like nothing they think they know is true. Mightn't nightmares be expected, both hers and yours?"

Amanda realized that her voice had been pitched higher than normal with an edge to it, and she consciously softened her tone. "I'm not sure, Lydia. She wants to go back to Boston to live. It's like she's afraid to stay here. It's true that if Nathan—" Her voice caught, and she had to clear her throat. "I'd already worked it out that the children would stay with my brother the next time Nathan went to sea, so I could go with him. If that had happened, Marion *would* have been living in Boston. Oh, Lydia, maybe we should leave, start over somewhere else, but if we did that, it seems like we'd be betraying Nathan. I know how irrational that must sound, but it's how I feel. I'm not sure what to do."

"Do nothing for now, I'd say," Lydia whispered, her eyes full of compassion.

Amanda stared at her hands. They seemed to have a mind of their own today, twisting and untwisting a bit of her skirt. She made herself stop, smoothed the fabric, and then looked up.

"Nathan would want you to do what you think best, Amanda. It's not only Marion who needs time. You do. Especially before you make decisions this important. When we lose people, it's a while before we accept they're not coming back." She watched Amanda's chin quiver and then continued softly. "I'm sorry, dear friend, but sometimes saying it out loud helps us know it's true."

Amanda nodded. "I feel like part of me is still waiting. I go out to the roof walk before I'm quite awake and stand there, wondering how his trip is going, how many whales they got, and when they'll be home. Then I remember." She paused and forced a smile. "I know it takes time. I just wish I knew what to do next."

"You'll go slow. You'll tend your children. You'll trust God, and you'll do whatever keeps body and soul together for yourself in the meantime. Sometimes that's all there is."

That's all there is, Amanda thought and then fought to speak past the lump in her throat. "Maybe you're right that I shouldn't make too much out of Marion's state of mind, but it's hard to tell what's important. One moment she's reasonable, and the next she's not; one moment an adult and the next a little girl."

"How old is she now, twelve?"

"Thirteen next month."

"Well then, she *is* between the two and will be a grown woman soon enough. Goodness, I was married and had Jamie when I was only a few years older than she is. You didn't marry quite that early, did you?"

"No. Folks at home were sure I'd be an old maid, and my father thought I'd never leave home. But I was waiting for the right man." She smiled, remembering Nathan as the dashing captain of his own ship. "And he found me." Amanda wished she could go back and do it all again, except that she would have gone with him on this last voyage. She wondered about Nathan. If he could go back, would he marry her again—and would he tell her about Keziah?

Lydia interrupted Amanda's thoughts. "Here, hold Matthew for a bit, would you?" She adjusted her bodice, stood, and arched her back. It had been a long while since Amanda held a baby, and the familiar smell surprised her. She inhaled and smiled. She was still smiling into the unfocused blue eyes when her friend spoke again. "I think it's normal for your Marion to bounce back and forth a bit, though you'll need to be firm about her behavior either way if it upsets you. At least that's my advice, though I know you already know all that. As for the child wanting to leave here, with all the memories this place has for her, I can also understand that. She's still young, and the young run when life gets hard. She'll learn to be strong, like all of us do, but right now it seems reasonable for her to want to be somewhere that doesn't remind her of what she's lost."

"Maybe you're right," was all Amanda said, still looking down at the little one in her arms.

"Well, that's enough worrying for now. Stay for supper," Lydia said. "I made bone stock this morning, so it won't take more than a minute to finish the chowder. The haddock's so fresh it's still swimming. I'll have the girls lay the table and get some biscuits going."

"No, really, that's not necessary. I think everyone we know sent us food when we got back, so we've plenty on hand. Besides, it's already late, and I don't want to walk the children home in the dark."

"Your food at home will keep a day. And don't worry

about managing in the dark. Silas and Jamie will help, probably saddle up the old mare and let Edwin ride, poor lamb. Won't take no for an answer tonight." She patted Amanda's arm, "We surely did miss you. Anyhow friends are for times like these."

Amanda sipped cold coffee to help her swallow back tears. She wished for the millionth time that Nathan was still here. She missed him desperately for all he was and all they were together, but most of all she missed who she was with him. But she would go on, and she would be strong for the children. Maybe someday she would talk with someone about the nightmares and the incident on the path. It might be that Marion needed to know about those things, though for now she would keep all that to herself.

As if Lydia heard her thoughts, she said, "Troubles feel bigger in the shadows, Amanda. I know there's somewhat you're not saying, thoughts you'll keep to yourself till you're ready to speak them." It was baby Matthew who broke the long look between them, reaching up a little hand to grasp the heart locket at Amanda's throat.

"It seems Matthew has an appreciation for fine jewelry," Lydia said, looking at the locket. "I do so admire silver, and that's a beautiful piece. I don't know that I've seen it before."

"A gift from Nathan, Spanish silver. He gave it to me right before he left, and I haven't taken it off since, but it's usually inside my clothes."

Lydia nodded. "Yes, against the skin is where lockets belong. What's in it, if you don't mind my asking?"

Amanda held the baby with one arm and undid the catch with the other. Then she leaned forward, lifting the open locket for Lydia to see inside. "That's Nathan when we were first married, and that one's me with Marion as a baby."

"It's a beautiful keepsake. An heirloom. A treasure you can pass on to Marion one day."

Amanda had a dark premonition then, of herself wearing that locket as an old woman with no hope of passing it on to anyone.

"So you'll stay and share our table," Lydia said. She wasn't asking, but in response, Amanda stood to hug her friend's narrow form, the baby gurgling happily between them. "Thank you, dear friend. Let me help."

CHAPTER 8

Marion—1859

MARION WAS SUPPOSED TO BE at the town wharf buying fish, but the winter beach was like a magnet for her. It had been snowing all morning, and though the salt spray melted the flakes as fast as they fell, the rocks were slippery. She didn't care.

Inching closer to the black water, Marion traced swirling eddies with one finger and imagined being on a ship that rose and fell with the waves. She was a tiny girl when she first learned to walk on a rolling deck, and her father had praised her for that. He valued steadiness in all things, and she'd always tried to please him. She still tried, even though he was gone.

Marion found herself thinking a lot about him lately, and this snow by the sea made her wonder about the way he died. What was it like to freeze to death or to drown in freezing water? Freezing didn't seem as bad a way to die as some, and neither did drowning, but her father and brother would have watched each other suffer. That would be worse than dying.

There was movement below the surface, and Marion imagined eels. Sometimes you could catch them here in the summer, three feet of muscle and slime. Eels fought like the devil himself when you hooked them, and they were unsettling to cook because the skinned pieces twitched and contorted as if still alive. But she wasn't fishing today; she was thinking about how short life could be.

First they found out that her father and her brother were dead, and then Zebulon Crowe killed himself. People said that meant he couldn't go to heaven, but she hoped that wasn't true. Zebulon was older than she was, but he was still young, and she knew him. Then she learned that a fisherman found Susanna Murphy drowned when they were in Boston. Marion knew her, too. And then there was 'Ginia. At first everybody thought Virginia would recover, but she never woke up. It was like she drifted further and further away until she couldn't find her way back. 'Ginia was her friend, not a close friend, but Marion didn't feel like she had any of those.

Five deaths of people she knew and then Edwin's "accident" six months ago. He didn't die, but he might have, and it would have been her fault. No one else was with them that day, so Marion knew she must have thrown that rock, though she couldn't remember doing it. Something was wrong with her. After all, hadn't her mother said that exact thing more than once, "What's *wrong* with you, Marion?"

She wasn't dying, but dying wasn't the worst thing that could happen to a person. You could disappear a bit at a time like 'Ginia had, and that's what was happening to her. Maybe "disappearing" was another way of saying she was losing her mind, and it started when they let her father and James sail without them two years ago. Two years seemed like a lifetime to feel this way.

In Boston it was better, like when somebody opens the curtains to let in light and air. She could breathe again there, she could sleep, and she thought the bad time was over. But when they came home, all the darkness was waiting for her.

Marion leaned down until her face was inches from the water, searching for the rocky bottom, remembering. After they put Edwin to bed the day he got his stitches, her mother wanted to talk. Marion told her as much as she knew about what was happening to her because she believed that she had to talk if she wanted to live. As Marion explained, her mother looked increasingly nervous, and got more so when Marion questioned her about her nightmares. Despite her discomfort, Marion believed her mother told the truth because the dreams she described were much like her own. Her mother said that in one dream, she was someone else, a woman who had lost everything and been left alone, a woman who was dying. Marion dreamed that too. When her mother admitted she sometimes woke up to the smells of smoke and rotting meat, Marion nodded, thinking for the first time in a long while that perhaps she wasn't crazy after all.

Then suddenly everything changed. Her mother

pulled back, closed up, and used words like *logical explanation* and *calming down* and *being sensible*, and *not getting carried away*. They looked at each other silently for a while until her mother looked away, her face genuinely calm. Marion realized then that her mother was somehow beating back the voices, something she hadn't been able to do.

For the next few days, every time their eyes met, they smiled awkwardly at each other. Her mother treated her like she was delicate or sick and refused any further discussion about the only things Marion could think about, the voices, the visions, and the nightmares. Instead, she told Marion to stop dwelling on unpleasant things and put them behind her the way *she* had. They were very different people.

Marion didn't tell anyone else because there was no one else to tell. Anyway, they wouldn't understand. "Maybe I *am* crazy," she whispered as she dragged her fingers though the icy water. Black, cold, deep, and with an undertow. Treacherous.

"Good heavens, girl, what are you thinking?" barked a gruff voice behind her.

Marion jumped and stood up too quickly, slipping on the wet rocks. She threw one arm behind her to break her fall and felt barnacles cut into her arm where her coat sleeve got pushed up. Then wiry fingers encircled her elbow, giving her a chance to find her balance as she looked up to see who it was—Clendon Royce, the lighthouse keeper for as long as anyone could remember.

"Surely you know better, miss. Even this little bit of

snow makes jetty climbing risky." He motioned to the scratches on her arm. "How bad you hurt?"

"It just stings," she said, pulling her coat sleeve down. Her blouse sleeve was torn, and there was blood, but she didn't want him looking. "I'm fine," Marion said as she straightened and stepped to a flatter rock. Only then did he let go of her arm. He'd scared her, and she didn't want him to see that either, so she brushed at her skirt until she found her mental balance. Then she flashed him a smile. "It's okay. I like it out here, even when the weather's bad. Thank you for the help, Mr. Royce."

"So then, you recognize me. Good you know I'm not some stranger." He shook his head. "Truth is I feel responsible. You were doing fine till I startled you, out here like a true Nickerson. Have to say that pretty green overcoat of yours looks none too warm for this weather though."

A true Nickerson? "I'm fine, really," she said.

"No, girl. Best you get to shore till things are a bit less slickery," he said, offering her a gnarled hand. "I owe it to your papa to see you get back safe. You shouldn't be here on your own, not with all that's been happening."

What did he mean by that? Was he talking about what happened to 'Ginia, what Zeb had done? But Zebulon was dead, so what was there to be afraid of? Mr. Royce was still waiting for her to take his hand, and since she didn't feel like explaining herself, Marion took a step toward him. She slipped again, but he caught her. "Steady there, girl, I've got you."

Steady. There was that word again. So maybe he was

right about the conditions, Marion thought. He moved her hand to the crook of his arm and held it there as they worked their way back down the jetty toward the beach.

"I've seen you down here before, you know, walking the beach and standing out here. When you were younger, I'd see you fishing all by yourself. Your father used to do that, you know. That youngster would be down here in all sorts of weather, out at the end of the jetty looking in the water like you were. I remember when he caught his first sea robin. He was no bigger than a minute and didn't know what he had." He smiled as he guided her down onto the sand. "Here we are. Good solid ground again."

"You knew my father when he was young?"

"Most certainly did. Knew his whole family going way back. That day with the sea robin, he was sure he caught some kind of insect instead of a fish. With all those legs, they surely look like something else. Well, I helped him take it off the hook, and he studied it real good before we threw it back."

"I remember when you'd come to dinner sometimes, when we were home between voyages. That was before—" She stopped and then lifted her chin before she continued. "Before my father died. You always brought your book of sketchings. Papa said you could draw anything, but I remember I liked the seashells and the birds best. And your lighthouse pictures, they were good."

"Sketchings. That's a sweet way to put it. I like that. And thank you, miss. It's a kindness for you to say that, just as much as it was kind of your father to show interest in an old man's hobby, especially since he could draw so much better than me. You know your dad was an artist, don't you?"

"We have carvings of his but no drawings I know about."

"My goodness, he could draw," Mr. Royce told her. "When your father was a young man, he drew mostly people and animals, but then after—" He stopped, and Marion watched a shadow cross his face, taking his smile with it. When he next spoke, he didn't look at her but stared over her head at the sea. "Well, he turned his talent other ways later on."

After what? What was he not saying?

"That beautiful house of yours," he continued, "he said he wanted to build a castle for your mother, and he drew the plans himself. It was those plans the builders used. He knew what he was doing."

Marion nodded. She knew her father designed their house but never thought of it as a castle before. Maybe the stone turrets were meant to give it that look.

"After he married your mama and they moved in, that was when he started his writing. I never saw any of his drawings after that," Mr. Royce told her.

Writing? She had so many questions for him, but he was still talking.

"Not that he would have shown me everything he did, and who knows how much he drew or wrote while he was away. You probably know better than me." His voice was gentler when he added, "I liked your father, young miss, liked him a lot. He was a good man, and I'm sorry he's gone so young. Sorry you lost your papa."

Marion didn't know what to say. Her mother would
have said thank you, but it didn't seem right to her, and she
was afraid that would end the conversation. She wanted
to hear more. "I remember sometimes he would visit you
at the lighthouse. My older brother and I always wanted
to go along, but Father never let us."

Mr. Royce looked up at the sky and smiled. "Aye, I
remember those visits too. "Your papa and I got to know
each other pretty well after some hard times both of us
had when we were younger. Hard times call for friends,
and that's a fact." Marion watched him gaze off behind her
again, obviously remembering.

After a moment he added, "I'm so sorry about your
brother, too. Such a shame."

But Marion didn't want to talk about that. She wanted
Mr. Royce to explain something he'd said. "What hard
times?" she wanted to know.

"Oh, just the sort of thing that finds most folks in life.
We all have sadness."

"What sadness did my father have? And what about
you?" she pressed. It wasn't polite, she knew, but she
wanted to know.

He didn't answer immediately, and Marion thought
he might not. "Please Mr. Royce, now that he's gone, I
want to know everything about my father. I can't ask him,
and I don't want to upset mother by making her talk about
him." It wasn't quite a lie.

When he finally spoke, his voice was almost a whisper.
"Well, I suppose there's no harm in that." He paused again.
"The truth is, both of us lost someone we cared for. Lost

them the same way, it turned out. We each knew what that felt like and I think that kinship helped us both." Then Mr. Royce looked uncomfortable and changed the subject. "Will you just listen to that wind howl?"

Marion wanted to hear more about the sadness and the losses they shared, and she said so, but Mr. Royce shook his head.

After another long pause, he said, "We both liked history," as if that was what they were discussing, "and sometimes I'd invite other old-timers to join us at the lighthouse. We'd all tell about what we remembered from the old days, and your father would write it all down in his book. He wanted to know everything people remembered."

History? She was disappointed but hoped that if she kept him talking, he would get back around to what she wanted to know. "Yes, I remember Papa liked history," she prompted.

"Indeed he did. Especially he wanted to know about the first settlers here, the ones that disappeared."

Disappeared? Marion was interested again. "What do you mean they disappeared?"

"Well, they didn't disappear, exactly. They either died off or they left."

"Because of Indians?" That was what she saw in her dreams.

"Maybe Indians, but smallpox and cholera spread like wildfire in those days, and other kinds of sickness as well. Sometimes it was just that folks couldn't grow enough food. Must've been six different settlements here starting in the 1500s. Didn't they teach you that at school?"

"I never went to school except a little while we were in Boston. Mostly Mother taught us. She never said anything about lost settlers or the old days here."

"More's the pity. Well, every couple of decades, a new group of folks would figure this would be a great place to live, and here they'd come. They'd use what they could from the last abandoned settlement and clear out the rest to rebuild over top. Then something else would happen, and they'd be gone."

Marion watched Mr. Royce get lost in his own thoughts for a moment before he said, "Your father collected the old stories because he thought people today should study them. That's why he wrote that journal. It was the old superstitions that interested him most, you know, ghosts and spirits and such."

It was as if a bell rang in her mind, making everything clearer for just a second. "Please, what stories, Mr. Royce?"

"Those tales aren't for child ears, and I've likely said too much already. It's best not to dwell on that sort of thing."

That sounded like her mother, Marion thought—*don't dwell on the bad thoughts … this too shall pass.* "I'm no child," Marion snapped, and his expression showed his surprise. "I'm my father's daughter, a true Nickerson, just like you said, and I've got my reasons for wanting to know."

He shook his head, but he was smiling, "Well, your mother's beauty and your father's pluck. You'll be a handful, sure, as some lucky lad's wife. Honestly though, there's not much to tell." Marion thought that while he said "not much" with his words, his sad eyes said something very different. She waited, her eyes never leaving his face.

Finally, he sighed and spoke. "Well, there's no harm in me saying that every old town has legends and rumors, and I think island towns are worst. There might be a snippet of fact in some of 'em, but mostly they're tales told in the dark. Best left alone, I say." Marion waited for him to say more, but he just winked. "My gracious, listen to me go on, and you standing there shivering. Best you get along now."

Clendon Royce knew something, and Marion needed to hear what it was. If *tales told in the dark* could explain the visions and what both she and her mother dreamed about, then maybe she wasn't crazy after all.

But he wasn't talking. "I think there was a massacre here," she prompted, "and it killed almost everyone. That wouldn't be a superstition, but more like history. Do you know anything about a massacre? And can you tell me?"

He hesitated barely a second before he said, "No, child. I've said too much already. I don't think me gossiping with his daughter about such things would honor my friendship with your father." Then he looked hard at her. "Unless you've got somewhat you'd like to say about your reasons for wanting to know. You're not having any sort of trouble?"

Marion stopped breathing for a second. Did "trouble" describe what she was going through? She considered telling him but decided against it. She breathed again. "Not trouble, exactly. It's just that I—" her voice trailed off, caught by the wind.

"Just what?" he asked.

"It's nothing," she said. Then it occurred to her that if she could get to know him better, show him how mature and reasonable she was, maybe he would be willing to tell her more. "Perhaps you'll come join us for a meal again, Mr. Royce. I'll speak to Mother. You could show us some of your new sketchings, your drawings, I mean. Edwin would love that too—and we could talk more where it's warmer."

"I'd like that," he said and then laughed a little. "Yes indeed, somewhere warmer would be better. Speaking of that, it's time you get home before you freeze to death." Though they couldn't see her house from the beach, Mr. Royce knew exactly where it was and motioned up the dunes.

Freeze to death, Marion mused, thinking again of her brother and her father as Mr. Royce's gentle eyes studied her face. "He was a good man, your father, and I'm so sorry he was lost to you." Then he nodded toward the dunes. "Well, go on, now. Get on with yourself, miss. It's blowing up quite a storm."

He knew she was a Nickerson, but she wondered now if he knew her first name. He'd called her "miss" and "girl" and "little miss" and "child," but never by her name. They all thought she was a child. She wasn't, and she'd find a way to show them, but all she said was, "Yes, sir. By the way, my name is Marion, and thank you again for the help out there. On the rocks, I mean."

"My pleasure, Miss Marion," he said and strode away down the rocky beach. She watched him go. Still standing where he left her, Marion saw him stoop to pick up something at the water's edge and put it in his coat pocket. Then he turned back and waved before continuing on his way, growing smaller and smaller until she was alone on the beach.

Marion hesitated, trying to decide whether to go straight home or do what she had been tasked to do and go buy fish. Either way she'd be in trouble. If she went straight home, she'd arrive without fish, and if she walked to the wharf, she'd get home with fish but very late, so it didn't much matter.

A shiver ran up Marion's back and goose bumps prickled on her legs. Pulling her coat collar up to cover her ears, she decided to get the fish. She would follow the beach halfway around the island, buy fish at the wharf, and then go home. Though Mr. Royce was completely out of sight, it was the way he'd gone, so if she got too cold, she could stop at the lighthouse to get warm and maybe convince Mr. Royce to tell her more stories.

Raising her shoulders so she could pull her head further down into her collar, Marion leaned into the wind. It was easier walking close to the water where the sand was firm, but it was still difficult. One gust after another buffeted her, and her face stung from the bits of ice and sand that the wind carried. Mr. Royce was right about the storm. Was this what her father and brother had experienced in the North Sea, only much worse? Was there icy wind to steal all their body heat and make their muscles quiver? She pushed on, trying to shield her face with her arm, but when an especially strong gust pushed

her backward and got sand into her eyes, she knew she
had to change her plan. Her mother would be angry that
she'd been gone so long without getting the fish, but that
couldn't be helped.

She sighed. So it had to be the path.

The last time she was on that path was the day she
hurt Edwin. She had felt "wrong" that whole day, missing
her father, feeling alternately sad and angry. There were
questions she could never ask him and ideas she could
never discuss with him. And if he'd come home, she could
have explained how she wanted go to school in Boston,
and he would have let her. But he wasn't ever coming
home. That saddened her, but more than that it made
her mad.

Being angry was the last thing she remembered that
day before she drifted into a daydream that felt real. She
was suddenly in the midst of a battle with people and
animals screaming and blood everywhere. The dream
ended with her throwing rocks at someone to protect a
baby. But in reality there was no baby, and no one was
attacking her. She was throwing rocks at her brother.
When he screamed, the dream vaporized, and she ran
to him. She been terrified he was dead, but she managed
to pick him up and carry him to the house. At home, it
all happened again, and she was back in that awful place,
alone and hurt trying to protect her dead child.

Not many times in her life had she seen fear in her
mother's eyes, but she saw it that day in the kitchen. When
she'd come back to herself and looked around her, Edwin
was bloody, her mother was afraid, and she was on the

floor with the choking smell of smoke in her nostrils. Since then her nightmares had been worse, but nothing was as bad as what she felt on the path that day, so she had completely avoided the path.

Today there was no choice. Marion turned and clutched her overcoat more closely around her as the wind pushed her back down the beach and then trudged up the dunes to the path. *Surely it won't happen again,* she told herself. *I'll be fine.* On the path, she was more protected from the wind, though walking uphill through the dry sand soon had her breathing hard. As she neared the pile of boulders at the midway point between the house and the beach, she thought about the dark water where she had imagined eels and wondered whether her father and brother were frozen solid on the ice floes or eaten by huge fish under the ice. She thought again about how she nearly killed Edwin, how she feared she would ever be normal again.

A thought flashed in Marion's mind then, a voice not her own, *You've found me!* Sarah.

Sarah knew this one. Despite the energy it took for her to climb out of the gloom, dark thoughts in this place always awakened her. People with such thoughts would understand and help her if she could reach inside them, make them listen and make them see. The reaching was mindless, instinctive, and desperate. Not all of those she tried to grasp could feel her and those left her empty, longing for touch, and even more desperate to be heard. This one, though, this one could feel her.

There was no evil in Sarah's intent, but the effect of her

presence could have disastrous consequences nonetheless. Whatever darkness was in those she touched, Sarah's presence amplified. If they were afraid, they became terrified; if they were sad, they sank in depression; if they were angry, they felt rage. Some did violence to others, and others harmed themselves. Some lost track of who they were or where or when. From Sarah's perspective, they all left her in one way or another. But while they remained, her influence on them grew.

Marion groaned as the smothering darkness enveloped her. "No, no, no," she moaned, "not again," remembering events from another time, suddenly desperate to find her children. With the last shreds of her self-control, Marion screamed and tried to run. If she could get away from here, then she might escape this! But she tripped on her long skirts and fell headlong into the sand. With Sarah's memories and emotions soaking into her, filling her, Marion covered her head with both hands and tried to hold on. She could feel herself crying, but they weren't her tears. She felt hot, even in the snow, with an awful pain in her shoulder, just like before. And she was hungry, hungrier than ever in her own life. Thirsty too, so very thirsty, with an acrid taste in her mouth, a taste like ashes.

Struggling to her feet, Marion fought to shake off Sarah's thoughts and feelings. She had to run away! But other memories battered her. *The baby! She had to bury the baby so the buzzards wouldn't find her!* She staggered back against the boulders and fell down, mind swirling. She could hear someone screaming, someone close, and finally she realized it was she who screamed, over and over.

But no one heard.

When the screaming stopped, silence enveloped her. Everyone she knew was gone, and no one was coming to save her. With so much pain and such loneliness, with no more hope, what was the use of going on? She found herself back on her feet, listening as the wind carried the sound of waves crashing. It sounded like breathing. She wasn't cold anymore, wasn't afraid. She was only alone. Marion turned, tasting the saltiness of the air, and took one halting step after another toward the beach. If anyone had been there to see her face, they might have seen contentment or resignation. Most of all, they would have seen intention.

But no one saw.

Marion felt like two people at once, one older and one younger, both heartbroken, both lost. *It will be better in the sea*, she thought.

Her first step into the frigid water was a shock, and she halted with the waves lapping her ankles, feet sinking deeper into the sand as each wave retreated. Her mind cleared for a moment, and she questioned this act, wondering if there might still be another way. Was this what she wanted? She looked up at the sky but saw only gray. Her answer was the second step, pulling her feet out of the sand and going deeper. That step felt as cold as the first but was less of a shock, almost a comfort. And then she took step after step as the water rose to her knees and then her waist, waves breaking higher. Faintly she heard barking far in the distance.

I've done this before, the last time sails disappeared over the horizon. Had she done that, Marion wondered,

or was that someone else? Her heavy green overcoat
soaked through, she went deeper yet. *How I love Tom!
Maybe he'll ask me to marry him, and maybe we'll have
children someday,* she thought. As she tasted the water,
she wondered who Tom was. Remembering, smiling, she
swallowed the water, welcomed it. *This is my favorite place
on the whole island* was her last thought.

Marion never heard the pitiful howling of the great
black hound that had heard her cries, arrived too late, and
tried to drag her to shore. Marion never heard anything
ever again, but Sarah remained, and so would Pharaoh.

CHAPTER 9

Byron Douglas—1943

S O WHAT IF IT WAS dark? What was wrong with going to the beach at night anyway? His father would have let him go, Byron was sure of it. But his father wasn't here. Maybe his mother was scared, but why should he have to suffer for what *she* was scared of? This wasn't like at home. There were no strangers here, no alleys for people to hide in, no bums and no big kids. This was a little tiny island where she said everybody already knew everybody else! What did she think was going to happen to him?

Coming here had sounded so exciting when she first told him, like a big adventure. But if it was going to be like this the whole summer, with her treating him like he was a baby when he was ten years old, then he'd rather be at home. Byron kicked at the wiry grass that grew in front of the cabin, trying to figure out what there was to do all by himself, something she would *let* him do.

He remembered how his father used to pick him up and swing him around when he was little. Thinking about how it felt, he tilted his head way back until he could see the stars, stuck out his arms straight from his sides, and started spinning. Round and round he went, getting dizzier and dizzier, until the stars were lines of light in his vision. When he fell, it felt like his head kept turning, and it almost made him sick. Almost. "Whoa," he giggled. The same as when Dad did it.

He missed his father, and knew it would be a long time till he saw him again. He was in the army, fighting the Germans somewhere overseas, and he had to stay there till they gave up. Byron tried not to think about some of the kids at school, the kids who knew their fathers weren't coming back. Not ever. And some of the kids got their dads back, but they weren't the same as when they left. Some were missing something, like an arm or a leg or part of their face, and some were blind. Evelyn Harmon lived on his street, and when her dad came home, he couldn't walk. He'd heard grownups whispering among themselves that his brain was messed up too. Byron didn't know that for sure, but he knew Evelyn's father never left the house. Mostly Evelyn looked sad and scared.

He flopped down on his back with one arm stretched up, covering stars with his thumb. He didn't know if it would be worse for his dad to come back different or not come back at all, but he tried not to think about that, because it scared him. Byron didn't like being afraid. A big, black ant crawled up his leg while he watched. Then the ant fell off, or maybe it let go. Last year his teacher kept an ant farm in the classroom, so he knew what ants did and wondered how the ants here could make tunnels in the sand without them collapsing, especially with people walking all around on top of them.

One time his father showed him a dead tree with ants climbing up and down it, and there was sawdust all around the tree. Dad told him that kind of ant lived inside the tree and made tunnels in there by eating the wood. He had a special name for them, but Byron forgot what it was. Sometimes he wanted to remember things, but they got away from him. He hated that.

Lying back and looking up with the whole sky spread out like his grandfather's maps, Byron could almost see his father's face, but then it was gone. He sat up and wrapped his arms around his knees. It was scary to think you could forget somebody's face, somebody like your own father. But then sometimes it would come back to him in dreams. Dreams about his dad were great, but Byron's dreams weren't always good dreams, especially the past couple of nights. When he was little, he sometimes had nightmares when he was sick, but since coming to the island, he was having them every night. He'd wake up wanting to run and remembering an awful smell, but he could never remember what the dreams were about. It was probably because he wasn't in his own bed or something stupid like that, so he hadn't told his mother. He knew if he did, then she would make him swallow cod liver oil or something just as bad.

His mother.

He sighed and broke off a piece of grass. There was a

way you could blow through it and make it whistle, but though he kept trying, the grass wouldn't do it. Byron threw it down. Either he was doing it wrong or it was the wrong kind of grass.

His mother. So it looked like it would be just the two of them all summer. She told him she used to come to this place on vacation when she was a little kid and that it was so much fun. He couldn't imagine his mother as a little kid, even though there were pictures that looked a little bit like her. Anyway, he wasn't sure her idea of fun was the same as his. It would be better if his father was here or even his grandfather. Byron thought his grandparents must have paid for some of this trip or maybe all of it, the way his mother kept thanking them without saying for what. They'd come to help his mom and him pack, making sure he took his trucks, his books, and a baseball. He didn't play with the trucks much anymore, but the other stuff seemed like a good idea.

So okay, he brought a baseball, but who was he supposed to play with? He couldn't throw the ball around with her, because she couldn't catch. Anyway, all she wanted to do was sit inside and read while she listened to that radio. They got here two whole days ago, and so far she hadn't let him do a single thing unless she was right there. Even when they went to the beach, she made him stay where she could see him. At home, he did stuff by himself all the time, so what was the big deal?

Byron got to his feet and dug into his pockets for the Butterfinger candy bar he hid this afternoon. Boy, did they ever taste great, and they were big enough to share too, if only he had somebody to share with. He had one friend at home, Davy, and Byron tried to convince his mother to let Davy come with them for the summer. She said they couldn't do that, but she didn't say why. He figured it probably had to do with ration cards, like maybe she thought that since he was kind of fat, he would eat too much. Or maybe it was because she thought Davy was "slow." She'd asked him about that once, but it was just that she didn't know him, and she didn't even try. Davy was a good guy. He never made fun of Byron, not for having red hair, not for being short, not for being a bad throw, not for liking books, not for anything. That's what made him a friend. Davy was the one who told him that you had to be careful never to fart, sneeze, and burp all at the same time, because if you did, you'd die. Davy knew lots of stuff like that, stuff nobody else knew.

But he wasn't going to see Davy until the summer was over. Instead, it would be just him and his Mom, just them—for the whole summer. What a gyp.

The sound of his mother's radio drifted out the open window, news about the war. The man's voice sounded serious and excited at the same time, listing strange names of places Byron had never heard before. She always had that radio on, whatever she was doing, like it kept her company. And when music came on, she always hummed. He looked back at the cabin and could see her sitting in the big chair under the lamp. Though he couldn't tell if she was reading or knitting, it had to be one of the two. As if she felt him looking, his mother raised her head. She didn't get up, though, and after a moment looked back down at whatever was in her lap. *Knitting*, he decided. *Why would anybody do that in the summer?*

Then he saw her get up and stand in front of the window. "Byron? Byron, where are you?"

"I'm right here, Mom, right out front." He tried not to sound whiny. Whining was for babies. But couldn't she leave him alone for a *minute*?

"Come in now, By." She usually called him By instead of Byron. That was okay, but he liked how his father always used his whole name. "Don't dawdle. It's getting dark out there."

Of course it was dark, it was night! Dark made it fun. Besides, he had his matches, but of course his mother didn't know that. "I'm right here in the yard, Mom, looking at stars and stuff." Again he tried not to whine, but he couldn't help it. "Can't I stay out a little bit longer?"

First she was silent, thinking, he figured, and then she gave in. "Well, okay. I'm going to take a bath, and you can stay outside till I finish. But you stay in the yard, okay?"

He didn't answer, because that way he didn't have to lie. She always took really long baths, so he knew he'd have time. As soon as he saw her disappear down the hall, he set off at a run down the path to the beach. He wouldn't be long. He wanted to see where the tide was and maybe find out what interesting stuff the last high tide had washed up. Before they came here, he never knew that the ocean water came up higher and then went back out like it did, over and over.

Though it was hard to run in the sand, he raced all the way. He kept sliding sideways, stumbling, recovering, and sliding again. His shoes filled up with so much sand that it hurt his feet, and he was tempted to stop and empty them out, but he was having too much fun running. It was *really* dark on the path where the big pile of rocks stood, and the path seemed to sink between the dunes. It got lighter again as he got closer to the beach. He kept running, sliding down more dunes, and then jumped with both feet onto more level ground littered with rocks of all sizes.

He had to dodge the bigger rocks on the beach, but that made it even more fun, and he kept going until his feet splashed in the water. There were rocks there too, worn smooth by the waves, and they were slippery. He slowed down and waded in just till the water covered his feet. He was afraid to go deeper, and when he started to get scared, he imagined he was standing a big mud puddle. Just a puddle. Sometimes fooling yourself worked.

Every once in a while, a surprise wave lapped up Byron's ankles, and he jumped back. He stomped in the water, ran from the waves, and then chased the water back as it receded, playing tag all by himself. *The tide must be going out*, he thought, *because the beach looks a lot wider than yesterday.* With the moon nearly full, there was enough light to see, but then Byron could always see better at night than most people.

Marking the highest place where the high tide waves reached was a line of seaweed, and he ran up to investigate. Byron knew there would be lots of other stuff mixed in with the weeds, what his mother called "flotsam." It all smelled salty and kind of like dead fish, and he always found interesting things. He picked through it, putting odds and ends into his pockets, like shells, legs from a crab or a lobster, and a couple of things he couldn't identify. One was rectangular and black, about three inches long, with curved spines coming off each corner. It was really light like it was hollow in the middle. What in the heck was *that*? He added it to his bulging pockets and kept looking.

Three times Byron thought he saw a flash of movement, but whatever it was scooted away when he tried to look at it. He thought about ghost stories he and Davy told each other when they camped out in Davy's basement, but his mother said there was no such thing as ghosts, so it was probably some animal. Maybe it was a dog. Again and again he whipped his head around, trying to get a good look at it, but it ducked out of sight. Maybe it *was* a dog, he thought, one that was afraid of people because somebody had hurt it. Maybe bad kids.

Byron stopped short, realizing he had no idea how long he'd been down here. If his mother got out of the bathtub before he got back and found him gone, "there'd be hell to pay." His grandfather always said that. Byron looked around, trying to decide. It was taking a chance to stay any longer, but he didn't want to leave yet. Not only was there more stuff to collect, but he wanted to see what he could find in the long pile of rocks his mother called a jetty. They sure had some strange words here, flotsam and jetty and who knew what else. When they first came down to the beach, he'd asked her how the rocks landed all lined up like that, but she laughed and told him people put them there to keep the beach from washing away. He didn't see how that could work, so he wasn't sure he believed her.

Whatever a jetty was really for, he thought it was a great way to get farther out without having to go into the water, but his mother said he couldn't climb out on the jetties until he learned to swim. She said it was high time he learned and could do that this summer, but until then he was to stay off the jetties. He told her he didn't want to learn to swim, but the truth was that the idea scared him. When people went in the water, it was like they were being buried. He was sure that if he ever went in, he would sink to the bottom and be down there forever.

Even so, the ocean fascinated him. On a jetty, he'd be able to see into deep water without ever getting wet. She'd never know. So Byron took a giant step up onto the first rock and then took them one by one. Before long he was even with the place where the waves broke. That was only halfway to the end of the jetty, but he started feeling scared and figured that was far enough for now. Looking out over the water, he imagined what could be rising up out of the waves, maybe a periscope! A periscope from a German sub! He would see it and then run up the beach to warn people, and he'd be the hero, the one who saved everybody. He stared and he stared, imagining time after time that he saw one. The first thing turned out to be driftwood, and once he thought maybe it was something alive. Whatever *that* was! It probably wasn't a periscope, but it was still really neat.

He reached into his back pocket and pulled out his book of matches. He tore off three and lit them all at once, standing on one foot and holding them up like a torch.

He'd seen pictures of the Statue of Liberty in a book at school, and he thought he must look like that.

While he was balanced on one foot, there was a loud splash behind him in the dark. Byron jumped and lost his balance. He yelled as he slid down the rocks toward the water, grabbing desperately for a handhold, dropping his matches and scraping his legs and his hands. When he came to a bone-jarring stop, his head snapped back and hit the rocks, making his vision all wobbly for a second. After things stopped spinning, Byron found himself hip deep in the water with his leg caught between two rocks. The cold was a shock, even though it was summer, and salt stung places on his knee and his shin that must be scraped. His head hurt really bad. Byron inched as far out of the water as he could, but his leg was stuck fast. No matter how hard he tried to pull it loose, he couldn't budge it. He was trapped! Tears stung his eyes, and he shouted nonsense. He always got mad when he got hurt.

He had to think of something. What if he was still stuck when the tide came in? What if a monster with big teeth found him stuck here? When he tried to yank his foot loose, it felt like he was getting cut even worse.

Byron swung himself around to one side and lowered himself a few inches back down into the water. Maybe if he tried pulling in a different direction. Then he yanked once more with all his might, and finally his foot came loose! He scrambled backward, all the while trying not to imagine the creatures rising out of the black water to grab him. Back on top of the jetty, he collapsed in a heap. His hands stung, and when he looked down at them, he could see blood, but not a lot. His leg was pretty scratched up too, and his shoe was gone, but there was no way he was going to stick his arm down there to try and get it.

Byron ran his hand over his leg. It really did sting, and it felt rough like the skin was all scraped. There were white things growing on the rocks down near the water line, things with sharp shells that looked like little volcanoes. He found a pretty good lump on the back of his head, but there was no blood. That was really lucky. He could have knocked himself out cold, and nobody would have known. Maybe ever.

Instead of standing all the way up, he made his way back across the rocks in a low crouch, crawling sometimes, afraid to fall in again. When he could finally jump down onto the sand, he took a better look at himself. Not only was his shoe gone, but his sock was all ripped, and he was more scraped up than he'd thought. Plus he was soaked. There was going to be no hiding the fact that he left the yard, and he'd get punished. "Oh, rabbits and squirrels!" he shouted. That's what his grandfather always said instead of swearing.

"Unless—" he muttered. Maybe he could get back and change before his mother got out of the bathtub! He took off his remaining wet shoe and both socks, picked his way across the rocky beach, and then started running when he got to the dunes. It went faster than he thought, but by the time he got to the cabin, he was wheezing, and his wet clothes were completely covered with sand. It felt like he might have scraped his shin and knee worse than he thought, because they stung as much as his hands did. And his head hurt worse. There'd be no hiding the injuries, even if he did manage to get changed before his mother saw his wet clothes. One problem at a time. That was also something his grandfather said.

Byron raced around to the back door and pulled off his clothes, even his underwear, and tried to shake off as much of the drying sand as he could. He hid his shoe and all his clothes under a thicket of sticker bushes in a back corner of the property, getting a few more scratches in the process. He figured his mother wouldn't find them before he could figure out what to do with them, either later tonight or in the morning. And maybe he could blame all his scratches on chasing some animal into the sticker bushes. The worst thing was that his matches were gone. He'd have to find some more. But his mother smoked, so that would be easy.

The radio was still on inside and seemed even louder than before. She probably turned it up so she could hear it in the bathroom. Good, that would make it easier to get inside without her knowing. It would be harder to explain coming in bare naked, so he eased open the screen door and sneaked through the kitchen to his bedroom and put on his long pajamas. They would make him hot but probably hide most of the scratches. He was still pretty sandy, but that couldn't be helped. He could make some excuse for that, take the lecture for getting sand in the house, and forget it. Gee whiz, why did things always get so complicated?

He heard the bathroom door open. "Byron? Did I hear you come in?" Wow, he'd made it just in time.

"Yup, I mean yes, Mom. I'm getting my pajamas on," he called back. She didn't answer. Maybe she was surprised he was getting ready for bed without her telling him twelve times. "I'm really tired, Mom. I think I'll go to bed. Good night." But he knew she'd come in to say good night.

He hid his scraped hand under the pillow as she tucked the sheet tighter around him and folded a light blanket at the bottom of the bed. Then she sat down next to him. "You might need that blanket later. This sea air does help us sleep better, doesn't it? But it can get chilly." Byron didn't know what to say. "I was thinking," she said. "How would you like to go to the wharf tomorrow? It'll be a long walk, but I want to get us some fresh fish. And—" She paused for emphasis like she did when she had a surprise. "Maybe we could get you some fishing gear, too. Would you like that?"

What? Fishing? It sure would be something different to do. "Really?" he asked. But wait, he'd never fished before. "Okay, but I don't know how, Mom."

"Of course you don't. Nobody does at first, silly. There are friendly people on the dock who are always willing to lend a hand. And I can fish too, you know. Haven't done it in years, but I used to fish here all the time. Think you might like to give it a try?"

His mother fished? His mother? "Sure, Mom!"

She stood and smiled down at him. "Love that big smile of yours, By. Get a good night's sleep then. It's a long walk, you know, all the way across the island. But we'll have fun. Good night, sweetheart. Sleep well," she told him and turned out the light. He hated when she called him "sweetheart."

Byron turned over, trying to get comfortable, but he was having a hard time. His hand, his head, and his legs all hurt, and his stomach had been feeling rumbly since he got back to the house. He felt like he might throw up. Probably it was because he got scared and then had to run so hard. Besides that, he was trying to ignore how guilty he felt about all the lies he would have to tell his mother tomorrow. Holy cow, did his head ever ache. *One problem at a time*, he told himself again. For now, he hoped he wouldn't throw up and that he'd dream about good stuff for a change.

CHAPTER 10

Byron and the Dog—1943

"So, DID YOUR MOTHER TELL you she used to spend her summers here? A little bit of a girl she was, came in regular with her dad. That's what we called her, Little Bit. Must have been what, twenty-five years ago, missus?"

Byron turned in time to see his mother laugh. "Let's just say it was a while ago, Mr. Swain, and not talk about how many years!" He didn't remember the last time he'd seen her laugh out loud like that.

"Nonsense, you're a youngster still," he said. "But it is true you've grown a mite since then."

The man was old, and he had a beard that Byron thought was thick enough for hamsters to hide in. He liked hamsters. Davy had one. "Yes, sir," said Byron. "She said on the way here that this was the exact same fishing store where she used to come." He hoped "fishing store" was the right name for this place, because he didn't know what else to call it.

"Yes, indeed," the old man said. "I taught that little girl to fish for scup and flounder. And here she is back, all grown up with a youngster of her own." He had already fastened a reel to Byron's new pole and was running the line up through the metal guides as he spoke. "Life certainly does go by, doesn't it? You're Mrs. Douglas now, am I right? And you're up at the old Nickerson property, same as back then?"

Instead of watching them, his mother was peering into the barrels and troughs that held all the different kinds of bait. "Yes, Mr. Swain. I was surprised but so glad it was still a rental. Makes me feel I've stepped back in time—in a good way. I loved that place, and the Nickersons certainly built it to last, didn't they?"

"Oh, that's a good place for sure, but it's not the house the Nickerson family built in the 1800s. Heavens, no. We islanders tend to use the old names is all, so that's still the Nickerson property to us, even though it hasn't been for near a century.

Byron watched his mother raise her eyebrows, her cue for people to keep talking, and the old man obliged.

"The cabin you're in is fairly new, built after a hurricane in the twenties made the original unlivable. The folks who had it then were kin to the Nickersons, I believe, and they tore down that big old place and put up your cabin. They were mostly summer people anyhow. Folks say that something happened to sour them on island life, but I don't know that for a fact. At any rate, one summer they didn't come back, and it's been a rental ever since. Imagine the property office in town could tell you who owns it now, if you've an interest." He waited for her to answer, but she shook her head.

"Anyways," he said, "I happen to know a little about the old place, the one the hurricane took. A whaling captain named Nickerson built it, and it must have been something to see, a sort of a mansion for those days, I'm told. It had turrets and balconies, and even an old-style widow's walk, mostly made from local field stone. Grand, it must've been. Course even I'm not old enough to remember it myself." Mr. Swain snickered at his own joke, and though Byron didn't know why that was funny, he didn't mind. He liked listening to the man talk. "I'm not *that* old," he said again, "but I've seen pictures of that house." He mumbled something Byron couldn't hear and then went back to work on the fishing gear.

"Do tell," was all his mother said. A few minutes later, she asked, "What about bait for today?" Then she answered her own question like she always did, something that drove Byron crazy. "A couple of lures, I think, and some squid if you have it. Could you cut some strips for us? I don't have a knife with me." She waited until Mr. Swain agreed and then turned toward a hanging rack. "These here, are they for mackerel or snapper blues?"

Snapper blues? Byron knew the word *mackerel* because it came in cans, but was a snapper blue a fish or some kind of turtle?

"Mackerel," Mr. Swain answered her. As Byron was about to ask about the snapper blues, his mother spoke again. "So, you said there are pictures of the original place, Mr. Swain?" Byron realized she'd jumped back one conversation. She always did that.

"No photos, but drawings, good ones. Talk to Edith at the historical society. She'll find them for you. She runs a little museum of island relics, some pretty surprising things."

"We should go," his mother said. "It would be interesting to learn about the place we're living. Wouldn't that be fun, By?"

A low groan escaped him, and though his mother didn't hear it, Mr. Swain did. He made a face that reminded Byron of how his grandpa looked when he said, "Best keep a civil tongue in your head." But there was a smile in the way he looked too, like they had a secret. Then the man turned to Byron's mother again. "You'll see how grand it was." Then in a more serious tone, he added, "But pay no mind to any silly tales Edith tells you. That woman seems to think every bit of superstitious blather is part of our history. Island jaw flap. I'm sure your family heard it years ago, living on that end of the island like you did."

"No," his mother said, "I never heard anything about island superstitions back then. But we don't believe in superstitions in our house," she said dismissively. "I love old legends, though, and have to admit I'm a little curious."

Byron was more than a little curious. "What superstitions?"

The answer was quiet, as if maybe the bait man didn't want Byron's mother to hear. "Just talk, boy, stuff and nonsense. Forget I said it."

"But talk about what? What nonsense?" Byron wanted to know.

"Never mind," Mr. Swain told him again.

"You think I'm too young, don't you?" Byron was whispering, but he was angry. "Nobody tells me anything." He was thinking about his father, about the war, about all the secrets that adults kept from him, how they all stopped talking when he came into the room. "Please," he begged.

"Well, it's only fairy tales, so I guess why not," Mr. Swain said, but he was still whispering. "People tell stories about happenings here, mishaps and catastrophes like the Grimm fairy tales. You know those, right? They talk about ghosts, even a ghost dog, and witches for goodness sake. That's the one Edith loves to tell people, especially visitors. She should know better, but some folks don't."

A ghost *dog*? This man might say it was nonsense, but Byron could see from his expression that he enjoyed talking about it as much as the people he said should know better.

Byron wanted to hear more, but his mother was holding up lures with a quizzical look on her face. The bait store man pointed to the one in her left hand and then held out the finished pole to Byron. "Here you go."

Byron tried to recall what his mother had called the man so he could thank him properly. It sounded like "stain," but he couldn't remember exactly. He didn't want to use the wrong name, but he couldn't keep thinking of him just as "the bait man."

When he reached out for the fishing pole, the bait man took his hand and examined the scratches his mother hadn't yet noticed. Then he lifted his chin, making his beard sort of dance. It was like he was asking about the scratches without saying a word.

Swain, that's it, Byron remembered suddenly. "Thank you for doing this, for helping me, Mr. Swain."

"Think nothing of it, boy," he said. "See this little doodad here below the swivel on the line, this catch? You open it. Then you can either attach a leader and a hook with live bait, or you can fasten a lure. Then, of course, you close it. If you want to use a bobber, you put it up here on the line, like this. How far up the line you fasten it makes the bait float at the depth you want. If you want to bottom fish, like for flounder, you would take the bobber off and fasten a sinker to the line here, like this."

It was a lot to take in, and half the words were new. Still, Byron thought he understood because the whole time Mr. Swain spoke he showed him the gadgets he was talking about. That made it seem like he really wanted to teach him rather than just show off what *he* knew. He liked this man.

"Thank you again, Mr. Swain."

"You don't need to call me Mister, young Byron. You can call me Jacob."

Byron had never been given permission to call any adult by their first name unless it was prefaced by Aunt or Uncle somebody. It made him feel good, like he was older and worth more.

"Oh, and by the by," Jacob said, leaning down to whisper, "if you're ever fishing off a jetty, you be careful. Barnacles get exposed at low tide. They look like little pyramids when they're all closed up, and those shells are some sharp! Scratches they give you get infected in a heartbeat, so mind you don't get cut up. But if you do, wash 'em out every morning and night with salt water, and they'll heal fine." He winked and walked over to help Byron's mother, putting back some of the lures she picked out and suggesting better options.

Yup, he liked Jacob, liked him a lot.

Later when they went outside to the public dock, Jacob showed him exactly what to do all over again. He didn't make him feel stupid for being a ten-year-old city boy who should know how to fish by now. The whole time, his mother stood there watching, and every once in a while, she smiled and nodded like she was remembering good things. Byron liked seeing her that way.

As they fished, Byron tried to get the conversation back to those stories Jacob mentioned. He wanted to know more about the "mishaps and catastrophes" Jacob spoke of and about the ghosts. All Jacob would say was that sometimes when loved ones died or when good people did bad things, those left behind needed to see a reason why. He looked like he wanted to say more, but he wouldn't.

While Byron had been thinking about the ghosts, he'd stopped paying attention to his fishing pole. It wasn't until he felt a tug that he realized he had a bite, and almost before he knew it, he pulled up his first fish!

By the time Jacob went back inside the shop to help another customer, Byron knew how to bait the hook, how to substitute a hook and squid bait for a lure, how to cast, and how to reel the line back in. And he'd caught two fish!

He knew he'd need practice before he got good at this, but it felt great to learn something he wanted to learn.

The walk home seemed so much shorter than the walk to the wharf had been, and besides the two fish he'd caught all by himself, his mother had bought a few more that she called "porgies." She said she could teach him how to clean them, but he didn't believe her. "No, really, By, I know how, and I'll show you. I don't remember how to fillet a fish, mind you, but I'm sure Mr. Swain would teach you and even give me a refresher course if we decide we want to do that."

She was smiling, looking happier than since before his father left, and Byron thought that being here was good for her. That was when it occurred to him that her decision to come here for the summer might be more about what she needed than about him like she claimed. She hadn't been in this good a mood in forever, and he decided this might be the right time to ask.

"Did you hear what he said about the ghosts?"

She looked at him like he was speaking a different language. "What? You mean Mr. Swain said that?"

"Yup, superstitions and ghosts. Even a ghost dog. Did you ever hear anybody talk about that stuff when you used to come here?"

She laughed, and he wished she hadn't, at least not that way. "Well, there were always dogs around," she said, "and now that I think about it, a lot of them looked similar, kind of like black greyhounds. But ghost dogs? Of course not. I thought you were too old to believe in ghosts, Byron. That's for little children and ignorant people."

He sighed. Well, bringing it up was a mistake after all. "Never mind. I thought it was interesting, that's all," he said half to himself and kept walking with his head down. When they finally reached the yard, she seemed to get excited again, but about what, he had no idea.

"You go out back and put your fish and these porgies on the fish table," she told him. "Over there, see? Then pump some water—there should be a bucket in the shed— and rinse the salt off the reel and the guide eyes on the rod so they don't rust. Then go ahead and wash up. Fish for dinner tonight!"

He hardly recognized her. Porgies? Guide eyes? Fish table? Even though he was still a little irritated with her for dismissing what he thought was interesting, he couldn't help smiling back at her.

In the back corner of the property was the thicket of brambles where Byron hid his wet clothes the night before. Since his mother took him to the wharf first thing that morning, everything was still there. The old shed she mentioned was right there too, with a hand pump and a sturdy wooden table that was almost chest high on Byron next to the pump. Last night when he hid his clothes, he missed all of this. That pump would sure come in handy for washing the sand out of his clothes when he finally got a chance. If he could just do it all without his mother seeing him.

The shed was nearly as big as the kitchen in this house with a door in the middle and a small window on each side of the door. Byron put his forehead against the glass on one side and cupped his hands around his eyes to peer in.

The shed looked *really* old, and there was lots of cool stuff inside, but he didn't see a bucket. He had to push hard on the door with his shoulder to get it to open enough to squeeze through. Inside it was much darker than he expected, but that was okay. He could see fine. He always felt a little calmer, a little safer in the dark. But the place smelled peculiar, a little like Davy's hamster cage when it needed cleaning and a little like a gas station.

After he found a bucket under some other stuff and was closing the door behind him, he thought he heard a squeak. Not a machine squeak, but an animal squeak. It was mice maybe, or even better, rats. That would be great! Then his mother would *never* come in here, and it could be his place. That also meant it was probably a safe place to dry his wet clothes. He'd tell her about the squeaking over dinner.

Maybe this summer would turn out okay after all. Today was all about fish, getting fishing gear, learning to fish, catching fish, cleaning fish, and eating fish! Tomorrow he'd figure out what to do next. Sleep came quickly.

The next morning, Byron woke as it was starting to get light, trying to remember the nightmare. Like all the other times, he couldn't remember much. This time he was drowning and a dog came, a really big dog with yellow eyes, and it barked like crazy. At first it scared him, but then it seemed like he could breathe again, and he wasn't scared anymore. He could still hear it barking, even now that he was awake, and that was confusing. If he was awake, and it was the barking in the dream that woke him up, then how could he still hear barking right outside his window?

He got up and tried to see outside, but it was like the whole house was stuck inside a cloud. Wisps of the fog drifted into his room, and he could still hear a dog barking. Pulling on jeans and a red striped polo shirt, Byron ran down the hall, through the kitchen, and out. The screen door slapped shut behind him.

At first he couldn't find it in all the fog, but then the dog moved. It was a dark color all over, maybe black. His grandmother had a book about Egypt, and he remembered a picture of a jackal that looked exactly like this dog. It was like the one in his dream too, but not as big. This one was regular dog-sized, and the way it moved when it darted behind the shed made him think that maybe this was the animal he'd almost seen on the beach the night before.

He hesitated. What if it wasn't a regular dog, but the *ghost dog* Jacob told him about? Whoa, maybe that explained a whole lot, like how it could move so fast, why he couldn't see it very well now, and maybe ghost dogs could bark in your dreams.

He was looking right at it then, and it was still barking. That was real. "It's silly to think it's a ghost," he told himself, but despite his logic, Byron was a little scared. He called to it anyway, "Here, boy." He wondered if maybe it was a girl dog instead. No matter. "Come on, boy. I won't hurt you." It ran away.

Byron kicked at the grass outside the shed, wishing he hadn't chased the dog away. His mother told him he could have a dog someday, whenever that was. Maybe she

meant after his father got back. After the war. It would be
great to have a dog right now to do stuff with, even if it
was only for the summer. Not many people he knew kept
dogs anymore, not like when he was little. Then it seemed
like everybody had one, but not now. People said they were
too expensive with the war and rationing and all that. It
would be so *great* to have a dog if he could find it again.

"You out here, By? What was all that racket?" His
mother leaned out the screen door, looking both ways like
she was crossing a street. She clutched a pink housecoat
tightly around her, hair all disheveled.

"Nothing, Mom. Just a dog. It's okay."

"Guess some folks let their dogs run, but it might be
a stray. Don't you go near it if it comes back, you hear?"

He sighed. "Maybe it's lost, Mom. We should find out
who it belongs to, keep it here until they come get it. Poor
thing is probably hungry and smelled the fish guts in the
trash. We should feed it." His mind was running fast. He
wanted a dog so bad, even if it wasn't really his. And if
they couldn't find the owner, then he could keep it forever!

"Don't be silly. We're not bringing any strange dog
into this house. It's not even our house, By. We're renting,
you know, and it's very expensive! You are not to go
anywhere near that animal if it does come back. It could
be sick, maybe have rabies, and it might be vicious. You
come straight back inside and tell me if you see it, do you
hear me? There must be a dogcatcher on the island. I'll see
if I can find out who to call."

Dogcatcher? Byron turned around so she couldn't see
him roll his eyes. Yesterday had been great, yesterday *she'd*

been great, but here they were back to that same old thing. "Byron needs protection. Byron needs to be told what to do. Byron's a baby. Byron's an idiot." It was driving him crazy! But it never helped to say stuff like that, and he usually got in more trouble. So he turned back, gave her a weak smile, and mumbled, "Okay, Mom." It was what she expected, so it's what he gave her. Otherwise she would keep at him. Besides, he wanted something from her today.

Last night at dinner, she told them they were going to town to see that history museum or whatever it was that the bait store man told them about. Byron didn't want to go. Instead, he wanted to stay here by himself. Maybe she would let him if he agreed with everything she said. He smiled a little bigger. "Okay, Mom. I see what you mean."

She looked surprised, and he felt a little bit guilty, trying to trick her like that. After she went back inside, he walked around the yard, kicking more dirt. It wasn't fair, how most of what he wanted to do was "not allowed." She was always keeping him from doing what he liked to do, always telling him how scared he should be about doing stuff other kids got to do. And the way she looked at him sometimes. Mostly it was frustrating, and sometimes it made him mad, but every once in a while, fear sneaked in.

What if there *was* something wrong with him, and that's why he wasn't allowed to do what other kids did? What if he was "slow" like his mother said about Davy, or his brain was bad like Evelyn's father? Or maybe he was a bad kid, like the bullies at school or the kids that hung out smoking on the corner near their house. Maybe the something that was wrong with him was why he made up so many stories. Really they were lies, but he thought they made him seem more interesting, more important, more grown up. What if the reason he thought danger was fun was because of that thing that was wrong with him? He didn't know if other kids felt that way, but he thought they probably didn't. Not the good kids, anyway, and probably not Davy. Maybe that was why most kids didn't like him.

Once he talked to his father about feeling like he was different from everybody else, and his father surprised him by saying that he felt that way sometimes too, that most people probably did. He told Byron that when he got older, he wouldn't feel that way anymore. But Byron figured his father was just trying to make him feel better because he *was* already older, and he didn't feel any better yet.

In what seemed like a few minutes, his mother came back outside, looking like she was dressed for church, gloves and all, except she wasn't wearing high heels. "Are you ready to go, By? I'm really curious about this place. It'll be fun, like a mystery, and Mr. Swain said there were drawings of that big house that used to be right here. You don't need to change your clothes. You look fine." She looked down at his bare feet. "Except you'll need shoes." Then she grinned at him, the kind of smile that made him feel good. "Only here a couple of days, and already you look like an islander!"

His shoes. He'd have to deal with that missing shoe soon enough, but if he was lucky, not right now. Speaking slowly and in a way he thought sounded mature, he took a chance. "I'd like to go there sometime, Mom. But today

I want to stay home. I know you don't usually let me stay by myself, but I'm getting older, and I think you should let me. So can I?" He was tempted to keep talking, but that was usually a mistake.

She opened her mouth like she was all set to say no, but then she looked him square in the eyes. "I'm not sure it's a good idea, especially with this being a strange place. But the island is pretty safe, and you might be right. I know I don't give you much room to be independent, and you are getting older. Truth is I was babysitting my little brother when I was only about a year older than you." She paused, seeming to size him up. Then she smiled a real smile. "Okay, By, we'll try it."

It was that easy? He couldn't quite believe it. Then she was gone, and he had the whole place to himself! She hadn't even given him a list of what couldn't do or places he couldn't go. Holy cow!

Though he felt like he wanted to run, Byron stood exactly where he was for a moment, trying to figure out what to do. Well, "first things first," his father always told him. His wet and sandy clothes needed dealing with. Then he had to figure out what was he could do about the missing sneaker. After that, matches. It wasn't that he really *needed* matches because he didn't smoke, though he and Davy had tried it once. It made him choke and feel sick and dizzy. Davy threw up. He didn't see why anybody would want to do that more than once, but he liked carrying matches around. The big kids all carried them. Besides, if he had matches, he could light candles if he needed to, or even a campfire. The idea of a campfire on the beach, maybe cooking hot dogs down there all by himself, was intoxicating. Okay, so maybe he'd make matches the first thing on his list. After that he wasn't sure. So *this* was the big deal about being grown up, that you could do anything you wanted, whenever you wanted to do it!

He knew his mother stored her spare packs of cigarettes in the cabinet over the refrigerator, and she always kept matches with them. Climbing onto a chair made him almost tall enough, but not quite, so he had to run and get some of his books to put on the chair. It was a little jiggly, but in no time he had two books of matches—one for a spare. Easy peasy.

Back outside, he headed straight into the thicket to retrieve the wad of clothes and the single shoe.

The shed door seemed even more stuck than the night before, and he had to throw his shoulder against it again. It opened with a squeal but hurt his shoulder, and he yelled, "Rabbits and squirrels!" He rubbed the sore place, figuring he must have hit a nerve or something like that because it was kind of numb. He'd probably have another bruise to explain, but right now he was just mad. He knew he always got mad when he got hurt, and it was something else he was afraid wasn't normal. Sometimes it helped him though, like when he had to fight back against the big kids. One of them told the whole school that Byron was nuts the way he fought back so crazy, but that was okay because now they left him alone. Mostly, anyway.

Inside the shed, there was still that smell of gasoline and dirty animal cages. "Oh, geez," he said out loud, "my clothes are gonna smell like that if I hang 'em in here. Rabbits and squirrels!" Well, he couldn't worry about that because he had to hang them somewhere, and this was probably the safest place. He told his mother about the animal noises the night before, so he was pretty sure she wouldn't snoop around in here until the "rat problem" was solved. But she might look through the window, so he draped his clothes over the handles of garden tools and put his shoe on a paint can, all out of sight. Then he explored.

The shed seemed bigger from the inside, filled with all sorts of treasures. Some of the tools he recognized, like shovels, a pick axe, and a rake. But he had no idea what some of the other things were. He reached up onto a shelf over the bench and took down item after item, lining them up in front of him. Who did all this stuff belong to, anyway? And why would they leave all of it at a rental place? Anybody could walk in and steal all their good junk.

Good junk, but it sure did stink, and the longer he was inside, the worse it seemed to get. Usually it worked the other way around, as he and Davy had found out at the dump, in the sewer drain, in the swamp, and lots of other smelly places. It was like your nose stopped working after a while, but in here the gasoline smell seemed stronger than ever.

Looking around, Byron thought it might be coming from two rusty gas cans under the bench, so he checked the caps and picked them up to look for leaks. He couldn't budge the caps and couldn't find any leaks, and when he

shook the cans, nothing sloshed, so they were probably
empty. He got down on his hands and knees and crawled
under the bench, where he found some old towels all balled
up and stained, like somebody had cleaned something up
and left them. Maybe that was what smelled. Thinking
there might be a mouse or rat nest in that mess, he poked
the pile with a screwdriver, but the only thing that ran out
was some kind of bug with way too many legs.

That was when he saw the lantern sitting in the corner
where the bug went. It was a candle in a metal base covered
by a glass tube. His grandmother had some of those for
when the lights went out during big storms, and she called
them "hurricane lamps." The glass tube was to keep the
wind from blowing out the candle. The glass thing on this
one had a hole in it, so it might not work, but besides that
one hole, it looked perfect. He set the lamp on the bench
and reached for his matches. Why not? When he had the
candle lit, he raised the lamp above his head, looking at
all of the spider webs on the ceiling, some complete with
fat, black spiders. Some of the spiders were humungous
and had webs full of dead bugs all wrapped up, waiting
to be eaten. Byron could see pretty well in dim light, but
the lantern made it easier to see into the really dark places
under the bench and behind stacks of old windows at the
back. There was so much *stuff* crammed in here!

Byron found more smelly rags in a wooden box behind
the old windows. Thinking maybe that was where the rats
lived, he pulled them out. They smelled even worse up
close and were all stained like somebody cleaned up a big
spill. With two fingers he held at arm's length what looked

like a man's undershirt with nasty-looking stains. Then he sat cross-legged on the floor and pushed one corner of the shirt through the hole in the glass lamp cover. It caught fire right away, so he pulled it out and blew out the flame. It was a good game until he cut his finger on the sharp edge of the hurricane glass. It didn't bleed much, but he decided to take the glass off the lantern so he didn't get cut again. When he tried to set the glass on the bench, it slipped out of his hand and fell into an open toolbox, shattering against all the metal. Oh well, it was already broken before he got there.

There was that sound again, that squeaking and a rustling. "Rats, rats, where are you?" he called in a singsong voice. Nobody could call him a baby, because after all, who was going to hear him? But now that he thought about it, he wasn't sure whether or not he wanted to find the rats. Maybe later he would, but for now, the game of lighting the rag and then blowing it out was fun. Light it, blow it out, light it, blow it out. Pretty soon all the edges of the undershirt were charred, and he had to try lighting places near the middle.

As soon as he did that, the whole rag burst into flames.

Byron blew on the rag and then shook it, but the fire wouldn't go out. He staggered to his feet, still trying to shake out the flame while he held the rag at arm's length, but the flames kept growing. When it burned his hand, he dropped it, thinking he'd try stomping out the fire, but then he remembered he was barefoot. He didn't know what to do!

Water, he thought. He could put out the fire with

water from the pump if he worked fast. At school they told everybody how open doors and windows made fires get bigger, but though he tried, he couldn't get the door closed all the way. It couldn't be helped, so he ran to the pump, glad to see the bucket was still on the fish table from the night before. But it was too late. By the time he'd pumped the handle enough times to start the water, he could hear a roaring from the shed. Orange light gleamed behind the windows and through spaces between the boards. How could it burn so *fast*? Then he heard a dog bark close by.

He pumped the handle harder, trying to get the pail at least half full, because less water than that seemed pointless. Smoke poured out from all around the shed. And where was that barking coming from? Byron hefted the pail and ran to the door, trying to get it open enough to throw the water, but it wouldn't budge. Choking in the heavy smoke that was coming from everywhere, he threw the pail of water on the door. He knew that would never work, but he didn't know what else to do. He ran around the back of the shed, trying to figure out how to get more water inside, and stopped when he saw a little tunnel in the dirt at the back. It looked like something had dug its way inside or maybe out.

He looked around, realizing that he couldn't do this alone. There were no houses close by, but somebody would see the smoke and come to help. If he could just slow down the fire! Something barked right behind him, and he finally saw it, the same dog from this morning, the one that ran away from him. This time it came right up, looked him square in the face, and then ran around to the front of the shed. Byron followed it, still carrying the empty bucket. The dog jumped at the door and then ran to the back of the shed again, barking the whole time. Byron ran too, and saw it digging furiously where the tunnel was. Dirt sprayed in all directions.

Then he understood, and his heart sank. Over the roar of the fire, he could hear whining and yipping. It wasn't rats inside. It was puppies, and this dog knew it! Probably this was the mother dog. Byron swallowed hard against the huge lump in his throat that threatened to choke him. He was still holding the empty bucket, and he ran to fill it again. He had to help her. Oh, God, why did he play with that lantern? When he got the bucket half-full again, he ran to the door and took a deep breath. No matter how scared he was, he had to get that door open, so he gripped the metal handle. It was so hot it burned his hand, and he jumped back again. His hand felt like it was on fire, and there was a mark like a brand in his palm. He wrapped the edge of his shirt around his hand and leaned hard against the door to try to get it open. Even the wood felt hot now, and he couldn't get it open.

The dog was standing beside him, looking up like she expected him to do something. But neither one of them had a chance. A window cracked and broke, and flames exploded out, forcing both of them to back away. Byron raised his arm to cover his face, coughing and sputtering as the acrid smoke filled his nostrils. The whole shed was burning now. What had he done?

He couldn't hear any more puppy noises from inside, but he ran around to the back of the shed, still carrying the water and found smoke billowing out of the tunnel. Flames licked the dirt at the edge of the little tunnel, and there was an awful smell. The dog stood next to him, not running or barking anymore, but she was whining, nose close to the ground. He shielded his eyes from the heat and looked more closely. Then he saw it.

It used to be alive, but it wasn't now. What was left of the fur was still smoking, and pieces of the skin had crisped and peeled back to expose red flesh. The poor little thing. Byron felt sick. What had he done?

Not knowing what else to do, Byron gently emptied the pail of water onto the little carcass. There was a hiss when the water hit it, and he was afraid for a moment that it was still alive, but it wasn't. The mother dog whined again and sniffed at the remains, and then she looked straight at him for a heartbeat before she began to dig. He realized she was still trying to get to the rest of them, right where the flames were coming out. Didn't that hurt her? Wasn't she afraid? She was braver than he could ever be, he thought. The mewling noises from inside had stopped a long time ago, and there was only the sound of the fire. He knew there was no use for the mother dog to dig, but how could you tell a dog that it was too late?

As if she heard his thought, she stopped digging, backed up a few paces, and sat down, panting. Byron thought her paws were smoking. He felt awful.

God, how stupid he was, such an idiot! What should he do now? It was bad enough that he'd set the shed on fire, but now he'd killed a puppy, maybe a whole bunch of them. He had no idea how many puppies were in there.

This was probably the last time his mother would trust him, the last time anybody would trust him. He was an idiot.

He wanted to cry and throw up and run away, all at once. What an awful thing for him to do. Awful. He did cry then, arms hanging by his sides, his chin on his chest.

This proved what he was always afraid of, that there *was* something wrong with him and now everybody would know it. When his mother and father found out about this, they might not love him anymore, and they'd probably lock him in his room forever. Other people would talk about him. There was no hiding this, not the shed at least. But maybe it would be less bad if nobody but him knew about the puppies. As big as the fire was, the ones inside would be all burned up, so if he got rid of that one by the tunnel, no one would know. He would know, and he didn't think he would ever forgive himself, but no one else would know. If he could just figure out what to do with it.

He couldn't bury it, because the shovel was in the shed. Then he knew. He could take it down to the beach and throw it in. Fish and crabs would probably get rid of it, but even if it washed up, nobody could know where it came from. He found a stick and tried to push the little body into the empty bucket without looking at it. He gagged when more skin came off, and he couldn't stop crying, but he got finally got it in. Then he took off at a run. He had to do this and get back before his mother came home, before people who saw the smoke came to see what was burning. He knew he'd have a lot to think about later, but right now first things first. Heck, if he didn't get back fast, his mother might get back first and think that he was still in the shed, all burned up. He had to get to the beach and then get back before she came home. How much longer could the stupid shed burn, anyway?

Byron pelted down the path, faster and faster. All he could think about was how big a mess-up he was. Everything was ruined. It was more proof that he was bad. That's what people would think, what they would say, that he was stupid and that he was bad. Did this make him a murderer? Maybe there was no use in even trying to be good. He was sobbing by the time he approached the pile of boulders on the path, wishing he could take it all back and start over, mumbling through the tears in time with his running steps. "I'm so stupid ... stupid ... stupid ..."

He knew his mother would pack him back to the city now. Then his grandparents would know, and his friends at home, few as they were, they would all know. And his teachers and the big kids. Everybody! And then his mother would write and tell his father. He'd be over there in France, knowing he had a son back home who was nuts. And his new friend Jacob would know the truth about him, would know he wasn't worth anybody's time or trouble. He was a murderer. And what did that make his mom? He didn't want Jacob or anybody else to think less of his mom because of him.

And it would never go away. Some things didn't get forgiven; Byron knew that. Some stuff you couldn't fix, undo, or make up for, sins that were way past "sorry." Permanent. He was sure this sin was the permanent kind, and in that moment, Byron felt completely helpless and hopeless.

And then Sarah awakened.

Like grunts of pain, shrieks of rage, and wails of hopelessness, some sounds and some feelings are universal. Whether young or old, male or female, strong or feeble, nothing mattered to Sarah except negative emotions strongly felt. Such feelings left a person blind, consumed in the feeling, with personality neutralized and rational thought impossible. Helplessness was one of those. Sarah knew helplessness, and so did this one. This one would understand her pain. She entwined herself in the self-recrimination that filled him, in the doubt, and in the fear. She recognized those feelings, even if the events that created them in the boy were different from her own experience. Only the feelings mattered.

Byron felt heavier, and it was suddenly hard to breathe, just like in his nightmares. One thought gelled in his mind, so clearly he almost heard it. *You came to help me! Thank God. But you can see I didn't keep them safe. I didn't try hard enough.*

Safe? Who, the puppies? He couldn't walk, and he fell on his face, dropping the pail. It was like someone had him all wrapped up in a sleeping bag tied shut over his head. He couldn't see either, partly because of the sand in his eyes, but that wasn't all. As he wiped at the sand, he coughed and felt grit between in his teeth, and all the while he fought for breath.

Struggling to sit up, thoughts and emotions he had no way of understanding filled him, sights he'd never seen appeared in his memory nonetheless, and thoughts that were not his were in his head all the same. *They're dead, and there's no one left but me. Even the baby. She died as I held her, and they tried to take her away. She's buried right here. See?*

Head whirling, still wiping his eyes and spitting out sand, Byron staggered toward the beach, but he fell back down to his knees. *It's all because of me*, Byron thought, *dead because I'm useless, because I'm not smart enough. Because I'm bad.* Something was weighing him down, holding him down. He was trapped.

Then he saw movement. It was a dog, and in the blurry fog he wondered if the dog from the shed had followed him. But no, this dog was much bigger and had gold eyes. The dog from his dreams! As he focused on the dog, Byron felt strength return to his legs, and he struggled again to gather his feet under him. He could breathe a little, too! When the dog vanished, Byron shot a glance down the path and then looked back up toward the house trying to find him, but the animal was nowhere to be seen. As he faced the beach again, a blur at his side coalesced into the form of the dog. Then it vanished again, only to reappear a second later ten feet up the path, moving toward the house. How could it move that fast?

Byron didn't feel as heavy as he had only moments before, but he was still confused. He knew that this wasn't the dog at the shed, the mother dog. That one was real— and the charred remains of the puppy in the pail were proof of that. This one was bigger, more muscular, and a male. But otherwise it looked the same, like one of those big black jackal statues in the pyramids. How could it keep disappearing and then come back? He must be imagining that, seeing things. He didn't think he hit his head when he fell, but maybe he had. Then his thoughts stilled as the truth dawned on him. This was the ghost dog Jacob talked about.

Was he imagining this? Was he truly crazy? In the distance, Byron heard sirens. Was that his imagination too, or were they real? Maybe he *had* hit his head, or maybe it was from breathing all that smoke. But since the dog appeared, at least those nightmare thoughts were gone, the ones about being trapped and about bodies all around.

Thinking about the dog seemed to help him focus, but he whacked himself in the ear anyway. He *always* got mad when he was hurt, and getting mad right now was exactly what he needed to do. He hit himself again.

Byron's thoughts cleared. He still had to get rid of the puppy, so he picked up the pail and took one step toward the beach. Suddenly the dog was in front of him again, this time snarling. He tried to go around the dog, but it kept appearing wherever he tried to go. Finally, Byron backed one step and then another. With every step he took back toward the house, the dog took one step toward him, and it had stopped growling. It seemed like it wanted him to go back home, but he had to get to the ocean. He looked down at what was in the bucket then and almost threw up. *Poor little thing*, he thought again. He'd done that. It was all his fault.

He started to feel woozy again, and visions drifted like

smoke, like he was dreaming, but then the dog jumped at him and looked like he was going to bite. He didn't, but the woozy feeling stopped. Byron held his breath and ran at the dog, racing headlong for the beach, positive the animal was going to attack him. But as he passed through the space where it had been, nothing happened except that he was sure of the dog's name. This was the dog from his dreams. This was Jacob's ghost dog, Pharaoh, and Pharaoh wouldn't hurt him.

CHAPTER II

Byron and Pharaoh—1943

BYRON AWOKE AFRAID, SURPRISED TO find himself already on his feet next to a bed in a dark room. His chest felt tight, and at first he didn't know where he was, but then he remembered: in his bedroom on the island having nightmares about dead stuff, the same as every night for the two weeks since the fire. Dogs were in the one he just had, lots of dogs barking all at once and sounding crazy. It made him think about the mother dog, about the ghost dog on the path, and then about how much he wanted a dog of his own. He wondered if they'd ever let him get one now. Probably not. He didn't deserve one.

More than once when he woke up, he thought he saw Pharaoh sitting in the corner of the room staring at him, but when he blinked and tried to focus his eyes, nothing was there. He wanted to believe that simply wanting a dog as much as he did was what made him see Pharaoh, but he didn't think that was it.

The day of the fire, he saw the ghost dog as clearly as if he'd been alive. Since then, he'd seen him only as a flash before he focused or out of the corner of his eye, and Byron wondered if maybe he wasn't there at all. Part of him wanted to believe that he'd imagined that whole day, that he hadn't started a fire, hadn't killed puppies, and that none of that awful stuff on the path ever happened.

He didn't want to think about it, but he couldn't help it.

Byron got back into bed and pulled the sheet up under his chin, even though it was warm in the room. Nothing could get you if you were under the covers. It was still dark outside, but out the window he could see that the sky was getting light. Here was another day, and all he knew was that he didn't want to get up. Maybe if he said he was sick, he could stay here all day.

Byron rolled onto his side, trying to get more comfortable, but his discomfort came from inside. Before, when he got in trouble, like at school, people would forget about it after a few days, and he got to forget too. It wasn't like that this time. Nobody was forgetting, he felt awful, his mother was sad all the time, and his nightmares were getting worse.

The worst of his bad dreams used to be the ones where he was trapped and the ones where he couldn't breathe. Now they were worse, like he was in a war with dead people, half decayed, everywhere he looked. Was that what his father saw where he was in France? He'd never thought about that before, but there had to be lots of dead people in a war. That was what his daydreams were about too, like the one he had on the path. People and animals screaming and the air full of oily smoke, like when the shed burned. There was a smell too, a nasty smell like a dead mouse in the walls, but much worse than that. He'd never smelled anything in dreams before, but now it happened all the time. He hadn't slept a whole night through since the fire. Thoughts kept spinning around in his head, making his stomach feel floopy, and all he could ever think about was that one day, playing it over and over again in his head like a horror movie.

His mother was already home by the time he got back that day, and he was right about what she would think when she couldn't find him. He hid and watched. Screaming that her son was trapped inside, she fought to get loose from the two firemen who held her back from the blazing shed. He felt horribly guilty watching her like that, but he was afraid to come out.

He watched the firemen working, mostly old men and some women too. They finally got the fire out, though by that time there wasn't a whole lot left. When Byron came out of hiding covered with greasy soot, his mother ran to him sobbing, and she hugged him so hard it hurt. But there had been that momentary flash of anger in her eyes that stunned him, a look he was sure he'd never forget. It didn't last long, and when she *really* looked at him, looked into his eyes, the anger seemed to drain out of her along with all her energy. She made a big deal out of his burned hand, and one of the lady firemen cleaned and bandaged it for him. That hurt, but it didn't matter.

Picking through the rubble as they searched for pockets of live coals, the firemen found what was left of four little creatures. The town vet was one of the volunteers, and he told everyone it was dog remains, just puppies really. *Just* puppies, the man said. Later that night, when his mother took his clothes to wash them, she found his matches. Byron thought she was going to yell or even hit him, but instead she cried and left the room, quietly closing his bedroom door behind her. The rest of the night, she seemed far away.

When she sat him down to talk the next day, he answered every single question she asked, and mostly he told her the truth. He admitted playing with the lantern and setting the fire accidentally. He told her how hard he tried to put it out. He told her about the mother dog trying to get to the rest of the litter and about the puppy, how sad and horrible it looked. They both cried about that. He said he threw it in the ocean and even told her about seeing Pharaoh. That was the only part she didn't believe, and she insisted it had to be the mother dog. He told her about how he got all confused on the path and "imagined" things, but he didn't mention the black feelings that wouldn't go away or the nightmares. He did tell her he smelled something dead in his room, but when they went in there, she said she didn't smell anything. She told him it was probably somebody burning trash. He was sure it wasn't trash, not like she meant anyway.

Standing there in his room while he told her about the dead smell, he thought she looked scared. Then she got quiet. The next day, a different kind of doctor came to see him, one who said he was there to help Byron deal with what happened. She must think he was really crazy.

Byron told the doctor all of it too, but that doctor didn't believe about Pharaoh either. He left a prescription for pills to help him sleep and told him that they might see each other again after he went home. He hoped he never saw that doctor again. It seemed like everything made him think about that awful day, and he wanted to forget instead of having to keep telling people what happened. That doctor asked him how he felt about the fire and the puppies, and that made him mad. How did he *think* he felt?

His mother gave him one of those pills that first night when she tucked him in, but his nightmares were worse than ever that night, and he couldn't make himself wake up. Since then, after she left his room, Byron would get up and throw the pill down the toilet. He didn't know if his mother had told his father or his grandparents yet about what happened. She probably did, but he hoped not. What a mess.

Nights were bad, but so were the days—worse for different reasons.

Other than his mother feeling so far away and never letting him out of her sight, things between them were okay otherwise. That wasn't the case with everybody else they saw in town. Every single person seemed to know what he'd done. Whenever he went somewhere with his mother, people stared, and not in a nice way. When they went to get new Keds, it felt like the shoe man didn't want to touch him. Then in the sandwich shop, he heard what two old ladies were calling him. It was a new word for him: "pyromaniac." He didn't even know what it meant, but "maniac" was part of it, and he knew what that meant. Maybe he was a maniac, maybe a criminal. Byron was afraid he might be both. He didn't want to leave the house anymore, and it seemed like his mother was okay with that. She looked sad all the time now, and he didn't realize how much she used to smile until she stopped. Everything was ruined, and it was all his fault.

At some point he must have drifted back to sleep, because when he opened his eyes, there was bright sunlight coming in his window, and he could hear someone talking with his mother in the kitchen. Who could that be? Nobody visited them. He wasn't sure he wanted to know anyway, because there was nobody he wanted to see.

His hand was throbbing again. It had gotten badly infected but seemed to be healing better now. The doctor told them he was going to have quite a scar. *Great, a souvenir to remember this summer by.*

The clothes he'd taken off last night were draped over the end of his bed, and he pulled them on. He didn't care if they were dirty. He'd go to the bathroom and then sneak a peek around the corner to see who was with his mother. But as he was going into the bathroom, Byron heard the screen door in the kitchen bang shut. After that he didn't hear any more talking, so he was too late to see who it was. Standing in front of the bathroom sink with his toothbrush in his hand, he looked at himself in the mirror. He thought he looked older, and there was something in his eyes that he didn't like. It was the same look he'd seen in Davy's eyes more than once. It looked like giving up.

He didn't want to look at himself anymore, so he rinsed off the toothbrush and tossed it behind the faucets. He'd have to put it away later, but right then he wanted to get away from the mirror. Just in case someone was still there despite the screen door slam, Byron peered around the kitchen door jamb. There was only his mother, sitting at the Formica-topped table alone, reading a letter. Her face was all twisted up, like she was trying not to cry, but tears were rolling down her cheeks anyway. Oh God, it was about his father.

"Mom?" He was afraid to ask, but he had to. She didn't seem to hear him, so he said louder, his voice squeaking with the effort, "Mom, what's wrong?" She looked up then, her eyes red and full of tears. He motioned to the letter in her hands, the letter that was shaking. He pointed to it. "What's that?" When he talked, it felt like he had a chunk of meat stuck halfway down his throat.

The seconds before she answered seemed hours long. Then she said simply, "It's from your father, Byron."

At least she said it was *from* him, not about him, so he had to be okay. Right? "Then why're you crying?" When she still didn't answer, he got scared again. "Mom, tell me! He's okay, right?"

"Come here, Byron," was all she said, holding out her arm like she wanted to put it around him, but he stood where he was, afraid to hear what she might say.

Oh, God, he thought again, feeling suddenly guilty that he hadn't been praying for his father to be kept safe, like his grandmother told him he should. His heart sank, and he felt like his feet were stuck in the wet sand where the waves broke, getting sucked down. He couldn't move. Without knowing it was coming, he was crying too.

Her face looked confused and then surprised. "No, no, no, Byron. He's okay. It's that he was, well, he's been injured, sweetheart. He's in France, in a hospital. Come over here." She held out one arm, expecting him to come and be hugged.

What did "injured" mean? Did that mean it was bad? "What happened?" He couldn't decide whether to whisper or shout, and it came out a little of both. He imagined his father with only one leg or with his face all mangled. Or like Evelyn's dad, with something wrong with his brain. He waited for her to explain, wondering if she had any idea how this felt.

She gave up waiting for him to come closer and dropped her arm back down to her side, the arm that wanted to hug him.

"Well, he doesn't say much, but it *is* his handwriting, so that's good. He says he'll be coming home in a few months. I guess if he gets to come home, his injuries could be serious, but I'm not sure. I'm just so glad to hear from him." She paused, folding the letter. "I didn't tell you, but it's been a long time since the last letter. There were gaps between letters before, but never this long, and this time I was worried." She smiled at him.

Byron was afraid that maybe she still wasn't telling him the whole truth. They never told him things. If his father was hurt bad, would he even be the same dad he remembered, or would he be like someone else? "But you're crying. Why are you crying?" he asked her, struggling not to cry himself.

"Oh, By, it's because I'm so relieved. Come here, son. I need to hold you." This time she held out both arms and stood. She hardly ever called him "son," so that convinced him he was right about her hiding something from him. He approached slowly. She waited for him, and when he finally reached her, she pulled him close. "Don't worry." She took a deep breath and then held him at arm's length so she could look directly into his eyes. "This hasn't been an easy time, not for either of us, and I know you're hurting. With your dad gone, us living in a strange place, and now this fire business, life's been pretty chaotic for us. That's not the right word, but you know what I mean."

He nodded. *Fire business* made it sound not so bad, but he still felt like crying.

"The truth is, sweetheart, a shed burning isn't the worst thing in the world, certainly not compared to what's going on in the world. I know you feel really bad about the fire and about … those poor puppies. But I know you didn't know they were in there, and I believe you that the fire was an accident."

One tear rolled out and plopped on his shirt, but he didn't want to cry, even though he felt like it. "Oh, Mom, those puppies… I know we don't have much money and now we have to pay for a new shed and all the stuff that got burned up." His grandfather was always saying how he had to respect other people's belongings. What did he think of his grandson now? "I'm so sorry, Mom."

"I know you are, By. Sometimes we all wish we could do things over, do them better or different, but we usually don't get that chance."

He couldn't help wondering what she wished *she* could do over, but he didn't ask.

"As far as the money is concerned, Grandma and Grandpa offered to help with that. You made a mistake, Byron, and we all make them. I know you feel bad about all of it, but it's going to be okay. *You're* going to be okay. Do you understand me?"

He nodded, tears now running freely down both sides of his face. He had, of course, cried before. Everybody did. But this cry felt different. It wasn't like little kid crying or mad crying or not-getting-what-he-wanted crying, and it lasted much longer than he expected. As he cried, he realized that he was crying for a lot of reasons. There was being without his father and disappointing his mother, not being able to stop the fire, killing those little dogs— and for being bad. By the time he stopped crying, his head hurt, and his chest was tight, and he had snot dripping on his shirt. Still, he felt a little better as he looked up at his mother.

She was smiling at him, but she didn't say a word, and he thought maybe she was waiting for him to get calmed down. Finally, he cleared his throat and tried to talk, but the words came out in a croak.

"I know—" He cleared his throat again and wiped his nose on his sleeve. "I know what you mean, Mom. I do. I think it'll be okay when we're home. Here, they look at me. They look, and it makes me feel ugly and nasty, like I'm a bug." His voice cracked. "And they look at you that way too. Oh, Mom, I really didn't mean it, and I'm so sorry. I was playing ... just playing." He didn't quite know how to say how he regretted making a spectacle of them both.

"I know, By, I know. This is a hard time for you, but you'll see, in time it really will be over. People get all involved in the latest crisis, the current drama, but then something else happens, and they get involved in that. As for what people say or think about me, I don't care." She smiled and pulled him close again, whispering in his ear, "I care about *you*."

Her breath tickled his ear, but he didn't pull away. He needed to hear every word.

"We'll get past this, dear. You'll see, no matter what it seems like right now." She held him for a moment longer before she let him straighten and pull back.

"I knew before you told me. It was obvious how uncomfortable you were whenever we went anywhere, and I could see how you felt, even though you tried to put on a brave face. That takes courage."

A slow smile spread across her face, and Byron thought it was the way she smiled when she had a surprise for him. He was puzzled, but he waited for her to explain, and she didn't make him wait long.

"So what do you say about the idea of us heading back home right away? Would you like to do that?"

What? There was more than a whole month left of summer vacation.

"Of course we have plenty of time before your father gets home, but he'll be back before we know it. We don't need to spend that time away. You could be with your friends for the rest of the summer." When he didn't answer, she prompted, "Well, what do you think?"

There were the tears again, and that lump in his throat made talking impossible, so he smiled his biggest smile and nodded.

"Good, then I'll make the arrangements. Could we be ready by the end of the week, do you think? I can call the rental agent today to let them know, though I know they won't let us out of paying the rest of the summer. No matter. We'll take that ferry back to the mainland and then catch the bus. I'll call your grandfather later today and arrange for them to meet us at the bus station. Sound good?"

"Mom, it's great! I'll go pack right now." As he was turning to run back to his room, she grabbed hold of his shoulder.

"Hold your horses there, kiddo, not yet! Let's have some fun today, shall we?"

Inwardly, he groaned. *Not another board game.*

"I think we've done enough moping around the house, and now we have two things to celebrate: your father's coming back and we're going home. Let's go down to the beach, shall we? We can walk, collect shells, and do whatever else we want. You could bring your fishing gear along if you want to."

Byron wondered about that little twinkle in her eyes. Another surprise? But what the heck, if it had to do with the beach, it had to be good! He was already halfway to his room when he heard her call, "Don't forget a jacket. There's a storm coming."

They walked side by side down the path, him carrying his pole, his little plastic box of lures, and the frozen squid they had left. His mother carried a couple of beach towels and a bag bulging with sandwiches, way too many for them to eat themselves, but that was okay. He thought they were probably peanut butter, maybe with some honey. The closer they got to the pile of boulders on the path, the more nervous he got. Though he tried not to, he clearly remembered a lot of stuff he didn't want to think about from the last time. It was like they were memories, but that was impossible. Maybe it wouldn't happen with his mother here. He thought maybe he wouldn't even be scared if he held her hand, so he stuck his box of lures, his pole, and the package of bait under his arm to give him a free hand. She looked surprised but squeezed his hand and smiled. Byron smiled back, thinking he probably wouldn't see Pharaoh again either. That part he regretted.

As they passed the rocks, Byron swallowed hard and glanced up at his mother. He felt okay, but he needed to see if her face changed. It didn't. She was smiling a kind of secret smile while the wind blew her hair all around her face, and he thought she must be thinking about his dad. Then he looked at the boulders. Somebody had left a doll there, stuck in between two of the bigger stones, a rag doll with a stitched face.

As they crested the last dune above the beach, Byron saw that someone else was already standing out at the end of the jetty—*his* jetty. Disappointment washed over

him when he realized they wouldn't have the beach to
themselves. And whoever it was would probably know
who he was and what he'd done. The day was ruined
before it started. But then the figure turned and waved. It
was Jacob! Byron started running, and before he even had
time to think about it, he was out on the jetty, standing
next to Jacob, admiring his string of fish.

"Well, good morning, young Mr. Douglas! Good to
see you." Jacob held his pole in his left hand and stuck
out his right to shake Byron's. His beard was the same,
but his eyebrows looked even shaggier than before. Byron
thought it was a good face.

It occurred to him that maybe Jacob had been his
mother's visitor that morning, and he nodded to himself.
That explained her suggestion that they go fishing today.
Probably Jacob's idea. "It's good to see you too, Mr. Jacob.
I see you already caught you some." Byron nodded at the
fish stringer, hoping his eyes weren't still red. The fish were
different from the ones he caught at the pier. These were
long and torpedo-shaped, a purplish-blue color with black
stripes. "Wow, you caught a *bunch*! What are they?"

"Mackerel, finally running, but really late this year.
Best you get your line in before the school passes us.
Seems like they're circling, but you can't depend on it.
Tide's about perfect, though." He shook his head when
he saw Byron unwrapping the squid. "Nope, save that for
flounder and scup. The mackerel are hitting pretty good
on lures today. Get that mackerel lure, the long one there
with diagonal cut metal pieces? That one with the really

long leader, see it? Yup, that's the one," he said when Byron put his hand on it. "You remember how to rig it?"

"I think so," Byron answered.

Jacob watched as Byron secured the lure and nodded when he looked up for reassurance. "That's right. Good memory! Now come stand out here so you have room to cast." Jacob stood in exactly the same spot where Byron fell in and got his foot stuck that night that seemed so long ago. His shoe was probably still down there if something hadn't already eaten it.

"You're miles away, aren't you?" Jacob said with a smile, and Byron realized he hadn't heard the rest of what his friend had said. But Jacob knew that. "I said this kind of fishing's a little different than what you did before. Throw your line out as far as you can, over there." He pointed. "Then right away start reeling in, slow and steady so the lure stays off the bottom. Mackerel this size swim a couple of feet below the surface. Jerk the pole back a little every so often, like I showed you that day at the dock. It makes the lure dance and track closer to the top. They can't resist that kind of action."

Byron was concentrating so hard on what he was doing that he jumped when his mother put her hand on his shoulder. Then he jumped again when she spoke. "You okay out here, By? He doesn't swim, you know, Mr. Swain."

Why did she have to say that? "I'm fine, Mom," he said and bumped her with his pole. He told her he was sorry, but he wasn't. It was obvious how she had tried to make him feel better earlier in the morning, and he appreciated that, but why did she have to tell Jacob about him being afraid to swim and make him look like a scaredy-cat little kid?

"He'll be hunky dory, missus." Jacob grinned. "Even if a big one pulls him in, it's not deep here. Anyhow, I'll take care of him, don't you worry. But with those leather soles you're wearing, you be careful not to slip. Maybe it'd be best if you move back a tad to make casting easier for us too. If you don't mind, that is?"

She smiled and nodded before she turned. Byron was glad to see her not simply back up but walk all the way to the beach and sit on one of the towels she brought, shading her eyes as she watched them. She was still smiling, so Byron figured he probably wasn't in trouble. Now he felt bad about bumping her with the pole. He heaved a sigh and looked at Jacob, feeling as if he should explain. "I never learned when I was little. To swim, I mean. And now I'm not sure I can. Like maybe I'm too old."

Jacob leaned sideways toward him as they both faced out to sea and said quietly, "Don't you worry none. Anybody can learn. It's not hard, and you're not too old." All the while he spoke, Jacob kept reeling and casting. "Nothing to it. You relax and keep your head above water. And you keep moving. That's it. Nature takes care of the rest. I'll teach you if you want, later this afternoon if that suits you. You'll learn the basics in a heartbeat, and then you can practice on your own. Practice is the best teacher."

"Really? You think I could learn?" Byron looked hard up into Jacob's eyes. "Really you do? We won't be on the island as long as we thought, probably only a few more days. But you still think I could learn?"

"Absolutely. Fact is, if you don't want to wait, we can start now." He reeled in faster until he could hold the lure out of the water and grab the line, and then he moved to set his pole down. "We can fish later."

"No, let's fish now." Byron looked back at his mother, and she raised her hand in a wave. He waved back to her as he answered Jacob. "Later, though, can we try to teach me swimming?"

"Fine, boy. Your choice," Jacob answered and cast his line back out.

For the first time in two weeks, Byron relaxed. Right now he felt like he didn't need to hide or apologize, didn't need to wonder what the person next to him was thinking. He and Jacob didn't speak for a long time, the only sounds the clicks and whirs of the reels and the buzzing of greenheads. Jacob explained how they didn't stick you like mosquitoes did. Greenheads had two crossed swords on their mouths. They made an X-shaped cut and lapped up the blood that oozed out. Those bites hurt bad and were worth avoiding, so whenever one landed on either Jacob or Byron, the other helped chase or kill it.

After Byron chased one off Jacob's back, he broke the silence. "Can I ask you a question, Jacob?"

"Sure can. In fact, I believe you just did." Jacob snickered at his own joke.

Byron didn't get it at first, but then he grinned. "Well, *another* question then? Was that you who came to our house this morning?"

The old man nodded as he continued reeling, not taking his eyes off the place where his line met the water.

"Surely was. A letter came addressed to your mama, and we all knew that news from your father was overdue. I didn't want her to be alone when she opened it, just in case ... well, in case it was bad news."

"But how did you know she got a letter today or that one didn't come for a long time?"

Jacob pulled the lure out of the water again and let it dangle as he regarded the boy. "Well, your mama mentioned last week to Mr. Evans over at the grocery that she hoped there was a letter soon and said it had been a long time. Folks at the post office already knew there hadn't been any Armed Forces mail for her since you folks arrived." When Byron looked puzzled, Jacob explained. "Small towns are bad when it comes to folks knowing each other's business, and small towns on islands are worse. But in hard times, we band together. Even for those not born here, there's a sort of kinship. Do you know that word?"

Byron shook his head.

"It's like we're all related, all like family. We don't always get along, and there's a good deal of judging and gossip that goes on, but when someone suffers a hurt, all of that stops. Then people gather around the one in trouble to help however they can. The postmistress, Marcia Louise, she saw your mama's letter and figured it might be bad news. She recollected your mama knew me from way back when." He grinned and shook his head. "Like I said, everybody knows everybody else's business. Anyhow, Marcia Louise figured I'd be the one to call. When she told me about the letter, I decided to bring it over to your mother myself and wait while she read it. Glad it was good news instead of bad."

Byron shook his head again, looking down as he worked the reel. Apparently that didn't always happen, that kinship thing. He hadn't felt any help or support since the shed fire, more like the opposite. But at least there was Jacob. And besides, how people here treated him wouldn't be important for long. Pretty soon be they'd be home, and his father was coming back. All he would miss about this place was Jacob.

When Byron looked up, he saw quiet concern on the older man's face, and he tried to remember where he'd lost track of the conversation. He realized Jacob might have misunderstood his head shake. "Yeah, it's great about Dad. But he's hurt, and even Mom doesn't know how bad, or at least that's what she says. I'm afraid it could be awful."

Jacob gave him a disapproving look, but there was gentleness in his eyes too. "Now don't you go borrowing trouble, son. He's coming home. That's all you need to think about. There's plenty of time to see the truth of the situation before you imagine the worst. Know what I'm saying?"

"I do, but it's hard not to worry." Byron reeled in his line, looked over his shoulder to make sure his mother wasn't there, and then swung the pole behind him for another cast. Then he whipped it forward, casting out as far as he could. As soon as the lure plopped into the water, he started reeling the line back in. "This fishing today, this was your idea." It was a statement, not a question.

"Certainly was. Thought it might be a kindness for

your mom as well as for you. I hadn't seen you after that first couple days and was trying to give you space. I heard folks talking, though, and figured you must be feeling bad about all that happened. It's time to let the past be the past. Hope you don't mind me sort of butting into your business."

"No, sir. Seems like forever since I felt, well, normal. Thanks, Mr. Jacob."

"Not sir and not mister. I'm just Jacob to you, remember?"

Waves slapped against the rocks, and two reels whirred. As they cast and reeled, cast and reeled, Byron watched the terns dipping and wheeling like fighter planes. Sometimes the larger gulls would sail through them and dive headfirst into the water, coming up with bait fish. Then other gulls would come out of nowhere and chase the ones with the fish. All the while he watched, he continued casting.

"How come I'm not getting any bites? Am I doing it wrong?"

"Not far as I can see. I haven't had a hit in a while either."

"Think I scared 'em away?"

Jacob grinned at him and teased, "Good Lord, boy, every little wrong in the world isn't your fault! You didn't do a darned thing wrong. Mackerel move pretty fast, sometimes circling back along the shore, sometimes not. Depends on the tide, the size of the school, and the bait fish they can find. Sometimes they go out farther than we can cast."

"Should we go someplace else, then? Farther down the beach? If they're moving, maybe they're down a ways." Byron looked down the long row of jetties, almost evenly spaced, as far as he could see. "Maybe it would be better down at that next jetty?"

"We could move, but we're probably better off staying here. We could lose the school while we're moving," Jacob said. Byron figured they'd already lost the school.

"*There* we go!" Jacob said louder than Byron ever heard him say anything. He yanked back hard on his pole, which was bent almost double and bouncing up and down as he reeled. Whatever he had was taking the line sideways, and fast! "There we go," Jacob said again more quietly as he maneuvered his catch in closer to the rocks. "Well, would you look at that. See 'em? Looks like we got a two-fer."

Byron looked down into the water, but the fish were so well camouflaged that he couldn't make out their shapes until they were right at the surface. There were two, just like Jacob said, and they were big! Each one was almost a foot long, shiny bluish-black shadows with black stripes across the top.

"Quick, throw your line straight out where mine was, as far as you can throw. Hurry now while I get these onto the stringer. Your lure in the water'll keep the school here."

Byron did as Jacob told him and was reeling back for all he was worth when he got a hit. He yanked back to hook the fish, but he missed it and stopped reeling. His face showed his dismay.

"No, don't stop! He'll hit it again, or another one will. Keep reeling. Keep reeling!"

The second time he felt the hit, Byron reacted faster, and the weight didn't go away. Reeling was much harder now, but he finally had one! He kept reeling and pulling back, but the fish didn't seem to be getting any closer. How far out had his lure been? Finally, it broke the surface of the water and he saw it. It looked huge!

"Keep reeling, Byron. Don't let up on him, and don't let him turn around. Get him in a little closer. Here, let me get hold of your line, and I'll flip him up top here so he doesn't get loose down in the rocks. Almost, almost. There!"

Byron looked at his fish, proud of himself, and smiling so hard his face felt like it would split wide across.

"Mind the other hooks while he's flopping around, Byron." Jacob held the fish down with one foot. "We don't want him to get himself back in the water. You should get him off the hook and onto the stringer so we can get our lines back out there. Or you want me to do the first one and you watch how?"

Byron nodded and felt his smile fade. He felt a little like a baby, needing to have somebody take his fish off the hook, but he was afraid of all the other hooks. Maybe he could learn. It was pretty cool how Jacob backed the hook out the fish's lip, and then held the fish and coached, "Here, lad, put your finger in through the mouth and out the gill, like I'm holding him. That'll give you a solid grip. Then don't let go."

"It won't bite?"

"Not so you'd notice. It's the dorsal fin spines you need to watch. But you're tough. Got him? Yup, that's right."

The fish was slimy in his hand, much more slippery than the ones he caught on the dock with his mother, and he had to hold tight.

As he worked, Byron heard his mother calling from the beach, "What'd he get, Mr. Swain?"

"You show her," Jacob said. "You're the one who caught him." Byron was afraid he was going to drop the fish, but he held it high so his mother could see it. She gave him her brightest smile along with a little cheer.

"Okay now, let's get him on the stringer," Jacob coached. "Remember, you put him on the same way as you got your finger in to hold him—the stringer leader through the gill and out the mouth, then push him down with the others, fasten the stringer to that rock again, and set the stringer back in the water."

Byron wanted to do it himself, but he hesitated. "Should you do it? What if I drop him and he gets away?"

"Well, that could happen, but I think you'll do fine. Anyhow, practicing's how you learn. You wouldn't believe how many fish I've accidentally thrown back! It's part of being a fisherman, and no mistake."

Okay, so he'd try. And what would be so awful if he dropped it anyway? He knew Jacob wouldn't make fun of him, whatever happened. As he bent down to pick up the stringer, already heavy with what Jacob had caught, Byron's foot slipped, and he gasped. He thought for sure he'd fall in again, just like that first night he was out here by himself.

But a big hand circled his arm and steadied him. "Whoa, now!" Jacob said with a big grin. "Thought we decided to save those swimming lessons till later." When Byron had his balance, he bent down and successfully added his fish to the stringer. Now that he could see all of them up close, it was clear that his fish wasn't as huge as it looked jumping out of the water, not nearly as big as the biggest one Jacob caught. But it was still good, and he felt even better when he saw Jacob's face, and heard what he said. "Good job, Byron! Now get your lure right back out there and catch another one!"

Jacob did catch another little one, and they each had a strike that they missed, but then the action stopped, and it was just the rhythm of cast and reel, cast and reel again for what seemed like a long time. Looking around, Byron noticed that his mother was walking up the beach, bending down to pick up things, probably shells or beach glass. Looking the other direction, he could see someone standing a ways down the beach. The person looked small, but he couldn't tell if it was a little kid or just somebody far away. For some reason, it made him wonder what Jacob looked like when he was little. As old as Jacob looked, how long ago was *that*?

"You said you were here when my mother was young, Jacob? And you were old enough then to be running that same store. Have you always lived here, then?"

The man didn't answer right away, and Byron thought he might not have heard. He was about to repeat his question when Jacob answered in a low voice, "Well, I was born here on the island, and I did grow up here, yes. That bait shop was my uncle's before it was mine, and one member or another of my family's run it for as long as anybody here can remember. But no, I haven't always lived here. I went away for a while, worked on the mainland. A long while, really."

"Why'd you leave?"

Again the answer was slow in coming, and Byron was all ears. Jacob had been quick to answer all his other questions. Why was this so different?

"Well, boy, it's complicated."

That was adult language for "you're not old enough to understand," but Byron waited. Only the sound of the waves slapping against the jetty rocks and crashing on shore broke the silence. Finally, Jacob turned to face him. "It's not a story you need to hear, Byron. I don't even like to remember it."

Now Byron *really* wanted to know the reason Jacob left the island, but it seemed like the man was done talking. "I'm not a little kid, you know," Byron prompted after a few minutes of silence.

"I know you're not. It's not your age. Well, maybe it is a little bit. But it's more that it's personal business, Byron. And it's not my way to talk about past sadness in my life. It wouldn't matter how old you were." He motioned to Byron's line in the water, and his tone changed. "Say, you didn't let that lure sink to the bottom, did you?"

Byron didn't realize he had stopped reeling until Jacob asked him, and when he'd stopped he didn't know. *Oh, no*, he thought. He forgot what Jacob was saying about sadness, pulled back hard on his pole, and started reeling. There was resistance, and at first he thought he had a humongous fish. The pole bent, and he tried to reel faster, sure he had a monster, but then he couldn't reel in any more.

"Best you stop. Looks like it might be hung up. Here, let me see," Jacob said as he held out his hand for Byron's pole. It bent when he pulled back on it and straightened when he let off the pressure. "Caught in the rocks on the bottom, I'd say, or maybe driftwood." He passed the pole back to Byron and pointed back toward shore. "If you walk around it, might be you can get it loose."

"What?" Byron had no idea what Jacob meant and felt stupid again. If his lure was stuck down there, then that meant he couldn't get it back. His mother had just bought it, and he'd already lost it! He glanced to where he'd seen her, but she was still beachcombing. Good. But what the heck did "walk around it" mean?

When he saw that Byron didn't move and then realized that the look on his face indicated total confusion, Jacob explained. "Looks like your lure's stuck there." Jacob pointed. "You might be able to get it free if you can get behind it so you can pull it back out instead of tightening it in same way it got caught. That's your best chance. Tide's running the right way too."

Byron still didn't understand, and he knew it showed on his face, but he didn't want to admit it. Did Jacob mean he should swim out into the water, out past where he'd cast the lure in the first place? He couldn't mean that. But Jacob smiled and put a hand on his shoulder, physically turning him so he was facing shore, and Byron was relieved. There was no impatience or irritation in Jacob's voice when he spoke—he was teaching. "It's kind of a trick. Course it's much easier in a boat, but sometimes you can do it fishing from shore, and I think that might work this time."

Byron still had no idea what Jacob was talking about, but it was sounding less intimidating by the moment.

"It's easy. Walk back down the jetty to shore. Then walk down the beach that way." Jacob pointed again. "Mind you, let out lots of line as you go, or the line'll break. Once you're opposite of where you are now—behind where it got hung up—try working it loose. Then as soon as it lets go, if it ever does, reel in like the dickens to keep it off the bottom."

A trick. Byron nodded. That made sense. In a way, it was what he did to get his foot loose when he fell in that time, pulling it a different direction. It might not work to free the line, but he could try. It would be better than losing his new lure without even trying.

"I can help you if you want," Jacob offered, "even do it for you. But I think you can do it by yourself."

"Yeah, I want to try it myself."

"Good boy. And Byron, if this doesn't work, that's okay. If a man doesn't lose a lure once in a while, he's no fisherman. You got it?"

As he reviewed Jacob's instructions and started toward the beach, Byron realized that he felt good, even though this was another kind of mess-up. Jacob had almost called him a man just then. He said "if a *man* doesn't lose a lure," and he was talking about him! Jacob wasn't making a big deal out of this and was teaching him a way to fix a problem instead of worrying about it. Well, not for sure to fix it, but *maybe* fix it. But he was still looking at that instead of at the problem. That felt important, like he should remember it.

He saw that his mother was back from her walk, sitting on her towel again. She looked like a little girl, he thought, with her knees pulled up to her chest, shading her eyes. When she saw him coming down the jetty, she stood up and called, "You finished already?"

"Nope, getting my line unstuck," he called back, jumping down to the sand. Even if it didn't work, he felt proud about trying and glad Jacob was letting him do it by himself. That was when he saw his mother approaching with her hand out like she planned to take his fishing pole and "help" him. "Rabbits and squirrels," he muttered under his breath.

Byron hadn't realized that Jacob was behind him until the man spoke. "Mrs. Douglas, how 'bout you and me take a stroll down the beach a ways and see what we can find. We can let young Byron do this on his own. Sound good?"

His mother hesitated for only a moment before she seemed to understand. "Surely, Mr. Swain. If Byron thinks he'll be okay, that is. By?"

"I can do it, Mom. Jacob told me what to do," he answered and watched the two adults turn and walk in the opposite direction from where he would go to walk around his stuck line. They walked slowly, looking down at the sand and talking like old friends as they went. Good.

Trying to get the line loose wasn't as easy as Jacob made it sound, but Byron kept at it. He felt it come free once, and he reeled in fast like Jacob told him, but it got stuck again. This time it was closer to shore but still too far for him to wade out and get it, so he kept working at it. It felt like maybe the hooks had snared something too heavy for him to reel in, and he was afraid he'd break the pole or the line if he pulled too hard. Byron looked back down the beach, hoping his mother and Jacob wouldn't return until he'd recovered the doggone thing. He was relieved to see them far away, looking as small as that figure he saw earlier from the end of the jetty, but in the other direction. He searched for the little figure, but whoever it was must have gone home or walked farther down the beach, because Byron couldn't see anybody.

Wading in up to his ankles, Byron continued trying to free the lure. When he held the pole up so the line tightened, he could see that it met the water only about fifteen feet from shore. The lure should be right below it, right? How deep could that be? Maybe he could wade out the rest of the way, reach down, and yank it loose. But what if he fell and went under? He shuddered and his vision swam. Maybe he'd never come up.

Byron took two steps back toward the shore and looked up at the sky. The cloud cover was getting heavy and it seemed windier. Maybe his mother was right about a storm coming. Deep breaths. He was okay. Nothing bad was going to happen. What was wrong with him anyway? Even little kids went in the water!

"Nooo!" the long, wavering cry sounded from down the beach, not the direction his mother and Jacob had gone, but where he'd seen that other person. He whipped his head around, searching for the source of the sound. "*Nooooooo!*" This time the voice was louder, frightened and pleading. Then he saw her, out at the end of the next jetty down the beach, a little girl wearing red shorts and a yellow shirt. He could see she had her hands over her face. "Go *away!*" she screamed as clear as anything. How could he hear her so clearly when she was so far away? Maybe it was the wind. And who was she talking to?

Out of the corner of his eye, Byron saw a flash. A dog! At first he thought it was the mother dog from the shed. He hadn't seen her since the day of the fire, but that was okay because whenever he thought of her, he felt awful. He hoped she knew he didn't mean to hurt her puppies. Maybe she was here because she belonged to the little girl. Then the dog disappeared, reappearing seconds later much farther down the beach, closer to the jetty where the little girl stood. Then it disappeared again. *Not the mother dog*, Byron thought. Dropping his pole in the sand, Byron took off at a run. The figure he saw couldn't be anything except his ghost dog, Pharaoh, and now both of them were headed toward the little girl.

By the time he got to the jetty where she was, the little girl was climbing down the rocks toward the water, and he could hear her sobbing. "No, don't go down there!" Byron shouted as he climbed out onto the rocks. "You'll fall in!" Pharaoh was appearing and disappearing at the end of the jetty, looking as if he was barking the whole time, but Byron couldn't hear a sound. "Wait!" he called to the little one. "I'll be there in a second! Don't move!" By now he could see her face clearly, and for a moment she seemed to see him. Then her eyes glazed over, and she turned back to the water.

He had almost reached her when he heard her say, "I can't find my baby," and then as she climbed down closer to the water, he heard "there's no one." That was the last thing she said before she sat down on a slanted rock, put both feet into the water, and slipped in. Then she was gone.

Byron froze. Maybe he should call for help. But who would hear him? He couldn't even see his mother and Jacob from this jetty. There was only him, and he couldn't swim. If he tried to help her, he could die.

Suddenly, Pharaoh was standing beside him, staring at him with those strange gold eyes. The dog was huge, his back even with Byron's waist. Byron remembered the darkness that enveloped him on the path and in his dreams, and for a moment got lost in those terrifying memories. But Pharaoh being here made him feel stronger. He wondered how could he be terrified of dreams but not of an immense ghost dog? Without thinking any more about it, he ran to the end of the jetty and threw himself into the water where he'd seen the little girl go down.

The water closing over his head was a shock, and he choked on what he inhaled. Coughing and sputtering, he remembered Jacob telling him to stay calm and keep moving his arms and legs. So he did. Jacob had also told him to keep his head out of the water, but it was too late for that. Then he felt something brush his leg, and he hollered. A shark or a crocodile must be trying to get him! But he pushed back the fear and reached down to grab hold of whatever it was. It was a little arm! He yanked hard and pulled her up, getting her head above the surface while he tried to keep from inhaling more water himself. She was tiny, but holding her up with one arm made it much harder to keep his own head above water. He couldn't let her go!

She wasn't struggling. In fact, she wasn't moving at all. Was he too late? He didn't know what to do, except that he had to keep moving if he didn't want the water to drown him. The current had carried the two of them away from the jetty, a little closer to the beach, but to Byron it still seemed like a mile. As the waves rose and fell, Byron knew he had to concentrate on staying calm, or they were both going to drown. And he had to keep moving. He kept kicking his legs as hard as he could, but he was already tired.

From far off, he heard someone calling his name—far away but getting closer. With one arm, he held the girl close to him, looking into the little face while he struggled to keep both their noses in the air. There was a blue color in her lips, almost purple. Lips shouldn't be blue. He *had* to keep moving! The voice got louder and louder, until all at once someone grabbed hold of them, carrying both of them toward shore. It was Jacob. "It's all right now, lad. I've got you. I've got you both."

On the beach, his mother examined him all over for wounds, her face pale from fear and anger. "What made you do that? You can't swim! I could have lost you. Why did you *do* things like this?"

Byron didn't answer her. He felt himself shaking all over, even his stomach, but he didn't know why, because he wasn't cold. His mother had asked him why he did it, and he had no idea. He thought about Pharaoh, wondering again how he could be scared of the water but not the fact that there was a ghost dog following him around. And how was he so sure that Pharaoh was the animal's name? It was crazy. Byron looked around, wondering where the dog went.

As Jacob laid the little girl on her stomach in the sand and turned her head to one side, Byron watched. Jacob was trying to make her breathe again, the way he raised her arms and then pushed down on her back, making a rhythm that was kind of like breathing. "Come on back, little one," Jacob said. "Come on. You can hear me, I know you can." At first nothing happened, but then water came rushing out of her nose and mouth, and she coughed and choked as Jacob helped her sit up. Her eyes were wild, darting looks at the three people in front of her. She didn't seem to know where she was.

Then she shook her head and heaved a great breath for such a little person, pushing the wet hair out of her eyes. At that moment she didn't look at all like the child she was but like a much older person, and what she said was very strange under the circumstances. "Thank the Lord you've finally come. I was all alone. But it's too late for the baby." Then Byron understood. Now he knew what she was trying to get away from on the jetty, the reason she hadn't seemed to hear him. Had she been walking the path in that same place by the rocks? He knew the answer was yes and was positive that it was her rag doll he'd seen there.

The little girl was crying now, her voice very different from what it had been just moments before. It was high and frightened, once again a little girl's voice. "I want my mommy. Where's my mommy?"

Still sitting next to her in the sand, Jacob smiled at her. "I don't know, little Miss Cheryl Anne, but we'll find her for you. Don't you worry."

When she stared at him wide-eyed, he patted her hand. "You know me, Cheryl Anne. From church. I know you do. I'm Jacob, remember?"

He took off his jacket and put it around her. When she finally met his eyes and nodded, he continued. "There you go. Was your mama down here with you?"

"I don't know," the little one wailed, overwrought and struggling to stand. "I don't know! I was just here, and I felt all black. And my dolly, I lost my dolly!"

"I'm not sure where your folks are, but we'll find 'em. You take it easy now. You're okay. You fell in the water is all, and this young man pulled you out. See young Byron over there? He's the one pulled you out of the drink."

The drink, Byron thought. What a strange way to put it.

To Byron's mother Jacob said, "She's Cheryl Anne Hopkins. Lives about half a mile inland from your place. That's a long way from home on her own, but she, well, I'm told she wanders a bit when things get 'loud' at home. If you get my meaning."

When Byron looked down at her, it seemed the girl saw him for the first time. In her eyes, he caught a look that made him very glad he'd be going home in a few days. It was the same haunted look he'd seen more than once on his own face in the mirror after one of those nightmares. "So she'll be okay? Really okay?" he asked both adults.

Jacob regarded Byron and then smiled down at Cheryl Anne. "She's fine, only scared. Right, little miss? We'll get you home straight away." He got her to her feet, and she wrapped both arms around his legs. Byron thought that meant she finally knew who he was and trusted him.

"You know you saved her, young Byron," said Jacob Swain. "You surely did. That was pure courage, going in after this little one when you knew you couldn't swim. Even folks that know how to swim would've hesitated, but you, you went right in after her. Pure courage, and that's for sure. I know your dad will be real proud of you."

His mother was smiling and nodding. "He will," she said. "And I am, too. That was very brave, sweetheart."

"I was scared," was all he could think of to say. His mother started crying then, but she did look proud, just like she said. She seemed to be waiting for him to respond. "There was no one else," Byron said. He was looking past Jacob at a figure materializing a little ways up the beach. It was Pharaoh, mouth open and panting, wagging that long whip tail of his. Byron wondered again how he could be so sure of the animal's name. It must be kind of like mind reading.

Byron started to point at him, wanting to tell what he was seeing, but he put his arm back down. He'd already tried that a couple of times with his mother and that special doctor, and neither one believed him. Anyway, maybe not everyone could see Pharaoh.

But if that was so, then why could he? Had Pharaoh ever been a real dog, he wondered, a dog somebody loved, a dog that protected somebody like he seemed to be trying to protect people now? Byron thought he knew what the dog was trying to protect people from. It had to do with the screaming and the dead bodies. But what did Pharaoh have to do with all that? He had so many questions. Of course he'd heard ghost stories before, but never one about ghost animals. What happened to make a dog into a ghost? Somehow he understood that he wouldn't see Pharaoh once they left this place. Pharaoh would be staying here.

Part of him wanted to ask all those questions, wanted to talk to somebody who would listen and help him figure this out. But maybe you had to wait before you could talk about some things, wait until you had a chance to think about them a long time. Probably some things you shouldn't tell at all.

He thought he would talk to Davy when he got home and later on maybe his father.

When I get home, he thought to himself. He thought he'd be okay at home, that all this trouble would stay here, and that it wouldn't follow him except for what he remembered. He hoped the nightmares would end and that he could forget about those puppies. Well, maybe not forget, but not have to think about them all the time. He hoped the sadness would fade. Yes, he thought he'd be okay, but as he looked back at little Cheryl Anne, he wasn't so sure about her. And were there others?

Chapter 12

Jack Doyle—2016

JACK WAS AT THE HEAD of the path when music started coming from his pocket, and it was a few seconds before he realized what it was. Hannah had laughed at him when he chose the most old-fashioned kind, what she called a flip phone, but he hadn't even wanted that. All these years he'd been fine without a cell phone. Still she insisted, "You're spending all summer in a house with no landline, Dad. You should have a way to contact people." She was probably right, but it felt like a leash.

He tried to answer the phone, but big as the buttons were, he couldn't see them. "Daggone thing," he muttered, patting every jacket and pants pocket before he finally found his glasses. The music stopped at the exact moment he put them on, and then the phone beeped at him. "Missed Call April 9," it said on the screen. "Yeah, I know," he told the phone. He'd figure out later who called, but it was probably Hannah checking on him. Nobody else would call.

Wind gusted up the path, spraying sand in his face. He didn't mind what the radio called unseasonably cool temperatures here on the island, but he didn't like it when sand got in his eyes or worse yet, his ears. He raised his jacket collar.

Harsh cries overhead drew his attention, a trio of gulls heading down toward the shoreline. It seemed like you could see more sky here than at home, and it was constantly changing. As he watched, heavy clouds piled up, blew apart, and then piled up somewhere else. *Windier up there,* he thought. *Mara loves windy days.* "Used to love," he corrected himself out loud.

It had been six months since Mara died, and the acute pain of her absence had eased some. What was left was a constant ache. Jack missed his wife, especially the little things that were just between two people who love each other, but most of all he missed the man he'd been with her. Now he wasn't sure who he was supposed to be or what he was supposed to do. That was why he was on this island, to try to work that out.

"Have to remember to call Hannah," Jack reminded himself.

Her taking-care-of-Dad behavior started shortly after Mara died, and though he sometimes wanted to tell his daughter to back off, he didn't. It was out of love, he knew, and he didn't want to hurt her feelings. Besides, at least Hannah was still talking to him. Near the end, when Mara had signed that paper saying she didn't want machines keeping her alive, Jack didn't try to change her mind. As far as their son Sean was concerned, honoring that wish was the same as murder. He blamed his father for his mother's death and hadn't talked to him since, though their relationship was never great to begin with. Hannah was a child of his sobriety, but Sean was old enough to remember the drinking years, just like some of Mara's friends did.

Jack sighed and shuffled his feet in the sand, remembering things that hurt. It seemed like the drinking came on slowly at first, but when it got bad, his wasn't the only life that got screwed up. Sometimes he wished people could shake themselves like wet dogs did and have all their regrets fly off like dirty water. He would love to do that, but life wasn't that easy. He sighed. All he could do now was stay sober and keep trying to do better.

When he told Hannah he wanted to figure out what was next for him, she thought he was making a bucket list. That wasn't it, but he didn't correct her because the real reason would frighten her, and it would hurt. He needed a reason to keep living.

The way Jack saw it, everybody was here to do some job in life, like a mission, and they wouldn't die till they finished it. Fine, he could buy that. After he got sober, he believed his job was to be a better husband and father, and he worked hard at both. But after sixty-six years of living, with Mara was gone and the kids grown, here he still was. If people were right about that mission thing, then he apparently wasn't finished with whatever he was supposed to do. By the end of the summer, he hoped he could figure out what it was. Then there might be a reason to keep getting out of bed every morning, a reason to go back to their little house and pick up the pieces. If he couldn't find a reason, well then maybe he was done.

It seemed to Jack that he did his best thinking when he was moving, so he'd come out to walk the beach this morning. Now his grumbling stomach reminded him he skipped breakfast. "So what do you think, Mara, some food first?" He knew she wasn't there, but talking to her like she was standing beside him made him feel less like he'd fallen between the cracks.

Jack turned around and started up to the house. It was Hannah who had found the ad for this "rustic island retreat" online, and the place delivered exactly that. Jack loved history—not the history of dates and governments and borders, but how regular people lived their lives. So he loved old homes, the ones with personality, and this patchwork of sections built by a series of owners was a doozy. The one thing he didn't understand was how different people could envision and execute all these additions without one of them recognizing that the house needed a front porch.

The real-estate agent claimed the oldest part of the house was the center, two small bedrooms and a parlor, with a kitchen attached at the back. Those were Jack's four favorite rooms. The gouges in the plank flooring and scars in the woodwork were much more attractive to him than the pristine surfaces in the newer rooms. Scars were signs

of living, and Jack wished he could go back in time to see
how they got there.

Despite the warm feeling of that older section, it was
there and in the back yard that Jack sometimes got what
he called a shiver or a twinge. For as long as he could
remember, he'd been able to sense things other people
didn't. Whatever you called them, spirits or ghosts, souls
or shades, phantoms or specters, they were all that was left
of people who should have moved on. When they didn't,
Jack could sense them.

It only happened occasionally when he was little,
and every time it had scared him. He thought it meant
there was something wrong with him, and he didn't tell
anyone. After a while, he decided the twinges weren't so
bad. The spirits he felt never did anything to him, didn't
even seem to know he was there. Anyway, it was kind of
interesting. He wondered then if this was one of the things
that happened to adults, one of the things like sex that
nobody talked about, and he'd asked his mother about it.

She thought he was making it all up, and for
good reason. As a kid, he had always made up stories,
embellishing them more each time he retold them. If he
jumped into a stream, then he made it a river and said
he almost drowned. If he saw a horse, he told people the
horse came right up to him and he rode it all around until
it kneeled down and let him get off. Really it was lying, but
it made him feel important.

When he told his mother about the spirits that he
sensed, she washed his mouth out with soap for lying. He
was telling the truth, and nobody believed him. He didn't

tell anybody about it for many years after that, not even his bride. Years later, after his drinking got bad, he started seeing things too. He expected the visions to stop when he got sober more than twenty years ago. They didn't.

It was only when Mara took sick and he understood she wasn't going to recover that the episodes ended. He thought it was over, until this past week showed him that wasn't the case. Though the feelings he was getting in the house were nothing compared to some previous experiences, Jack felt definite sadness and longing there. At least he thought he did, but he wondered if it was his own memories, rather than some restless spirit, that echoed in the stillness. He didn't think so. Sometimes he would enter the parlor or one of the little bedrooms and feel like he'd surprised someone crying, someone who wasn't there. The feeling never lasted for more than a few heartbeats.

An especially strong gust felt like it went right through his jacket, and he turned his back to the blowing sand. That was when Jack felt his stomach rumble again, and this time he heard it too. "Okay, okay," he said aloud, "coffee at least, and maybe a couple of those chocolate doughnuts. Anyway, my girl, that'll give the sun a chance to warm things up out here." And there it was, that pang of missing Mara.

Jack walked around to the back of the house where the door opened right into the kitchen. It felt strange to simply open a door and walk in, but apparently nobody locked anything here. That was quite a difference from back home where everybody was afraid of everybody else.

Keeping doors unlocked would take some getting used to, but he liked the idea. At least for the summer.

Inside, Jack put his hat on the table, surprised at how much sand fell off. If he didn't pay attention to that, he'd end up sleeping in grit. Then he hung his jacket over the back of a chair and glanced at the coffeemaker, but he filled the steam kettle instead. "Instant coffee," he mumbled. Mara would have crinkled up her nose and brewed some real coffee for him.

He had to find his glasses again so he could read the marks on the stove knobs. It had been a long time since he used a gas range, not since their first apartment, and it took him a few moments to get it lit. The oniony smell of the gas took him back to their newlywed days, before his drinking got bad. Good times. How long ago that seemed, yet not long at all. Time was so slippery.

While the water heated, Jack paced around the kitchen, opening cabinets and drawers, making a mental catalog of where things were. He liked to be able to put his hand on what he wanted without having to search, and being in a new place made that a challenge. The house was advertised as completely furnished, and it certainly seemed to be. The only trouble was that some things were stuck in such odd places that it took him forever to find them, like the soup ladle hanging next to the wood stove and the flashlight in the bathroom. Of course, he knew that the "right" place for something was arbitrary, and where he wanted silverware or a bottle opener might be different from where other people kept them. Still, maybe he should rearrange the place, at least the kitchen.

"Nonsense," he said out loud and shut the silverware drawer hard enough to make everything rattle. What was the use of worrying about things like that? He was a renter, for goodness sake! "Still," he whispered, "order is a good thing." He pulled his notepad from his back pocket along with the small mechanical pencil he kept in the spiral binding. Maybe order in the minors was a comfort when the majors in life were upside down or unsettled. "Reorganize kitchen," he said out loud as he jotted it down. Then he returned the notebook to his pocket so he'd have it next time he looked for it.

"Unsettled. That's it exactly, Mara. That's how the house feels." Then he sighed. "I know, there I go talking to myself again." If Mara was really here, maybe they could have talked about it. "But you never believed me about any of that, did you, dear heart?"

Jack's spirit twinges, his shivers, usually started with the certainty that someone was staring at the back of his head. Then some emotion would wash over him—fear, love, loss, anger, hope, loneliness, confusion, hostility, joy, sadness, jealousy. Many were negative, but not all. What all the feelings shared was that they were strong enough to overwhelm him, weaken him, and after the feelings hit, he sometimes saw the people.

More than what he saw, it was the memory of the emotion he felt that lingered. He assumed those emotions were the last thing those poor people felt before they died. That was puzzling, though. Surely everyone felt some strong emotion when they were dying, but most spirits didn't hang around, so what kept the ones he saw tethered to Earth? After the first few times he saw things, Jack wasn't afraid, but sometimes the hairs on his forearms or the nape of his neck would stand up. It was like his body was telling him he *should* be afraid.

He tried a few times to tell Mara about the spirits, like what he saw on Monomoy Island in Massachusetts, where a number of shipwrecks had occurred; in the foyer of Dahlgren Chapel in Maryland, where some of the faithful had been killed; at Woodlawn Cemetery in New York, the site of a Civil War prison camp; all through Walter Reed Hospital, especially at night. All were places where people had suffered and died. He'd tried to tell her, but those light-blue eyes of hers showed only concern for him and fear that he was drinking again. So he stopped talking about all of that, but it saddened him. It was something else they couldn't share because he'd broken her trust. The only other person he ever told about the spirits was his AA sponsor, and he had chalked them up to alcoholic hallucinations.

A sudden noise made him jump. *These daggone phones don't ring right*, he thought, but at least this time he already had glasses on to find the talk button. Maybe later he could figure out how to change the way it rang. "Yes. I mean, hello?"

"Mr. Doyle, good morning! Glad I caught you. This is Kelli Gregson."

Jack paused. Kelli Gregson? Oh, yeah, the real-estate agent. "Morning, Miz Gregson. What can I do for you?"

"Touching base to make sure the rental was all you expected. You getting settled okay?"

Was it the nasal quality or the pitch of her voice that made him mentally wince? "Absolutely fine."

"I also wanted to alert you about an inspector coming out this week. The owner is considering a sale of that property, but it won't affect your rental. She's looking toward the end of the season to make her final decision."

"No problem. Want me to do anything special, like leave the door open or police the area extra well?"

"No, no. They just need to confirm there are no termites or carpenter ants. The inspector will knock, of course, but he has a key in case you lock up. That's why I wanted to give you fair warning."

"As I said, it's not a problem. While I have you on the phone, can I ask you where the property lines are? I wanted to look around and don't want to trespass."

"Oh, feel free to wander. Folks in that part of the island won't mind you walking across their property. But you know, if you take that path out your kitchen door, you can walk that whole ridge and still be on either your own property or park land. The dunes between your place and the water are part of a beach-protection initiative, but you're free to use the path, like I told you when you first looked at the place."

"From what I can see, that path is the only way to get down to the shore, at least if we're supposed to stay off the dunes." She didn't respond, so he continued, "I saw the signs, so I assume the dunes are planted to combat erosion?"

"My goodness, how did you know that? But yes, replanted, actually. Historically the grasses were quite thick, but that was before dune buggies and motorcycles. We're trying to restore them and preserve the dunes. By the way, you told me you were interested in the family graveyard. Have you found it?"

Good God, that voice was like cutting Styrofoam. "No, ma'am, not yet. You said it was past those pines in the back, right? I assume it won't be hard to find."

"You'll have no trouble. And if you like history, be sure to visit our museum in town. It's attached to the library. Since there's only so much room on an island, pretty much everything here used to be something else or was built on top of something from before. It's a grim thought, building in the rubble, but I guess progress is progress. That hill where your cabin stands has apparently been a home site going back to early Native American settlements, layer built upon layer."

"Such a shame to lose all that history," Jack said. In the moment of silence that followed, he thought she was about to say good-bye, but she wasn't done being a sales brochure.

"Which is why we have such wonderful old stories and legends, to fill in the blanks. You really should visit our museum. There are real treasures there—lithographs, diaries, clothing, paintings, books, whaling records, and so much more. They have a sales ledger from a 1700s general store that was here, listing who bought what and for how much. Fascinating."

That voice. "Yes," he answered her, "I'll definitely look into it, and—"

She cut him off. "Whoops, I'm getting another call.

If you're okay there, I'll let you go. Happy to have you as a tenant, Mr. Doyle. Call me if you have any questions."

The connection was broken before Jack could respond. He shrugged at the phone in his hand, thinking his life experience with real-estate agents was pretty consistent. Then he took out his notepad and wrote, "Pest inspection. Vacuum."

He considered calling Hannah then, but the kettle started to whistle, and he turned off the burner. That whistle was a good sound, like so many other kitchen noises. He spooned the instant coffee into his mug and poured in water almost to the rim. Mara needed room for lots of sugar and milk, but he preferred the bitter taste of strong, black coffee, even the instant kind.

Though he sipped the steaming liquid gingerly, it still burned the roof of his mouth, so he sat down, holding the mug between two hands, blowing on the surface to cool it before he took a second sip. Jack decided he really didn't feel like chocolate donuts. "Maybe later. Well, beach or cemetery first?" he asked Mara and himself. He really was talking to himself more often, and he hoped he shouldn't be worried. "Not likely a problem," he mumbled. "Lots of people talk to themselves. Anyway, it's nothing new with me." Then he let his thoughts drift, staring out the window at the swaying tree branches, thinking of many things and thinking of nothing.

Jack had resolved to gift himself this time on the island, to ignore what anybody else thought about it being a waste of good money, just like he'd ignored what Mara's friends had said about how he should have let the doctors keep her alive regardless of what she wanted. His son wasn't the only one who thought he'd as good as murdered her, and though he could ignore what her friends had said, it was hard ignore his own son.

If only Sean would talk to him. Jack wanted to explain that he had wanted Mara to change her mind about the machines too, wanted to talk her out of giving up. But it was her life, and if she was ready to let go, nobody else had a right to make her stay. At least that was what he believed, though it broke his heart.

He wished Sean would let him explain other things, like how he understood why their relationship was difficult even before Mara's death. He'd been a drunk when Sean was young, and he remembered once when Sean told him he wished he had a different father. Jack got really angry at the time, but he understood now and wanted Sean to know that. Why wouldn't a kid want someone who was around more, someone who paid more attention to him in a good way? And why wouldn't he want a father who was a better provider? Money wasn't the most important thing, but Jack could see how different Sean's life trajectory might have been with a little more money at key points early on.

It wasn't that Jack lacked intellect or talent, but until he got sober, all he wanted to do was drink, and even cheap whiskey cost money. Mara had worked all during those years, for a while at a bookstore in town, and the rest of the time she cooked for a little luncheonette. Neither job paid much, but at least her income was steady.

He worked menial jobs because they were easy to get and never required much of him, but he never kept them for long. He'd done maintenance work, yard work, and all sorts of odd jobs. He'd been a night watchman, a substitute lighthouse keeper, a grave-digger, and a janitor at Walter Reed Hospital. He'd carried stone to repair jetties in National Seashore sites from Cape Cod to Cape Canaveral. Sometimes he was gone for weeks. Maybe Sean was ashamed of him for doing that kind of work when most of his friends' fathers were white-collar men. Jack wondered how much more ashamed his son would be if he knew about other things, like the strange women Jack had found in his bed when he came to some mornings. He wondered if Mara ever guessed.

In spite of his being gone and what he did for a living, Jack believed that if he'd shown an honest interest in the boy when he was young, all the rest would have mattered much less. He couldn't change the past, but maybe they could find a way to get along. If only he could get Sean to talk to him.

By the time Jack focused again, the coffee left in his cup was cold. He downed it anyway, rinsed the cup, and dried his hands on his pants. How long had he been sitting there woolgathering? *Woolgathering.* One of Mara's words.

When he tried to stand up, Jack stumbled as his hip and knee both caught, tight from sitting too long. He held on to the chair and stretched until they loosened and then stood up tall. "Well, shall we go see if we can find this graveyard? Time we got to know the folks who used to live here." Then he grabbed his jacket and hat. Hopefully it had warmed up some outside, but it wouldn't hurt to be prepared.

Outside, he found it much warmer, and the wind wasn't blowing so hard. The clouds had thinned, and he could see the sun. Sun on his face always made him smile and pay attention to what was going on around him. What was it about that warmth that made it so different from other kinds of heat?

Between the house and the pine grove where he was headed was a broad expanse of ground that passed for a lawn, with wiry grass that was more brown than green. It crunched when he walked on it. There was a bench set just beyond the drip edge of the trees that bordered the yard, and it struck Jack that there had to be a better place for it. Maybe he'd move it out front.

As he strode toward the little forest, Jack's attention was drawn to what sounded like a sewing machine overhead. A small plane was flying low, probably headed for the tiny airport he knew was at the north end of the island, and Jack wondered if they hired out for tours. He'd arrived by ferry and thought he'd love to see the island from the air, get a better idea of how it was laid out.

Ducking under low branches, Jack pushed in among the trees. The layer of pine needles was thick and soft under his feet, and he thought this would be a great place to put a tent. The needles were sharp, though, and he wondered whether they would poke through the tent floor. To answer his own question, he squatted down to feel the ground and then decided to lie down. Yes, they were a little stickery but comfortable nonetheless. From that position, he could see the tops of the trees swaying in wind that he couldn't feel on the ground. With a sigh, Jack relaxed, closed his eyes, and listened.

Once he'd told Mara that he could hear the trees. It wasn't hearing, exactly, more like being aware of a sound that was beyond what his ears could detect. The trees sang. When he thought about it, he sounded crazy even to himself, but he told Mara anyway. He remembered that she agreed with him and how much he'd been shocked by that and excited. Then she explained what she meant, how you could hear creaking when trees leaned against each other. It turned out they weren't talking about the same thing at all.

So he'd described what he could hear, the single note that all the trees of the same kind seemed to sing, especially if there was a whole group of them together, and especially in the wind. He told her he couldn't always hear it but that he suspected they were always singing. He described how different kinds of trees sang a different note. He was going on about how he thought if a person could hear all the trees on earth singing their single notes at the same time, it would be every musical note possible. Then he saw her face, stopped talking, and never mentioned it again.

Reclining in the pine needles, Jack could almost hear the high, sweet note the pines sang. Maybe this hearing was related to feeling spirits. If he had some kind of heightened sensitivity to various vibrations, maybe that would explain both the spirits and the tree songs. They were there all the time but imperceptible to most people most of the time. *Lucky me*, he thought. Or maybe it was all in his imagination, like people always told him.

"Maybe I'm just nuts," he mumbled as he stood to brush himself off. Out of the corner of his eye, he saw a flash of movement. At first he thought it must be a rabbit or a squirrel, but it was much bigger. A fox? He'd love to see a fox or any kind of wildlife, for that matter, and he hoped he'd see it again.

The farther in among the trees he pushed, the thicker the forest seemed to get, and the darker it grew until it seemed like dusk. The air was still. Then between one step and the next, Jack found himself at the edge of a clearing with the sun in his eyes once more. The air felt lighter and easier to breathe. All through the clearing, large boulders were scattered over that same wiry grass that grew at his house, but here the ground was speckled with wildflowers he didn't recognize. Near the center was a grouping of grave markers, surrounded by a ring of white stones. Jack approached the markers and stepped carefully into the circle, wondering if it was the spirit of one of these people that he felt in the house.

He saw movement again, this time at the edge of the clearing, but again he wasn't fast enough to see what it was. With hands clasped behind his back, Jack stood in front of the largest marker, the remains of a gray stone cross. It was broken below the cross bar, and the top piece was lying on the ground. The words on the base were hard to make out, but he mentally filled in the missing letters to read the name, *Amanda K.* The last name was unreadable, and the dates might be *1818–1862*, but he wasn't sure. When he worked out what he thought the inscription said, the words chilled him, *loved them too dearly whom the sea claimed.* Words or names were written after that, but Jack couldn't read what was there.

A few feet from the cross was a marker stone only about a foot tall and more difficult to read than the cross. It was sitting crooked, the way headstones get after repeated freezing and thawing of the ground. Jack bent down to clear the grass from in front of it to read *John,* and then *infant soul,* but the rest was indecipherable, including any dates. *No last name readable on this one or the cross,* Jack thought. *Who are you folks?*

On the other side of the cross was a larger stone leaning slightly to one side. In deeply chiseled block lettering Jack could make out the whole inscription: *Edwin Nickerson 1851–1864 Beloved son and brother. Killed in battle.* Jack did the math then. God, he was young, but lots of young boys had served in the Civil War. "More's the pity," Jack said out loud. He looked again at the dates on Amanda's stone. "So are you a Nickerson too, Miss Amanda K?" Jack asked aloud. "It looks like you'd have been the right age to be this young man's mother. Were you?" Opposite the cross and facing it was a fourth headstone, not the typical granite of which the others were made. This one looked like the rock used to build the jetties here—water smoothed with what looked like barnacle scars. What he could read said *peace, daughter. Marion Ni … 1846–1859.*

It struck Jack as odd that of everything on the markers, it was the dates that seemed most deeply inscribed and the most readable after all this time. He would have thought the names more important to chisel deeply. Odd, indeed.

The only last name he had was on Edwin's

stone—Nickerson. It was reasonable to assume that the
Ni fragment on Marion's stone had been "Nickerson" as
well, and Marion might have been Edwin's wife. *No,* he
thought, *not his wife. They were too young, and both died
at thirteen. His sister, maybe, or some other relation.* It
was a leap to assume the others were also Nickersons, but
it was possible. Given the dates, it was also possible that
Amanda was the mother, and these others her children.
Certainly this graveyard had the look of a private burial
place, consistent with the way families handled things at
the time these people lived.

If they *were* all the same family, and if Amanda K was
the mother of at least some of them, it seemed the poor
woman had outlived all her children except one, Edwin.
All the children died young.

Jack searched the rest of the clearing for more markers,
but he didn't find any. Then he took his notepad from his
back pocket and revisited each stone. He sketched them
and recorded what he could read on each one. It was like a
puzzle, a history puzzle, and Jack loved those. There was a
lot of information here, but unanswered questions as well
and his mind swirled with them. If Amanda K. had lost
loved ones at sea, did that mean her husband died, or had
he abandoned her for a sailing life? There seemed to be
no marker for him here, but Jack decided he would look
around again to be sure. Apparently she lost more than
one person she loved. "Loved them," the inscription said,
not "him." Jack shook his head and smiled to himself. He
did this all the time, had done it since he was a boy. He'd
get some little pieces of information about a person or a

situation, and he would come up with a whole story. It got to be kind of a family joke, but it didn't bother him. Everybody had a story. Stories were all a person really had.

His knee twinged, and he reached down to rub it. There would be a price to pay for all the walking and standing on uneven ground, but there was no way he would settle for being sedentary. Still, it might be a good idea to rest. It didn't seem right to sit among the gravestones, so he stepped outside the stone ring and lowered himself to the ground. Then he leaned back on his hands and tilted his face up to the sun, closing his eyes as it warmed his face.

Jack's eyes snapped open when something touched his back, and he whirled around to see what it was. Whether he expected a spirit or a living human, he didn't know, but what he didn't expect was the quizzical expression on the face of a half-grown black dog. A second almost-identical animal stood about five feet behind the first, watching. They were in that adolescent stage, not puppies but not fully grown—gangly and rangy rather than pudgy and bouncy. "Hey, guys," Jack said holding out one hand, palm down. Whatever they were, they were handsome animals. The closest one sniffed him from a distance and then took a step backward. "That bad, huh?" Jack smiled. The eyes that met his were arresting, somewhere between brown and yellow in color, and a look of intelligence was evident.

Slowly Jack rearranged himself to push up to a standing position, thinking it was a much harder task than it had been only a few years ago. He kept his eyes on the dogs, and they watched him, tensed to bolt. The one that touched him moved backward until it was beside its twin, but they didn't run.

Neither one had a collar on, and as thin and scruffy as they were, it was likely they'd been fending for themselves. There wasn't a single hair except black on either of them, and they were so identical that he didn't think they could be a mixed breed, but what were they? Jack could recognize quite a few dog breeds from his work at various kennels, but these two had him stumped. They were greyhoundish in body shape, but not the face or the ears. Not Malinois or Tervuren because though their ears were erect and the body looked almost right, these guys had short, smooth coats and longer muzzles. What they looked most like was the Egyptian god Anubis. Whatever they were, it looked like they were going to be big when they finished growing.

Straightening, Jack extended his hand again, but he must have looked scarier standing than sitting, and the two ran off. Too bad. Maybe he could coax them closer if he saw them again. He watched until they disappeared into the pines, and then he brushed himself off. Looking back at the grave markers, Jack decided to revisit each one and make sure he hadn't missed anything he wanted to remember.

Stooping down on one knee in front of the broken cross, Jack cleared more of the tall grass from the base. "Well, Mrs. Amanda K. Nickerson, I'm pleased to meet you and yours." He half expected to feel a presence or a pressure. There was nothing.

One by one, he visited each of the markers, checking his notes against what he could read of the inscriptions, and then he scouted the rest of the clearing in case there was a marker outside the circle. He found none. Last, he returned to the gray stone cross.

"I'll be back with a weed trimmer and some flowers," he said. He'd negotiated a lower rent in return for keeping the grounds around his cabin tidy, and he figured it would be easy to add this little area to his list of chores.

"Well, let's go home, shall we, Mara?" he muttered and decided maybe he'd have some of those chocolate doughnuts when he got there. "And I have to remember to call Hannah."

CHAPTER 13

Jack and Sarah—2016

J ACK SAT UP WITH A start, expecting to see someone in the bedroom with him, someone who'd been watching him while he slept. "They call that paranoia, Jacko," he said to himself, trying to straighten out his tangled pajama bottoms. There was the shadow of a nightmare as well, one he couldn't quite remember, but the heavy feeling it left was hard to shake off. If Mara had been in the bed with him, he would have spooned her and gone back to sleep, but she wasn't there.

He needed to get up but he felt awful—disoriented, vaguely nauseated, and foggy-brained. It was like he'd been up all night drinking, but his last drink was twenty-two years and seven months ago. Feeling like this again for no reason was unsettling, and he thought about calling his sponsor. "Yup, just like a hangover, but I'm clean," he'd tell Preston. Maybe in the dream he was drinking, because he could almost taste whiskey. Almost. When he was first getting sober, he'd have drinking dreams fairly often, but it only happened a few times after that first year.

"Oh, for Pete's sake, quit your bellyaching and get up," he said, but when he tried to throw back the covers, his shoulder caught, and he grunted. There was that same sharp pain he'd felt every morning for the past week.

The first day it was bad enough to make him think about heart attacks. They could present that way, he knew, pain in the shoulder. But by lunch that day, the pain was gone and didn't return, so he dismissed it. He'd been doing a lot of yard work and probably pulled a muscle. When the pain was back the next morning, he wondered if his hiatal hernia was flaring up, because that sometimes hurt in weird places, and he wasn't being careful about what he ate. A couple of hours later, the pain eased again, but he propped up the head of his bed anyway so he could sleep on a slant. The next morning, the pain was back just the same, and what concerned Jack more than the way it hurt was the sense of foreboding he felt. That was supposed to be another sign of impending heart attacks in some people.

He rubbed his shoulder, cautiously trying to roll it around and then massaging it more purposefully. If he could find where the pain was centered, he could work on it. Mara had done that for him, rubbing his shoulders and his neck to find the sore places. "Feels like you've got knotted rope in there," she'd say. Then she would knead out the hurt. He wished she could do that now, wished he could feel her touch again. But he didn't believe this pain would respond, even to Mara's touch.

He shifted in bed and winced. It was much worse this morning. If he were at home, Hannah would see that something was wrong and pester him till he saw somebody about it. But she didn't know about this, and he wouldn't tell her. The truth was that he couldn't face seeing the inside of another doctor's office or hospital. Not yet. This pain would pass, and if it didn't, maybe that was okay.

"Enough," he said out loud and threw back the covers. "Up and at 'em, Jacko!" That was how his father used to wake him up when he was little, and thinking of his dad made him smile. The love he had for all six of his children had been palpable. He laughed a lot, touched a lot, and he loved playing with words. *Jacko*. It sounded like a dog's name, and Jack would never let anyone else call him that, but he liked when his father did.

He thought if he ever got a small dog like a Scottish terrier or a West Highland white, Jacko would be a perfect name. But he preferred bigger dogs, like the two at the graveyard. He'd seen them a couple of times since that first day but only from far off. Neither one of those looked like a Jacko, that was for sure.

Throwing his legs over the side of the high bed, Jack decided he really would think about getting a dog when he got back home. "Hmph, haven't thought about that in quite a while," he mused but thought it wasn't a bad idea at all. *Not till I get myself straightened out, though. Not till I know what I'll be doing for the rest of my life.*

So far this "vacation," he hadn't spent much time thinking about his future like he intended to do. Instead, it was the past that occupied his thoughts, all the things he'd done wrong, all the missed opportunities, and everything he wished he could do over. He felt stuck, his will stalled, with keen knowledge of his own shortcomings and the hole left in his life by Mara's absence. Moving forward seemed impossible. What if, like Mara, he was ready to let go?

Jack stretched his arms one at a time over his head, feeling a catch in the sore shoulder, but it was better than when he first woke up. *Best to get moving, and it'll loosen up like all those other times*, he thought. He went to the bedroom window, continuing to stretch as he walked. He always left the window open a crack at night, but he raised it all the way and watched a wisp of morning mist drift into the room. You could taste the salt in the air here.

The air coming in the window felt chilly, so he chose jeans and a flannel shirt, even though he knew he'd end up having to change later in the day. Hannah always teased him about wearing blue jeans at his age, calling him an old hippie. But she also told him he looked good in them, whether or not that was true. It didn't matter; he felt like himself in jeans. He grunted when he bent over to lace his running shoes so he loosened his belt and tried again. Maybe he could stand to lose a few pounds.

"How about a big breakfast this morning, Mara?" Thoughts of losing weight would have to wait. Although he hadn't been hungry the past few days, Jack pulled waffles and a package of sausage from the freezer. "Good excuse for maple syrup," he said with a grin. Used to be that a meal like that took half an hour to put together, assuming you knew how to make waffles, and then cleaning the iron afterward was a chore of another level. These days, you popped the waffles into a toaster, cooked the sausage in the microwave, and poof, it was all done. No cleanup either. It didn't taste quite as good as scratch, but still a blessing when you were hungry. "Still a blessing." That was something else Mara used to say. However many times it happened, he was always surprised when her words came out of his mouth, and at the same time it felt good, it also made the loss of her feel fresh.

While the microwave hummed and he waited for the toaster to pop, Jack leaned against the counter and looked outside. It was hazy out there, but maybe the sun would burn it off. He wanted to get down to the ocean today before it got too late. The beach in the morning was his favorite time, but he'd only made it there a couple of times since arriving. As each day started, it seemed like he got going on one project or another, and then the day would be over. He'd spent time in town looking around and doing a little shopping, time at the wharf talking to people, time reading on the bench, time tending the gravesites and grooming the yard, and too much time rearranging the kitchen. Today would be different. First he would go outside to eat his breakfast, and then, by golly, he was going the beach. And he intended to take his new fishing gear.

A couple of days before, Jack had succeeded in dragging the bench from the back yard to the seaward edge of the property where the path downhill began. That's where he sat with his plate of toaster waffles and sausage, his mug of coffee beside him. Maybe after he was done he would sit a little longer, look around, and appreciate all this. But no, he told himself, that was how whole days managed to disappear. He could "appreciate all this" just as well from down on the beach, throwing his line in the water!

With his shirt cuff, he wiped a drip of syrup from the corner of his mouth and looked down the narrow path winding through the dunes toward the water. Its sides were steep in places, V-shaped where the dunes slanted sharply up on both sides, with fragments of snow fence showing through. "Wonder why the wind doesn't fill that in with sand," he wondered out loud. A person could stand in those deepest places and be invisible from either uphill or downhill. Though he could see the expanse of blue water above the dunes on the horizon, he couldn't see a bit of the rocky beach or the jetties that jutted out from the shoreline like whiskers. It was a longer way down than it seemed.

Well, up and at 'em, he thought again as he got to his feet to take the dishes inside. There was no one here but him, so he'd worry about washing them later, but he had to go back in anyway to get his fishing gear, and with that in hand, he started downhill to the beach.

In minutes his old Saucony walkers filled with sand, but he kept going in increasingly heavy shoes until they were too uncomfortable. "So much for shoes," he muttered and tried to stand on one foot and take them off one at a time. But his balance wasn't what it used to be, and finally he had to drop all the fishing gear and lean against one of the boulders piled up where he'd stopped. In that position, he tried rubbing the heel of each shoe off with the other foot, but he kept losing his balance anyway. Finally, he gave up and sat down on a rock. It was when he picked up his shoes and stood to dump out the sand that the memory of other sand-filled shoes hit him, one of the memories he wished he could burn out of his brain.

It was right before he first tried to stop drinking, a late August day when the kids were little and the whole family was visiting Mara's brother in Point Pleasant, New Jersey. Her brother's place was a couple of blocks off the beach, near the end of the boardwalk, and it would have been wonderful if it hadn't been charity. The only way they got to take vacations back then was if a family member gave them a place to stay and fed them.

Jack was just coming back after being at a bar all afternoon, a place that had quarter beers as a promotion. Those were the days. The beer was awful, but if you drank enough, it got the job done. He was covered with sand from a couple of falls, and though he didn't remember being on the beach, his shoes were full of sand too, so he tried to take them off. It wasn't that he wanted to keep sand out of the house, simply that he wanted to sneak in and go up to bed without anybody knowing. That was when he saw Mara come out the back door, and having her catch him like that made him mad.

He was dumping sand out of the shoe in his hand when she walked up to him, and there she was with that look on her face, half sympathy and half disappointment.

So he hit her with the shoe. Hard. In the face. She didn't fall, but she stumbled backward with a stunned look, more sad than anything else. Then he hit her again, and that time she went down. To this day, he didn't know why he did it. She hadn't said one word to incite him and didn't say a word after he hit her. He had never done that before—not that he remembered.

When her brother and his wife came out, nobody shouted, nobody touched him, nobody did anything to him. They gathered her up like they were expecting this and took her inside. Him they left outside in the dark. When he tried the door as quietly as he could, he found it locked. He spent that night in the car.

She left him after that, or rather she and the kids stayed in New Jersey with her brother's family, and they told him they didn't care where he went. He went home. It was the worst time of his life. He loved Mara despite what he'd done and how he sometimes acted. Drunk or sober, working or not working, she was the center of his life. The problem was he forgot that and hadn't told her in a long time how important she was to him. He couldn't remember the last time he told her he loved her and had to admit that the way he lived conveyed quite the opposite message. He was frightened then, afraid he'd understood too late, afraid he'd lost her forever.

That was when he decided to stop drinking. Of course he knew about AA, but he told himself he wasn't a joiner, hated listening to other people whine, and was sure he could quit on his own. He figured he could do whatever he put his mind to. When that didn't work, he tried setting different kinds of limits for himself, like only drinking on weekends, then letting himself have just one drink a day, and finally he tried drinking only beer. None of those tricks worked either.

When he heard one of the guys on a job he was working say he couldn't go out with the others because he had AA that night, Jack asked if he could go along. He didn't even know he was going to ask till after it came out of his mouth, but the guy said, "Sure," and Jack went with him. That was the beginning of sobriety except for a couple of slips in the first few months when he got cocky. He'd been sober since, one day at a time.

Getting work was even harder than getting sober, though, and he could get only sporadic and short-term jobs. Sometimes he had to choose between buying food and paying rent. He always chose rent because he thought he'd never get Mara back if he lost their house. The house wasn't really theirs, not till years later, but they'd lived in it a long time, and he believed that little place mattered to Mara. For him it was a sort of touchstone.

Not drinking, doing whatever jobs he could get, going to AA meetings, and working the steps, little by little the fog cleared. He never touched another woman except Mara after he got sober. Finally, after a year of begging for another chance, Mara came back, but only after he convinced her he'd stopped drinking. He really had.

From the day she came back to this one, Jack hadn't taken another drink, and he never again raised his hand or even his voice to Mara, but he never forgot his shame. The first day she returned to their little house, she said she forgave him and that she loved him. After that day, neither of them ever mentioned the incident in Point Pleasant again, not one word. In a way, it was as if it never happened, but he remembered, and he knew she did too. When he was honest with himself, he had to admit it was never the same between them. What a loser he was. He had hurt the love of his life, betrayed her trust, and spoiled what they had. He would have spent the rest of his life trying to make it up to her, showing her how much he loved her, but now he couldn't. She was gone, and she wasn't coming back. Regret choked him.

For a split second, Jack felt someone watching him and whirled around to see who it was. No one. Then it was like something crashed into him. He grunted and fell to his knees, feeling a suffering presence all around him, a woman in pain. He realized what was happening then, another spirit, but never in his previous experiences had it felt like this. This was like an assault. He couldn't see her; instead he seemed to be seeing through her eyes. Images from someone else's past came into focus behind his closed eyelids. They remained even after he opened his eyes, overlaying the present like a double-exposed photograph. Never had he experienced anything like this, and never had he been this afraid.

Jack registered his own adrenaline response—heart beating harder, breathing faster, muscles tensed—but he felt other sensations that puzzled him. His throat was dry, and he ached all over while the pain in his shoulder seared him. It felt like he'd been branded. Jack fought to stand and then locked his knees and leaned back against the rocks, allowing his chest to collapse. He gagged, feeling a hand tight around his throat, and all he could think of was the baby. *What baby?*

His mind swirled with images of people he didn't recognize, but he knew each one of them. Friends. Family. First there was the furor of a battle, and then stillness, sorrow, and finally total aloneness. Rather than solitude, it was isolation, and there was a voice calling. Jack leaned deeper into the rocks, letting his chin drop, barely breathing. The rocks held him upright, cold and hard.

His own memories intertwined with Sarah's. He had hurt the only woman he ever truly loved, hurt her deeply, pushed her away, and now she was alone somewhere, bodies all around her. He could hear her calling, but he couldn't reach her. Even if he could, how could she ever trust him again? He'd left her and the children, and he didn't deserve to be loved. He was alone, forever alone.

Sarah burrowed deeper inside him and became him as he became her. They were all gone now, except for the friends lying butchered among the charred remains of homes and barns. There was no one left, no one to hear the voice that was hoarse from crying. Helpless, hopeless, grieving. The baby was buried right here in these rocks. Right here, poor little lamb.

Jack felt weak, and the big muscles in his legs shook. But of course he was weak; she had lost a lot of blood when she was shot. *She'd been shot? She?* He sank to the ground again and pulled aside his jacket and shirt to examine her wound, the flesh around it putrid and rotting like the carcasses of massacred friends.

Her wound? She?

Why was she still alive when all the rest were dead? What was the point of her being alive if there was no one else? And she was so thirsty, it was maddening—not hungry anymore but thirsty beyond all explaining.

She?

And hot. She was hot even with the wind and the sea as cold as ice.

But how could he be "she" when he was Jack Doyle? His vision was blurry and sepia-toned, brownish-red like dried blood. Maybe he should end all this. It would be better then. No pain and no tears.

Jack's own mind clawed to the surface, clutching for reality, struggling to shake off what wasn't his. That was when he heard the barking. Closer, louder, more threatening, deep-voiced barks interspersed with snarling. It sounded like a dogfight, or like the alarm the dogs had raised when the Indians attacked, dogs fighting for their lives and defending their masters. But no, he was confused again—that never happened, not to him. Jack tried to put his hands on his temples, trying to focus, but only one arm worked. He fought for control and tried to take a deep breath, desperately trying to shake the feeling of a stranger sitting on his chest. The smell of charred wood and rotting flesh was in his nostrils, and clawing fear still threatened to choke him. But Jack mustered all the force of will he'd ever had and pushed her out. For just a flash, he saw her, badly scarred face streaked with dirt, long skirts tattered and bloodstained, and looking exhausted. But when he tried to focus on her face, the image faded, leaving in his mind one thought: *I am Sarah.*

Sarah? Was he Sarah? Of course he wasn't, he was Jack Doyle. Jack fought to collect confused thoughts. *But it felt like I was her,* he thought. The barking sounded closer, but considering what he'd just been through, Jack wasn't sure what he thought he heard was real. He shook his head, trying to remember where he was and how he got here. He felt himself breathing fast with his mouth open. He wanted to vomit, but he had to get away from here!

Jack tried to stand up again, but his shaking legs wouldn't hold him. He was still more frightened than he'd ever been in his life, and he wanted to run, but there would be no running, not for a while. The pain in his shoulder was intense, and when he yanked his jacket and shirt aside to inspect the wound again, he expected to see it green and purple, oozing thick, gloppy pus. There was nothing there, and with that realization, the pain evaporated.

Must've hit my head, he thought and felt all over his scalp for a cut, positive his hand would come away bloody, but he didn't find even a bump. His vision was blurry, like he was looking through frosted glass, and he could hear his own pulse pounding in his ears. It was still hard to breathe. "Easy, easy," he told himself. He was okay, and he had to calm down. Over the years, he'd learned to regard his spirit experiences as sometimes disconcerting but nothing to fear. This was different. Never before had he been so physically affected, felt so shaken. What if this was something else? Was this what a heart attack felt like, or a stroke? "Oh, God," he murmured. No one would find him here. Maybe he should make his peace—unless there were people with those dogs he heard. Wait, he had a phone!

He tried to call 911 but couldn't get a signal. As he held the phone overhead, he caught a flash of movement out of the corner of his eye. Someone must have found him after all, by accident or miracle or whatever! But all he saw when he turned toward the movement was a gigantic dog the shape of a heavy-bodied Great Dane. It looked a lot like the two young dogs at the graveyard, except this one was huge. When it lowered its head and approached him, Jack was sure it was going to attack. Closer and closer it came, staring directly into his eyes. *I shouldn't meet his eyes*, Jack thought, but it was too late. The dog was almost touching him when it simply disappeared. Jack blinked in confusion. Moments later the dog reappeared, sitting by his side with its tongue out, silently panting. He could hear other sounds around him, the surf, birds, an airplane, but the dog made no sound.

"What is this?" he breathed. Was this more of Sarah? He reached out to touch the dog, to assure himself that it was really there, but his hand passed through it. Jack held his breath. The dog was still there, looking quite content. There were no ghost animals, at least none he'd ever encountered, so what was this?

Was he dead? That would explain why the pain in his shoulder was gone and he didn't feel sick anymore. But no, he was tired and dizzy, and he didn't think dead people would feel those things.

He heard more barking and turned to the dog at his

side, but it wasn't him. The snarling and barking got closer and closer until finally around a bend in the path came those two black dogs from the graveyard, rolling in the sand, yipping, and play-biting. They jumped back and forth over each other like they were playing leapfrog, fighting over the dead gull one of them was dragging. Both dogs froze when they saw Jack, staring at him for a moment before scampering back toward the beach, the dead bird suspended between them.

So the barking was the pups. One bit of reality, but he could still see the dog at his side. Maybe the question of what it was or wasn't could wait. Right now he might be having a heart attack, and he needed to somehow get himself home.

He felt something on his face and reached up to touch it. At some point he must have fallen on his face, because one cheek was encrusted with sand, and there was definitely more of it in his teeth. That made him pretty sure he wasn't dead. He brushed at the sand but only managed to get it down the neck of his shirt. No, he wasn't dead.

It took Jack a long time to get home because he couldn't keep his balance and lost track of how many times he fell. Sometimes he forced himself get up right away, but sometimes he lay there with his head spinning. "Stay down." Jack remembered that line from a movie about a man who didn't know when he was beaten. One of the guys who fought him kept saying, "Stay down, man. Just stay down." Maybe it wasn't a movie where he heard it. Maybe it was bar fights, and the man on the floor was him. That was how Jack felt, like he was up against a strong adversary, one he couldn't beat. Even that was different. Never had he considered the spirits to be adversaries.

Stay down, he thought again. But he'd never figured out how to stay down in those bar fights, and he would keep getting up now. He thought he'd left the dog ghost behind, but every time he looked up, he saw it a little farther up the path, as if it was waiting for him.

By the time Jack got to his bench at the top of the path, the sun was setting. But how could that be when he'd left in the morning? He couldn't have been down there the whole day, unless he'd passed out, maybe more than once. He didn't know, but Jack counted himself lucky to have made it back at all. Maybe later in the tourist season there would be more people around, but even then his place had no close neighbors. It might have been weeks before anyone found him down there. Up here, he knew he could get a cell signal if he needed to call for help. Right now, all he wanted to do was rest.

Jack hauled himself onto the bench and slumped forward with his elbows on his thighs, his head hanging. He was still breathing harder than he would have liked, and his heart was pounding, but the situation was what it was. "Breathe," he told himself. "Easy does it." It occurred to him that people who used that AA slogan probably didn't have situations like this one in mind. When his breathing had slowed a little, he sat up straighter on the bench and looked around. He remembered the feel of those hands on his throat and shivered. The hands had been large and calloused, not Sarah's hands. His neck felt like it needed to crack, but he was afraid to try it. "The phone," he said, pulling it out of his pocket. Yes, he had enough bars to call someone now, but he changed his mind and put it down on the bench.

That dog, he thought looking around. Turning first to one side and then the other, Jack searched, but it wasn't with him. The sun was low in the sky, the heavy clouds lit with purple and orange. Jack shook his head. "What a thing to notice," he said. But then, wasn't the world always supposed to seem more beautiful after a brush with death? He believed that's what this had been.

Jack swallowed hard, realizing that for the first time in a couple of decades he wanted a drink. He didn't want one, exactly, more like he realized how good a drink would feel if he were the old Jack. *Feel*, not taste. He never drank for taste. "Whoa, there," he told himself. "Not an option, Jacko. There's nothing that a drink won't make worse." Another AA saying.

Though Jack wasn't seriously considering a drink, it had been a long time since even the thought had crossed his mind. Maybe he really should call his sponsor in the next few days, maybe hit a meeting. Those simple measures worked to get him sober and to keep him that way. You stuck with what worked. "Yeah, maybe later I'll give Preston a call," he told himself. Anyway, thinking about his AA program gave him a chance to step back from thinking about Sarah, and maybe thinking about something else was a good idea. Step back for now and think about it in a little bit.

What he wanted most at that moment, he decided,

was coffee. Anyway, making coffee would keep his hands busy. He'd go inside, make coffee, sit at the table, and talk out loud to himself about what had just happened. "Whatever all that was," he said. "And if I'm gonna be talking to myself about spirits, better if it's behind closed doors." Before he shut the front door, Jack switched on the outside lights and looked around one more time for the figure of a large black hound, but he was gone.

Standing with his hands on the counter, watching the coffee burbling into the pot, Jack let himself remember. That presence, the feelings, the images, believing he was someone named Sarah. She had identified herself, given her name. None of the spirits Jack had seen in the past even seemed to know he was there. She had not only seen him, but she told him who she was. Strange. And that dog. He had continued to see the dog long after all the other images and feelings from Sarah had faded. In fact, he hadn't seen it until he was coming out of that *episode*, or whatever it was, and that started happening when he heard the two young dogs. But the barking was the pups, the real ones, not what he'd begun to think of as the phantom dog. That part of it was confusing. "That part?" Jack laughed. "Only that part is confusing?" But imagined or not, he believed that phantom dog had helped him get back home.

Jack poured himself a cup as the last drops of water hissed on the hot surface of the coffee maker. He was almost afraid to make himself review the details of the experience, afraid it might start all over, but he needed to do it.

Okay, he thought. *Headed for the beach, not worried about anything because I'd walked down that path before. Just walking along, shoes filling up with sand. Stopped to take them off.*

Sand in his shoes made him remember that bad time, the time he'd hit Mara. The reason she left. The memory slammed him, exactly the same way it did after he got the booze out of his system and realized the enormity of what he'd done. With two punches, he'd betrayed the person who cared most about him in this life, destroyed the innocent trust he so loved in her, innocent despite all he'd put her through before that. He'd killed something delicate and precious, something he didn't value until it was gone.

So he had remembered all that, felt all the guilt and self-recrimination he'd ever known, and then his hold on reality slipped. There was the awful pain in his shoulder, like after the recent nightmares but so much worse. Then he saw the visions like he was looking through her eyes, felt a powerful and terrifying presence. Sarah. The spirit didn't feel evil, but it was desperate, utterly and completely lost, and it threatened to drag him away with it.

Not it, her, he thought. *Sarah.* It was obvious she was stuck here, just like those others he'd seen and felt in the past. But never before had he been sure of a name. Never did he feel yanked out of his own life and dropped into someone else's. Remembering the force of her presence made his insides quiver, and when he fished in his jacket pocket for a cigarette, he found that his hand was shaking, too. But of course he didn't find any cigarettes, because he'd quit years ago. "Old habits die hard," he muttered and folded his hands on the table in front of him.

Those times in the past when he felt or saw spirits, he'd sit down wherever he was and smoke. It seemed like a way to say, "Well now, that was interesting." It reassured him that he was okay, that the experience was no big deal. He didn't have anything to smoke now, but he remembered times when smoking helped.

There was the little boy he'd half seen, standing in front of the chimney in a third-floor bedroom. It was in an old house his friends were renovating in Maryland, a place that started as a one-room cabin in the 1700s and had been added to piecemeal by a dozen families. The boy looked about seven years old and was wearing homespun. He had big, dark eyes, and he was crying. When he vanished, Jack smoked a cigarette.

Then there was the old man in the lodge at Tanner's Mill. He was sweeping in the loft offices and saw the man sitting at one of the desks, a figure so filmy that Jack could see the grain of the chair right through his crossed legs. He was dressed in jeans, boots, and a red plaid shirt, eating a sandwich. Jack knew it was liverwurst and onion. Jack went down the stairs and outside and smoked a cigarette.

There were no wounds visible on those two, but there had been others. In the entryway of the Dahlgren chapel, he'd seen a woman sitting on the floor in a corner. She looked so real that he went over to help her up, but when he got closer, he saw a gaping wound in her neck, like her throat had been cut. There was blood all over the blue lace of her collar. Her expression was so sad, and then all at once she wasn't there. He'd had to wait till he got back to his car to smoke that time, because he'd left the pack in the glove box.

Once, at night on a Monomoy Island beach, he saw a group of men pulling a boat out of the surf. Each one of them had bone showing though some part of their flesh—one side of a face laid open, a hip or a rib cage exposed, a shoulder blade sticking through. It was like something had been eating them. Those were the only ones he'd actually heard make any noise. They moaned, but maybe it was the wind. Another cigarette.

The worst ones were at Walter Reed, where he was a janitor. Some things walked the halls at night there, some things were in the closets, and other things seemed like they were in the walls. The hospital had been there a long time, under one name or another through multiple wars, and he imagined lots of people died on those grounds. Besides ghosts who looked like patients, Jack saw doctors and nurses as well. Perhaps they were still here, restless and mourning, because they couldn't relieve the suffering they saw, or maybe because they stayed too long trying. Whatever the reason, more than a few of them were still there. It was at Walter Reed that Jack started smoking cigars.

There was a time when Jack feared death, wondered if heaven was a fairy tale and our real fate was the wandering existence he'd glimpsed. It was only after Mara died that he got his faith back. Strange as it seemed, it was because he never saw her, never had one inkling of her presence, that he could believe again. Then he knew beyond questioning that he only saw the suffering ones, the ones who never found their way "home." His Mara was at peace.

Jack shivered and swallowed against a queasy stomach as memories from the path came back to him. Never in all those times had he seen or smelled their memories, never felt their wounds as if they were his own. But this time was different. And this time he'd been given a name.

Through an entire pot of coffee, trying alternately to calm the fear that kept rising in his throat and to clear his head, Jack tried to piece the facts together. He didn't know enough, though, and decided he was probably running circles around whatever the truth was. Finally, he wandered back outside to the bench in the dark.

He had always loved the night, and for him the silver light from the stars and moon was even better than the yellow light of day. Now he leaned back and watched the tiny twinkling pinpoints that had been there for eons. The caffeine had done its job. His mind whirled, memories surfaced and sank, interpretations presented themselves and were accepted or rejected, and the time sped by. At some point he dozed.

When he awakened, chilled and tasting the sourness of unbrushed teeth, he was surprised to realize he'd been out all night. It wasn't quite dawn, but it would be very soon. He tried to get up, but he was stiff and imagined the imprint of the bench slats would remain on his hind parts all day. Finally, he managed to stand, knowing that if he gave his legs a minute, they would straighten. Meanwhile, he rubbed at the seat of his pants to get the circulation going. He needed a pit stop too.

"First things first," he muttered, thinking there was another AA saying. Then he walked into the house, rocking from side to side a bit as he walked, doing the best he could.

This was certainly a different kind of "out all night" from the old days. But this time, no one was disappointed in him, no one had feared for his safety, and he didn't have any regrets about what he'd done or said. No one else even knew. That made it lonely, but there was also a freedom in having nowhere he needed to be and no one to answer to. The shadow of fear remained, but he stuffed it into a mental box and closed the lid. He would look at it again later.

"Have to remember to go back and get my shoes and my fishing gear," he mumbled but realized that at the moment he'd rather have somebody steal everything than go back down to those rocks. "Right now, more coffee," he said aloud and wondered if he was drinking too much of it lately. No matter. *Coffee, and after the coffee, food, lots of it*, he thought. Figuring out what all this was about could wait. Everything in life made better sense when the sun was up and you had a full stomach, even this.

CHAPTER 14

Decisions: Jack—2016

WHILE HE SWUNG THE STRING trimmer back and forth to clear weeds from around the headstones, Jack mentally nodded to the soul who rested beneath each one. He kept waiting for something to happen, but he felt no spirit twinges here, no shivers. Everything felt pleasantly mundane, a pine-scented breeze, the surging sound of surf on the beach below the point, the good feel of working outside. There was nothing else, and whatever it was that had happened to him on the path had nothing to do with these people, Jack was sure.

He stopped the trimmer and scanned all around. Maybe he'd see those two dogs again today. Their resemblance to the phantom dog was unmistakable, and he wondered about a connection. *Certainly related*, he thought and then muttered, "Didn't know animals could come back." Then he started the trimmer again. Hopefully the battery charge would last till he finished.

Questions. He wanted to know what happened to Sarah. It must have been horrendous, and from the look of the old scars he saw on her face, whatever killed her wasn't her first violent experience. What she did to him some people might call possession, but he didn't like the idea or the word. Anyway, this wasn't his idea of possession. Instead, he thought of it as being hit by the impression of a person, an impression so strong that emotions, memories, and even the personality came through like a fire hose turned on full blast.

Still, he knew that whatever he chose to name it, it was dangerous. At least that was what his inner voice kept whispering, and he'd learned long ago not to ignore those warnings. The most intelligent decision was probably to high-tail it off the island and never look back. But he was intrigued. In the days since the incident, he'd reviewed and dissected every detail he could recall, because he wanted to understand. The upshot of all that analysis was that he didn't know any more now than he had that first night.

When he finished the trimming, Jack pulled his notebook from his jeans pocket to record what he'd done. Today, besides the weed whacking, he tried to reset all the crooked markers. He did the best he could, but there was nothing to be done about Amanda's broken stone. Maybe Kelli Gregson could speak to the property owner about having it replaced. It seemed like the right thing to do. *Cemeteries*, he thought. *After enough time, they could provide you with interesting bits of history, but until then they were simply monuments to grief.* Sarah had no monument here, and he didn't know yet what she had to do with these people, if anything. He might never know. But he understood that she grieved, and grief could do terrible things to a person.

Jack heaved a breath and looked up at the sky. The plan after his summer here had been to go back to the home he used to share with Mara, and to start over there, this time alone. With all his jobs in all those different places, starting over was nothing new, but it was bitter.

Starting over meant you'd failed again. It meant stepping back and trying to see what you got wrong the first time around, if you could. You had to get small and keep your eyes down after you embarrassed yourself, burned bridges, and made mistakes you couldn't fix. Starting over meant trying again to get something right, however many times you got it wrong, even when you didn't think you could. Practice, practice, practice, like a sport or being in school. That's what life was, Jack thought, a school where you kept getting the same lesson over and over till you understood.

But what was this lesson about?

More questions. What if it was no coincidence that he chose this island where Sarah was for the place to think about his next steps? After all, how many people could have sensed her presence? Was it part of some plan that he was here, the weird guy who'd been sensing spirits his whole life? But then what was the plan? Sarah was suffering, that was obvious, and there was no telling for how long. Was he supposed to help her somehow?

Not once had he considered "helping" any of those other spirits, and thinking about doing it now made him anxious. He suspected that if he tried to help Sarah, he might not be around long. It wasn't that he was afraid to die, but he wasn't eager to check out yet either.

And what if something worse than dying happened to him?

This time he knew immediately what the out-of-place sound was, the ringtone he'd set on the phone to replace that awful sound it made. Fleetwood Mac's "Dreams" still wasn't quite right, but it was better than what he started with.

He cleared his throat before he answered, "Hello?"

"Dad, hi! It's Hannah. You okay?" Her voice was always pitched a little higher when she talked on the phone. She sounded worried.

"Hi, sweetheart. Yup, I'm hunky dory with not a care in the world," he lied. "You okay there?"

"Yeah, no. I don't know, Dad, I had one of those feelings. Anyhow, it's good to hear your voice." She paused, and neither of them spoke for a moment before she added, "Any excuse to check up on you, right?" He could hear the smile he couldn't see.

It seemed like she'd been getting feelings about people since she could use whole sentences, and though she was sometimes off base, most of the time she was spot on, scary accurate. Like now. Jack wondered if his kind of sensitivity could be hereditary. If it was, he hoped all she got was this kind of talent and not the rest of what he had. What an awful trait to pass on to your child.

"So what are you up to today? Fishing, reading, or what?"

He couldn't tell her the whole truth. "Well, doing some yard work right now, but yeah, I decided I want to read that Braudel book I liked again. Thought I'd find a good spot on the beach and start it this afternoon."

"Fernand Braudel? The one about the Mediterranean, right? You recommended that one to me a few years ago. Pretty heavy for a beach read, isn't it, Dad? You and your history!" He thought her giggle sounded the same as when she was four years old. God, he loved this kid.

"Well you know me. I brought along the new Stephen King too. But I'm outside mostly, weed whacking at the moment, and I was about to head back to the house for a meal. This place was a great find, by the way, sweetie." Was this Friday or Saturday? It mattered because she would be home on Saturday, and maybe he could talk to his grandson.

"What, not fishing?"

"Maybe later. And probably I'll do some sitting around, you know, watching the birds and such. After all, it's a vacation, right? What about you guys? How's Herb? And what about little Jack? Thought you were taking him to the shore this weekend. Or did I misremember?"

"No, yeah," she said again. "You're right, but it's pouring here and supposed to be like this all weekend, so we decided to postpone."

He grinned every time he heard her say that "no, yeah" thing. It always tickled him.

"As for your namesake, he acted like his heart was broken when we told him we couldn't go, but five minutes later he was running off doing Jacky stuff. Four certainly is an active age! Maybe we'll get to the beach next weekend, but Herb just took him down to that covered Pitch 'N Putt to keep him occupied while I grade. Seems like I should get paid for working at home, you know?"

He nodded and smiled, not thinking about how she couldn't see him do either one. So it was Saturday, but he still wouldn't be able to talk to Jacky. Maybe he'd call back later tonight.

"So anyhow, Dad, how's it really going?" She pitched her voice a little lower, her tone serious. "Made any friends there yet?" She knew he had no close friends anymore, no one except his sponsor and a few of the guys at meetings. Hannah was concerned he was isolating, worried he was lonely.

"Not seeing many people to speak of, sweetheart. Did talk with some folks at the public dock and the produce store, but I wouldn't say I've made friends exactly. To tell the truth, I find myself thinking mostly about your mama. What I wish I'd done different for her, and for you and Sean."

Hannah was quiet for so long that he wondered whether their connection had broken, but she was still there. "You know Mom loved you like crazy, right? And so do I. When it comes to Sean, well, he's got his own issues. As for changing what's already happened, you know that's like shoveling smoke, Dad. It's pointless."

Hannah had spent a lot of time in AlAnon while he

was staying sober in AA, and sometimes the slogans came out of her mouth too. She was probably right, but he still had regrets.

"It's like you used to tell me," she said, "we try to make amends for what we did or wish we didn't do. Then we have to let it go, even if the other person doesn't forgive us. We've got no control over what somebody else does. Right?"

She was waiting for him to answer, he knew, but he didn't want her to hear how choked up he was. Why did age make tears come so easily to a man who probably hadn't cried enough when he was younger? Jack cleared his throat.

"Yeah, you're right," he finally answered and then changed the subject. "So, no beach for you guys this weekend. You know, I told you before, but I'll repeat the invite. You should come here for a couple of weeks, or a month even—you and Herb and little Jack. The island is beautiful, and it's nothing *but* beach!"

Hannah laughed. He loved that sound.

"Maybe after school gets out, Dad, but for just a week. I'll talk to Herb and see what his work schedule looks like. The fact is, Jacky's been pestering me about seeing his PopPop. He misses you, Dad." Jack could hear her swallow hard and wondered if she was thinking about the person little Jacky wouldn't ever get to know because she wasn't coming back. He decided he was right when he heard her clear her throat the same way he'd done moments before. "So, you really think you've got room for us?"

"Absolutely! There's a huge master bedroom I'm not

using and another little one I've hardly been in. Come whenever it works for you guys. Supposedly the ferry runs three times a day after the first of the month." He paused. "Please do come, hon? I'd love to see you guys."

"We'll try, Dad. I'd better get a move on now, but I needed to be sure you were okay. I love you, Dad."

"Love you, too, Hanna-Banna. Hug that little guy for me, will you? And regards to Herb?"

"Sure, Dad. You have fun now."

When the line went dead, the silence around him was loud. It was surprising how much simple contact with another person added to a day, even when it was only a voice and a mental picture of them.

That phrase resounded in Jack's mind, *simple contact with another person.* What if someone were denied that?

From what he'd seen of Sarah's memories, there was a massacre, and she was left alone. Her hold on him had felt desperate, and he could still feel that wash of aching loneliness. There was something about losing her children too, maybe in that same massacre. God, how awful that would have been.

Simple contact with another person.

Would human contact help Sarah? And what exactly would constitute contact? Even if he could figure out exactly how to help her, he wasn't sure how wise it would be to try. Letting her in, this time voluntarily, and allowing himself to stand under that fire hose of feelings was probably a major risk, and not just to his body. He would be open and vulnerable. Jack remembered the strength it took to wrest his mind back from her that first time. It wasn't possession, but it was close enough, and he'd seen *The Exorcist* more than once.

If he couldn't pull away, what would happen to him? Given how contact with her had affected him the first time, he supposed he might die from a heart attack or stroke. The worst scenario, what he couldn't help thinking about, was that the contact would cost him more than he was willing to risk, like his soul. Jack didn't know if soul was the right word—he wasn't sure what he believed anymore. But whatever made him who and what he was, what if he stayed alive but lost that? Anyway, he didn't know if he had the courage to open that door to her again. And besides, what made him think he could help in the first place?

Back and forth. Good idea, bad idea, both, neither. He couldn't decide what to do or what to think, and he hated waffling. He wanted to forget the whole thing, but he couldn't make himself do that. He felt stuck. "What do you think, Mara girl? Am I supposed to do this or not?" Then he remembered a quote. Whether he'd read it or heard it, he didn't know: *If you can't get out, go in deeper.*

Jack tried out the words in his mouth, "If you can't get out, go in deeper." Then he nodded to himself. He came here to figure out what he was supposed to do with the rest of his life. Maybe this was it. *Go in deeper*, he thought again, the decision suddenly made.

On the way to the path, he stopped at the house, stacked his yard tools next to the back door, and went inside for some water. Standing at the window over the kitchen sink, he watched the hand that held the glass shaking just enough to disturb the surface of the water. That was odd. He set the glass on the counter and held both hands out flat in front of him. Both hands shook, but the right was worse. It could be there really was something physically wrong with him. Calmly he took stock, thinking he was doing that a lot lately. Breathing was okay, pulse was normal, no unusual pains, and other than the shaking hands, he felt fine. *Go in deeper?* Sure, but maybe not right now.

Picking the glass up again, he downed the water and washed his hands. He'd been considering a visit to that museum, and if he was having some kind of health issue, being closer to civilization was wise. Besides, he could ask about the early island settlements, maybe get more data about any massacres that happened on the island.

Outside, he started walking toward town. He didn't have a car here, but maybe he should find a used bicycle. They said you never forgot how to ride, and he might need to test that old adage.

Chapter 15

The Museum: Jack—2016

A LITTLE BELL CHINKLED WHEN HE pushed the door open. For someone who loved history as much as Jack did, this sort of museum was a find. It was housed in a renovated federal-style brick home with high-ceilinged rooms and scrollwork in the crown molding. Standing in the foyer, Jack faced a central staircase that L-bended to the second and third levels. He got out his notepad, twisted the mechanical pencil to expose fresh lead, and turned to a fresh page.

Every bit of floor space held a cabinet or a display, and all the walls were covered with paintings, quilts, and maps, but it didn't feel cluttered. Jack wanted to see it all. As he closed the door behind him, the bell over the door sounded again.

"Good morning and welcome," a quavery voice greeted. The voice belonged to a tiny bird of a woman who looked so old she made Jack feel young. The papery skin of her face and neck was a network of wrinkles, but her back was straight, and she moved with grace. Behind her, Jack could see glass cases with clothing from different times in history; the woman herself wore a high-collared long dress ballooned by petticoats, lace at her throat and her cuffs. Period dress, Jack knew, though from when he wasn't sure. He loved history, but he knew nothing of women's clothing.

He smiled at her, hoping she was a living, breathing resident of the present and not something else. "Good morning to you, ma'am," he said. "I'm visiting for the summer and was told this is a place I need to see." Her answering smile exposed teeth that were the yellow of a lifelong coffee drinker, but the smile assured him she was no spirit. None of them had ever smiled.

"It's nice you're interested. Seems like fewer and fewer folks are these days. You staying in town, then? At the Narragansett Inn, mayhap?"

Mayhap, he thought. An old word. "No, ma'am, not in town. I'm renting a property on the ridge near the old lighthouse. From the cemetery there, I'd say the house might have belonged to a family named Nickerson. Do you know it?"

"Well, Nickerson's a common name around here, but yes, I know the place. That isn't the house Captain Nickerson built, though. Let me see if I can find you those pictures." With that, she walked into the next room calling, "Come along," over her shoulder. Jack followed her through a maze of rooms until they came to one with a row of what looked like painter's files against the long wall. Each one held a stack of framed and glassed items leaning on end against each other. Some were paintings or prints, and others seemed to be documents. They looked old, and Jack couldn't help wondering if this was the best way to store and display them.

The woman interrupted his thoughts. "I'm Constance Amberson," she said.

Jack offered his hand. "Jack Doyle. Pleased to meet you, Mrs. Amberson." Her grip was stronger than he'd expected.

"It's Miss, but no matter. Let's see, I think it must be in this group," she said and flipped through the framed pieces one by one until she found what she was looking for. "Here we are. Have a look."

Jack stood next to her amazed at the amount of dust raised by her sorting. It looked pretty in the sunlight from the window, though, kind of like galaxy pictures through the Hubble telescope. He wondered if maybe they could use somebody to help clean the place.

"Now *this* is the original Nickerson house, drawn by Captain Nickerson himself," Miss Amberson said. "See his signature right there, and the date?"

"Yes, 1842," Jack answered. The charcoal sketch showed what looked like a stone castle with a balcony-ringed turret, more like someone's dream of a house than an actual dwelling.

"That was the house he had built," Miss Amberson told him with pride in her manner, "and his work is signed

N. H. N. for Nathan Hawkins Nickerson. Like I said, it was the captain himself who drew this."

"How could a charcoal survive all that time, and in such excellent condition?"

"Who's to say? It seems to have been coated with something before framing, and it doesn't touch the glass because of those nested mats. I'm sure it's partly because of the paper he used," she said. "It's rare, made from sail cloth. Of course he had ready access to sail cloth, though we don't know if he had this paper made to order or if he simply purchased it."

She paused without breaking eye contact, and Jack thought she was waiting for a signal from him to continue. "He had ready access?" Jack prompted.

"Yes, indeed," she said quickly. "Captain Nickerson owned and operated his own bark, you see, unusual for here in those days. Most whaling was done by companies then, companies that owned the ships and hired captains and crew. But the Nickerson family had money, so he had options. I'll say this for him: he kept good records, and it seems he had a talent for finding whales. His name shows up in newspaper articles from the time. We've been publishing our own newspaper here since the mid-1700s, you know."

"You don't say?"

"Anyway, rag paper is more durable than wood pulp and is likely one reason some of these pieces survived. Of course, parchment is even better, the original type made from animal skins, not what you get these days. Besides the question of material, I believe there's a good bit of luck in what survives and what doesn't. We've got more of Captain Nickerson's work, if it interests you."

"His work, you say? I'd appreciate seeing anything you have from that time, especially about the Nickersons." Jack thought about the little cemetery.

The entry bell sounded again. "My goodness," she said, "no visitors for a week, and already two today. Feel free to browse through these. You should find other works with Captain Nickerson's mark, and of course there's a good deal else to see." With that she turned and left, her long skirts swishing.

Jack sorted through the other stacks, unclear about how things were grouped. It seemed logical that they be arranged by date, but they weren't. Eventually he found more pieces with the N.H.N. initials, all dated, most of them amazingly well preserved for how old they were. He found sketches of the house from different sides, complete with measurements and some details of decorative work on doorways and window frames. They were house plans, Jack realized.

In another rack, he found a beautiful sketch of a three-masted ship, *The Gull* written underneath in flowing script. Then he found a large frame holding four small drawings, all with Nathan's initials. One was of a lighthouse, one of a different ship, and one a scene of ice and snow with seals resting on floating ice. The man had been quite talented, he thought. The fourth sketch was the face of an attractive young woman, signed with his whole name and dated 1826. Even from the picture, her eyes smiled. *So this was what Amanda looked like*, he thought. Then he saw the name written in calligraphy at the bottom, Keziah. He leafed through his notebook to where he'd recorded the inscriptions on the gravestones until he found what he was looking for. "There," he muttered. "That's what I thought. Amanda K. 1818—1862. This can't be a sketch of Amanda. She would have been only eight years old in 1826, and the woman in the picture is an adult. So who was Keziah?"

At the sound of skirts, Jack looked up from the sketches to see Miss Amberson's face alight. "That was my nephew's son, Jackson," she offered. "He has a history project to do and wants it to be about the 'Indians' of this area."

"What tribe?" Jack asked.

"The island was supposedly sacred to the Wampanoag before the first settlers came, maybe a burial ground, but it's not clear if any of the native people lived here when those first colonists arrived. Of course, there was a thriving mixed community here in the 1800s, mostly whalers and their families. Lots of folks settled here for that, Portuguese and Hawaiians, besides Native Americans from the mainland."

Jack thought of Sarah and his visions of what looked like a massacre. He wanted to talk about the Indians. "I imagine there were conflicts. Battles were fought here early on?"

She nodded. "In the early years, settlements kept sprouting up and then disappearing all over this region. There were some issues with First Nation peoples, there were pirates, and disease was always a factor. One outbreak of smallpox could wipe out a whole colony. On the islands, a couple years of bad weather could starve people out and force them to go elsewhere. It's hard to tell what happened to each of the settlements, because the chronology is spotty."

Chronology, Jack thought with a smile. Spoken like a true historian. For him it wasn't hard to tell what happened to the settlement where Sarah and her family lived. That wasn't famine or disease; it was war. He was reminded of a Braudel quote, "Happiness, whether in business or private life, leaves very little trace in history." He almost quoted it out loud, but he didn't want to sound pompous. No, there was little trace of happiness in history. It was the violent and disastrous events like what Sarah experienced that left the scars we call history.

"Besides the Nickersons, I'm interested especially in anything about the earliest colonies," Jack said.

"That would have been the 1600s, about four hundred years ago, and I'm afraid we don't have much. On an island, you understand—"

"I know," he interjected, "with the limited space, new buildings replace older ones, built right over the ruins."

"Yes, even if it's not ruins, and so much is lost that way," she said with an expression of authentic sorrow. "We do have some items that stand time and weathering." With a wave of her hand apparently including the entire museum, she said, "We've got horseshoes and candleholders aplenty, and more than a few crane and pintle assemblies. That's what supported the cook pots in a fireplace, you know. And of course weapons, like muskets and musket balls, arrowheads and spear points, even knives. But very little evidence of the colonists' everyday life survived. What you see here of the clothing," she indicated a mannequin in a long simple dress, "are reproductions." She looked down to smooth her own skirts and then smiled up at him. "There's always something new showing up, though. I read that an old journal recently surfaced, one kept by an early islander. Likely some rich collector already snapped it up, because I haven't heard a peep more about it. What a crime to keep such a valuable resource in a private collection."

Jack opened his mouth to agree, but he didn't get the chance.

"With my own eyes," she enthused, "I've read trade records and journals kept by preachers trying to plant certain brands of religion in these islands. There are holes in the history, though, stretches of time with no written records, maybe lost if they ever existed. All we have from some periods are stories passed word of mouth down the families. Of course we know much more about later years. If you're interested in the whaling trade, for instance, I've studied a good bit on that."

"Well, I thank you, Miz Amberson. I'd love to hear all that you know about that, maybe the next time I visit. For now, I'm intrigued by the Nickersons and the very early years. Do you mind if I look around a bit on my own?"

"No, not at all. Call out if you have questions. I'll be here." And with that she swished away toward the front of the building, leaving Jack in the hush of old things.

That was when he saw them in their own display case, beautiful old flasks, some plain and others ornate. A few of them were glass, but most looked like silver or pewter, and they reminded him of the stainless steel hip flask he used to carry. He didn't remember what became of that flask. Probably Mara put it in the attic when he got sober, or maybe she'd thrown it out. Looking at these, he could almost feel the reassuring curve of that old friend, could almost taste the whiskey.

"Whoa, Jacko," he said to himself. "Tasting it? Dicey territory." How long had it been since he'd had a drink? When his sobriety time had been measured in weeks or months, he'd known the answer with hardly a thought. These days he had to remember the year he quit and subtract. "Let's see, not quite twenty-three years." That was a long time, but only one day at a time, he reminded himself. "Just today." But here he was thinking about drinking again, and the other night dreaming about it? It *would* be a good idea to give Preston a call later on. Better to nip this in the bud than go where he never wanted to go again.

As he was leaving, Miss Amberson appeared on the stairway and the way she looked Jack had to remind himself she was flesh and blood. "Thanks so much," he said. "I'll be back."

"Wonderful," she told him. "And you be careful up there. That end of the island can be dangersome." *Dangersome*, Jack thought. He loved the old words, but before he could comment, she turned and disappeared up the stairs again.

CHAPTER 16

Putting It All Together: Jack—2016

Hearing Preston's gravelly voice on the phone, Jack was instantly relieved. He'd been sitting in that parlor chair for close to an hour, debating whether to call his sponsor or put it off again, and he was glad he decided to call. Preston Lake wasn't his first sponsor, but he was the one he'd had for the last eleven years, and he was a good man. Jack could almost see him, his unruly beard and his white hair pulled back into the ponytail he'd probably had since his motorcycle days. He was walking more bent over these days, but he still got around.

"So, what's up? You doin' okay, Jack?"

"Yeah, I'm okay. Needed to touch base is all," Jack said. "Trying to be smart."

"That's two different things, buddy, two different things." The old man said it deadpan, but Jack could imagine the wry grin on his face. "And 'smart' can be a little slippery, you know."

"No lie," Jack said, feeling like they were across a table at the Big Boy Diner, drinking coffee instead of talking on the phone with a few miles of ocean between them. It seemed like forever since they'd been face to face.

"Besides touching base," Preston said, "you got something you want to tell me?" Jack imagined Preston cleaning his nails with his pocketknife.

No nonsense and right to the point, Jack thought, two of the reasons the man was the perfect sponsor for him. "If you mean have I gone back out, then no, and I'm not considering it. Had passing thoughts about drinking a couple of times is all. Dreamed about it once too. But I haven't done either of those things in so long that it scared me. Don't want to go there again. Anyhow, haven't found a meeting here and wanted to stay honest."

"Haven't found a meeting or haven't looked?"

Preston's frank question surprised Jack, and he laughed. He hadn't looked, and Preston already knew that.

"More support might be a good idea, my friend. By yourself where nobody knows you, you're asking for trouble. All the time you've got in, you know you have to build your base before you need it."

"You're right. I need to find a meeting."

"Have to say you sound kind of off. You okay otherwise?"

Jack hesitated, wondering whether the whole truth would be a good idea. He remembered what happened early in his sobriety when he told Preston about the spirit thing. Since Preston was one of those who'd had alcoholic hallucinations, he thought that was Jack's problem and told Jack his ghosts would disappear if he stayed sober.

Jack's ghosts never went away, but he kept that to himself and still managed to stay sober.

"You still there?" Preston asked.

"Yeah, just trying to think how I want to say this." The bottom-line question was would not talking about the nightmares and what happened on the path make him drink? The answer was no. Nothing could "make" him drink. He'd nursed Mara through that cruel illness, watched her die, buried her, and grieved her, sober the whole time. That meant he could go through anything without a drink, as long as he remembered to control the only thing he could, himself. Maybe he'd share the whole mess with Preston at some point, but not right now. "Haven't been feeling all that well," he said, "and to be honest, it's hard being alone again. But otherwise I'm good. Lots to do here, with fresh air and space to consider what's next for me. Doing lots of thinking."

"I hear you, but easy does it. Over thinking everything made it tough for you to get clean in the first place, you told me. Paralysis of analysis. We have to remember our wrongs so we can make amends to those we've harmed. Then we gotta make peace with ourselves and close that door. Too much dwelling on mistakes, why we did what we did and what we should've done different, that's a sure way back into the bottle."

"I know," Jack said but didn't add how that was hard when the past kept pushing its way back in. He was thinking about both Sean and Sarah, as well as his own painful memories. "We don't ever get clean starts, Pres. It's not that easy."

"Nope, and nobody promised easy. We deal with today the best we can. We plan and we hope, but we can't worry about what's ahead. It all needs time to play out."

Time to play out. The phrase snicked into place in Jack's mind like the tumblers of a well-oiled lock. *Time to play out* and *simple human contact.* Then the connection broke for a second before Preston spoke again.

"Hey, I'm getting a call from a new pigeon, Jack. Mind if I sign off for now? We can talk more later on if you want."

Jack smiled at the odd AA term for a new sponsoree—pigeon—and then said, "I'm good. You gave me what I needed."

"You already had what you needed, but anytime, buddy. One day at a time, right? And get to a meeting!"

Then, almost before he knew it, Jack was standing at the head of the path, looking down toward the sea. He had thought about the idea of "simple contact with another person" up in the cemetery, and then a few minutes before Preston said, "It all needs time to play out." It was as if two puzzles assembled in different places at different times were fitting together, just as two lives were touching across the centuries. So had enough time passed for things to "play out" for Sarah? Should he offer himself as that human contact—and if he did, what would be the price?

Jack took one huge breath, held it for a moment, and then let it come rushing out. He knew it was dangerous but had to try. "Okay, here goes," he said out loud and started down the path.

Resolute was the way Jack thought of himself as he slogged his way through the dry sand. The effort soon had him breathing hard and his knee aching, so he slowed down but kept on. At least now he wouldn't have to worry about whether or not to go ahead with this. Whatever happened, it would be done. Sometimes action was its own reward. Approaching the sheltered place where the rock pile was, he slowed his pace a little and then slowed even more when it came into view. He stopped about fifteen feet away, giving himself one last chance to change his mind. Then he stepped forward.

He waited for the onslaught. When nothing happened, he took two steps closer to the boulders and stopped. Still nothing. Step by step he approached the rocks and hesitantly reached out one hand to touch them. Jack steeled himself for the rush of memories and emotions, holding his breath as he rested his weight on his outstretched hand. It was just a rock. Releasing the breath, he relaxed. What was wrong? Was he doing something different than when it happened last time? Well, he'd been leaning into the rocks then, so maybe that was it. He straightened and stepped closer, finally turning to rest his back against the cool surface of the boulders. But he smelled only surf and heard only gulls. Why was it different today?

Jack pushed back and turned to examine the rocks, wondering how long they had been here and how they got piled up this way. Maybe it was a glacier. Certainly they were already here in Sarah's time. He tried to imagine them from the perspective of other times in history, tried to envision them as she would have seen them. He got nothing. It was exactly like the blank feeling at the graveyard—there seemed to be no one here, but he knew there had been.

Thoughtful, he took another deep breath and backed down the path toward the beach, still looking at the rocks. Was she gone? Maybe all his worrying about what he should do had been pointless. Maybe that one time was all there was, and the whole thing was over the same way it happened to him all those other times. In a way he was relieved, but he also felt cheated. All that turmoil and upset for nothing. "Guess we might as well go walk on the beach, huh, Mara?" he said. That was when he saw his fishing gear arranged against one of the boulders on the beach side of the stack. Someone had set his shoes there too, all nice and neat. "Well, I'll be..." he said, resolving to retrieve his things on the way back to the house.

The surface of the water was calmer than he expected, with waves that were more like the waves on a lake than what he was used to. He knew it probably had to do with wind direction or air pressure, but whatever the reason, the lap-lap-lap sound was soothing. Jack stooped down to pick up a few of the stones that littered the beach, some quartz, some granite, some conglomerate. Most of them were smooth, and he picked some up to hold as he walked. This beach was nothing like the white-sand beaches along the mainland shore farther south. Here the sand was brown, and there were countless rocks of all sizes and shapes dotting the shoreline, in many places more rocks than sand. You couldn't walk without paying attention here, or you'd turn an ankle for sure.

The stones he held made him remember skipping stones on the pond near his house when he was a boy, but he hadn't done that in years and wondered if he could still remember how. None of the rocks he picked up seemed suitable, so he walked a widening circle with his head down, looking for smooth, flat ones of the perfect size. With one in his hand and half a dozen other likely ones in his pocket, Jack strode down to the water. He didn't consciously remember how to hold the rock, but his fingers did as he leaned back and side-armed the first one. It plopped in the water. Not a single skip.

Flick your wrist, he thought as he palmed the second one, a little bigger, steel gray with green veins. *Not the arm. It's all in the wrist*, he reminded himself as he threw. Three skips this time. Better! Another one, three skips again. Then another, and then another. It was almost mesmerizing—find a stone, lean back a little, toss it, watch it, count the skips, find a stone, lean back, throw—over and over again. His shoulder was starting to complain, but he didn't want to stop, and for a long time he didn't.

The rhythm of the actions was almost a meditation, calming for the most part, but it called up memories of something he regretted, something he hadn't thought about in years. When Sean was little and Hannah not yet born, a church friend of Mara's let them use her camp on a nearby lake, and they all went fishing. Mara and Sean dug worms. Mara rigged Sean's bamboo pole with line, bobber, and hook. She made lunch, and she remembered the bug spray. Jack brought beer. While she kept Sean from falling in, baited and rebaited his hook, and tried to get across the idea that he had to hook the fish before he tried to pull it in, Jack got drunk. Not sloppy drunk, because a little beer didn't do that for him anymore, but drunk enough to be an ass. That was the day he tried to teach Sean how to skip rocks, the day he dislocated his son's shoulder by holding his arm and throwing for him.

It happened a long time ago, but the memory made it seem like that morning, and he didn't feel like skipping stones anymore. Dropping the rest of the stones he'd collected, he turned back toward the dunes. He hadn't remembered that incident. How many more were there, the good reasons Sean had for hating him? How could he ever patch up what was between them when he couldn't even remember all he had to be sorry for?

The AA Serenity Prayer that he said with the others at the end of a meeting supposedly made it clear: *God grant me the serenity to accept the things I cannot change, the courage to change the things I can, and the wisdom to know the difference.* But was the situation he'd created with Sean something he could change or something he had to accept? Either way, that didn't help Sean at all. All the amends in the world couldn't possibly make up for all his father's wrongs.

Jack's feet felt heavy and awkward as he trudged over the dunes, heading home. Maybe he could try calling Sean again. He hadn't responded to Jack's message asking him to consider letting the kids visit when Hannah and her family came. Sean had married late, but now he had a son and a daughter that Jack had only seen a couple of times on holidays at Hannah's house. Sean knew he didn't drink anymore and should know that Jack would rather die than hurt those kids. On the other hand, why should Sean trust him? Calling again probably wouldn't make any difference, but he should try. What a mess he'd made of everything.

As the path wound up, Jack leaned forward, breathing harder and feeling his heart rate climb until he could hear blood pounding in his ears. "Probably not a great sign," he muttered, thinking again about strokes and heart attacks, but he kept walking. He was aware he was nearing the boulder pile but didn't give it a second thought. The Sarah spirit was gone.

Sometimes he thought he would give his life to go back, to have the chance to do it all over again without the drinking, without the horrible mistakes. Other times, the whole situation made him angry. Lots of children and lots of wives had it worse. Mara had seen the change in him and forgiven him, so why couldn't Sean give him any credit for the changes he made? Didn't there come a time when people had to let go of blaming, especially when somebody worked so hard to change their ways and begged for forgiveness? Sure he'd been a stinking father back then, but he tried to do so much for Sean after he got sober, tried to do what he could to make up for the earlier years. Jack felt like he'd been punished enough!

As he drew even with the rocks, he had that old, familiar sense that someone was behind him. Then he was hit by a rush of pain, emotions, and memories that he knew belonged to Sarah. She wasn't gone! "No," he choked out as the unexpected onslaught drove him to his knees, shouting unintelligible words and pounding the sand and rocks with rage. She wasn't gone. She was right here, and she had him.

Chapter 17

Face to Face: Sarah and Jack—2016

IGHTING WITH EVERY SCRAP OF intellectual and emotional strength he had, Jack tried to force Sarah out like he had before, but he couldn't. Over and over he tried, but she seemed stronger this time, or maybe he was getting weaker. He thought of Mara, sure this was the last time he would have the chance to think of her before he died, but when he called up her face and her laugh in his mind, he felt Sarah weaken.

In that split second, Jack did something that he could only describe as pulling his mind aside from Sarah's. From that viewpoint he simply observed. Something like this happened to him once before, when he was nineteen. Stationed at the navy base in Spain, he went to a party in a nearby town, where he was promised his first marijuana experience. What they gave him instead of marijuana that night was opiated hash, and he spent the rest of the evening floating in a corner of the ceiling, watching the party.

This felt like that. He saw himself on his knees, face contorted, pounding his fists into the sand as he howled with rage.

The spectator piece of his mind wondered, *Why rage?* That wasn't what he felt the last time Sarah found him. That time it was sadness he felt, her own and his, overpowering. He'd been remembering that time he hit Mara, feeling the remorse all over again, and the loneliness of life without her. That was what he felt from Sarah—remorse, loneliness, sorrow. But not anger.

This time on the path he'd been angry, angry that Sean wouldn't forgive him, and those feelings had grown into a rage that had him pounding the ground. Could it be that Sarah was an amplifier, a magnifier of whatever he was feeling?

The man in the sand stopped for a moment and appeared to be listening for something. He stared off into space and then turned on his knees to face the rocks. He didn't look angry anymore. He looked empty. In Spain that night, Jack had eventually found himself whole again, standing on an airport runway without remembering how he got there. He hoped he would find himself whole again after this. That separate part of him was still observing, but not from above. He was the man in the sand. Sarah was still there, but he was holding her at arm's length in his mind as her presence swirled through him.

Shadows changed as the sun moved across the sky, and the air began to cool. As the time passed, Sarah alternately

pulled at him, showing him over and over again what had
happened to her and then loosened her hold as he pulled
back from her. Each time he pulled back took more energy
and more will, and Jack didn't know how much more he
could take, how long it would be before he lost the ability
to keep himself separate from her. But then all at once it
changed. It was no longer Sarah's horror that Jack saw
but something else. It was a parade of people—women,
children, men—all of them in distress.

There was a young woman in long skirts, crying as she
ran. Then came a boy with a black eye and a cut on his
forehead, walking slowly with his head down. After him
was a sad-eyed young girl in a green coat, and then a man
with one arm, thin and sickly looking. The next one was
a soot-smeared boy with a bucket, and then a little girl
with a doll. A girl with bruises on her arms followed them,
and then a young man with bloody knuckles. What was
she showing him? Person after person marched through
his field of view as if through time. The line of unhappy
souls seemed endless. Finally there was a man, an old man
with a limp, a man broken by memories of how he treated
people he loved, a man who was angry about how his son
treated him. It took Jack a moment to recognize himself.

All at once he put it together, realized what he was
seeing, and knew who these people were. These were the
people Sarah had found over all those years since she died,
people whose strong negative emotions had drawn her
to them, the ones whose lives she forever changed. "So
many," Jack whispered.

Then he saw her, or rather he saw two images

superimposed, and he knew the truth of them both. Both were slender women with scarred faces, but one was smiling and confident in her healthy strength, while the other was injured, emaciated, bent under the weight of pain and hopelessness. Both women were Sarah.

Slowly the healthy image dissolved, and the other Sarah met his eyes. Her look of anguish changed to one of disbelief. If he'd had any doubt about her having seen him the last time he encountered her, that doubt was gone. She saw him.

Mind racing, settling on and then discarding possibilities, Jack registered the sound of his own pulse in his ears, an irregular rhythm. Maybe he didn't have long. Sarah's eyes bored into his, holding him as if he was her one tie to life, pleading with him. She wasn't threatening, wasn't frightening. She was simply more alone than she could bear. He had intended to help, but what could he do?

Jack gathered his own personality tightly around him like a shell. He wanted to reach out to her, but he didn't know how to do that, so he simply talked. "I see you, Sarah. I see you." He remembered the parade of people he'd seen and wondered how long Sarah had been here waiting. How awful to be alone all that time. "You're not alone now," he said. "I'm here."

You came! In his mind it was a shout, but there was no sound at all. Then a burst of images flooded into his mind like a movie fast-forwarding. The noise was deafening. People and animals ran through thick smoke, some fighting and some trying to escape. Jack heard Sarah's anguished wail as she held a child scarcely more than a baby, a child who wasn't moving. He also felt that wail come from his own throat. He saw that she held her little one with one arm, while her other arm dangled useless, and in his own arm was searing pain. An Indian wrenched her to her feet by her throat and tried to take her child. Jack gagged. He watched her fall back down, watched her frantic efforts to drive him off with rocks, trying to keep him from taking the baby. That lifeless little baby.

His whole body ached. "I'm still here," he said with great effort and watched her move among mutilated bodies scattered all over the hill where his house now stood. She was calling for children who weren't there. He watched the bodies decay in a jumpy time-lapse, saw as Sarah wasted away, watched her walk into the sea and then struggle back to shore. But in all this he saw no one else alive. No one but Sarah.

"You were totally alone," he whispered, tears running down his face. The movie slowed and then stopped, and he could see the look on her face. He couldn't tell whether he was seeing her only in his mind's eye—in the flow of images she showed him—or whether it was the ghost of Sarah whose eyes showed such pain. At that moment, Jack understood what he could do for her, but he wasn't sure he had the strength.

If you can't get out, go in deeper, Jack remembered. He might have said it out loud, but he wasn't sure. He never prayed much, only the Serenity Prayer and the Our Father at meetings, but at that moment he wished he had. Praying now, in trouble, seemed disingenuous. Instead he said, "There must be a reason you made me this way, God.

Must be a reason I can feel and see like I do. I know I don't deserve anything from you, but maybe she does." It wasn't a prayer, but it was all he had.

He knew what he had to do. He stopped breathing, not exactly holding his breath, but listening in the stillness. It was such a risk—but he opened his mind to her, opened it completely. Time seemed to stop. Then Sarah's movie began again, moving more slowly this time. Jack felt alternately as if he were looking through Sarah's eyes and then standing next to her as it all unfolded. Back and forth. She took him again through it all, the shock of a murderous attack, violation of her home, fighting back, massacre of her friends, death of her baby, loss of her children, her own physical suffering, and finally her death right on this spot. And through it all he felt the waiting, the aching need for someone to come for her, someone who never came. All that she saw and all that she felt became his until it all stopped at the pile of rocks. And then it began all over again.

"It's a loop," he realized. People sometimes found themselves in loops of memory, loops of behavior, and loops of feelings. But they eventually lived their way out. Sarah couldn't, so she was stuck. The images continued to roll again and again in his mind, Sarah's memories.

But why couldn't she let go? All she suffered was tragic, yes, but tragedy was the stuff of life. Though the details were different, every single human being lived through their own horrors, felt those same emotions that Sarah felt. The events were different, but the feelings were universal. Why couldn't Sarah move on?

Jack felt the loop restarting as all the dogs in the settlement barked an alarm. Could he stop the replay? He reached out to her, and as he did, he remembered an event from his own life. He'd half awakened in a rat-trap hotel room to find three men whispering quietly as they rummaged through his meager belongings. He pretended he was still asleep, knowing he'd be no match for them in his half-drunk state, and he watched them carry what little he owned out the door with them. Sarah's memory movie slowed, and he felt her watching. Different events, much less traumatic than hers had been, but they evoked similar feelings—violation, loss, helplessness.

Jack felt his heart racing, felt the pounding in his throat, but he held on. Sarah had been through so much more than he had, but perhaps they shared more than he realized. People always thought their own pain was unique.

Sarah's memories rolled forward to the moment she saw her husband's rifle in the hands of someone else and realized he must be dead. Jack knew what that was like. He remembered holding Mara's hand in the hospital when the treatments they tried had caused their own kinds of suffering and still had failed. Jack showed Sarah all of it. He showed her he knew what having no hope felt like, understood the pain of being forced to live on without the one he loved most. He showed Sarah things he'd never had the courage to face himself. Jack felt Sarah notice, saw her movie pause. She knew he was there. She saw. And he knew she saw him crying.

He showed her his grief, the way he still mourned for

Mara, how lost and alone he felt. His mind reeled with the force of what she threw back to him, images tumbling over each other—her utter aloneness, all the death she saw, her fears and grief for her children and husband, her anguish over the loss of her baby.

He and Mara hadn't lost a child, but their close friends had lost their baby suddenly and seemingly without cause. Disbelief, anger at the injustice, sorrow, sympathy—all who gathered to support them felt those things. Maybe that was the important piece. As awful as some things in life could be, when you shared the pain with people who understood how you felt, then you could bear those things. Simple contact with another human being. Contact.

Jack pulled back to assess his physical condition. He was very weak, but he thought he was still okay. As he returned to Sarah, events began to replay, but this time there were pieces missing, and Jack realized they were the ones that corresponded to the bits of his own life he shared with her. If he could share more, maybe she could let go of more pieces of her loop. If she understood that someone heard her, perhaps she could be free.

As Jack continued to offer his own experiences, his own feelings in response to what she showed him, more scenes were left out of Sarah's memory movie with each replaying. Finally only one seemed to be left, her utter loneliness near the end. He knew that feeling, had known it since the day he struck the love of his life in the face, knocked her to the ground, and could never take it back. Sometimes you could be the loneliest right next to a person you loved but had deeply hurt.

Jack didn't know if he was speaking out loud or simply thinking, but it didn't matter. "I think we're all lonely for most of our lives. But we share wonderful experiences too, no matter the details of our lives. I know you suffered horribly, but you're not alone. You never really were. And there were good things in your life, I know there were."

He remembered then that the hospice workers told him to tell Mara it was okay for her to go, that the dying often need to know that those who love them are ready to let them go. It was the hardest thing he ever did when he told Mara he would be all right alone, that she could go. That time it shattered him. This time he said it without tears but with just as much compassion: "It's okay to go, Sarah. You can let go."

But she couldn't. There was something more, he sensed, something he hadn't seen in the repeating loop. Something else. She looked right at him then with her scarred and soot-streaked face. He didn't hear the sobbing, but he could see it. Then words that were all run together formed in his mind, words that had to be from her. *I didn't keep them safe I vowed I vowed I vowed but I didn't they depended on me to protect them but I didn't I didn't I didn't keep them safe.*

Exhausted, Jack struggled to stay with her, trying to understand. Then he knew. Sarah's children.

He knew what it felt like to break vows. When they married, he vowed to cherish Mara, to love and protect her, and to forsake all others. He'd always loved her, but as for the rest, well, he could empathize with Sarah's anguish. Now it was too late for either of them to make good on their promises.

Jack felt himself failing and didn't think he had much time left, but he thought he could do this one more thing. He showed Sarah his shame then, his helplessness, the cold place inside himself that nothing seemed to reach, the part that believed he was a failure at everything that was important, everything he'd ever tried. He had let down those he loved, as Sarah believed she had let down her children, but his wrong was greater. She was given no choice. He had choices. It pained him, raked him, burned him, but he showed her everything. He held up for her to see all the times he'd failed Mara, disappointed her, hurt her, the ways he'd failed his children, the vows he had all but vomited on. He showed her his regret.

Jack could hardly keep his eyes open, but he kept his gaze fastened on the filmy figure before him. Then it felt like the world tunneled in around them, leaving them suspended, facing each other in total silence. The spirits Jack had seen before never smiled, but he saw a smile form on Sarah's lips, watched her scars fade as she stared off behind him, waving as though she recognized someone she loved. And then she was gone.

A tremendous sigh began deep in Jack's belly, inflating his chest until he thought it would burst, but then leaking out of him like water through cupped hands. Sarah was truly gone, safe now. He knew that without a doubt. And there would be no future incidents here on the path as a consequence of her spirit. She was with those she'd lost.

He collapsed onto his side, arm crooked beneath his

head, wondering if he was dying. Whether he passed out then or he slept, Jack didn't know, but when he came back to himself, the stars shone bright in a moonless sky. He was dizzy and didn't have any idea how much time had passed. *Well*, he thought, *I'm still alive*. He must be—there was no way his hip or his head would hurt this bad if he were dead.

Afraid to try standing yet, he pushed himself to a sitting position and leaned back into the rocks. There was no danger here now. Sarah was finally home. "All those people," he murmured, thinking of the parade of souls he'd seen. He wondered if they were at rest now too. He hoped so. Then he closed his eyes and smiled. When he opened them, he was surprised to see the black hound curled up beside him, and even more surprised when the animal laid his great head on his leg and looked up at him. He couldn't feel the dog's head, but he could see the peace in the animal's golden eyes. All his agitation and urgency were gone.

For a lot of reasons, Jack didn't believe that Pharaoh had been Sarah's, most of all because she always seemed so afraid of the barking. Nowhere in the parade of people in her "movie" had he seen a dog like this one. Where Pharaoh came from would probably always be a mystery, but his intent to protect was clear. Jack accepted that he wouldn't ever know the whole story, though he wished he could. The dog stood up, open-mouthed and tongue lolling to one side, looking perfectly happy. Then Jack watched his image slowly dissolve. He suspected that he'd never see this one again either. Whatever had kept him here, he was free now, just like Sarah.

***

For the next few mornings, Jack stayed late in bed after sleeping all the way through the night with no nightmares. He woke with no pain and felt better than he had in years. In fact, he wondered whether something about the experience with Sarah had helped him as much as it did her. It was as if seeing her pain and guilt and then sharing his own with her allowed him to finally let go of his worst regrets. He still had amends to make, but that gift of relief was an unexpected one.

He knew Sarah was gone, but twice since that day, he'd felt his "shivers," once when he was standing in the back yard and the other time while he read in the little parlor of his house. But a shiver was all there was. He hadn't seen or felt anything more. "Well, seems like I haven't lost anything. Still the same old Jacko," he told himself after a few moments of anxiety passed each time. Time would tell.

This beautiful morning, he wasn't thinking about any of that. He was sitting on the bench at the head of the path, legs crossed, a cup of strong coffee in the one hand and his other arm draped along the back of the bench. The sounds of seabirds filled the air, and it promised to be another gorgeous day. He had a pack of hot dogs beside him, not for himself but for the two half-grown pups, both males he'd determined, who had visited him about this time the past couple of days. The first day he shared his breakfast sandwich with them, and the next day each of them got a hunk of his cheese, so he figured they might show up again today to see what was on the menu. He loved their energy and the hopefulness in their eyes. If they came again today, he would work at getting closer, maybe even touch them if they'd let him. He had to start somewhere.

Even his thinking seemed clearer since the night on the path, and for the first time since Mara died, Jack felt hopeful about his future. He didn't know how many years he had left, and of course he would have preferred to have Mara at his side, but he knew he'd be okay. His memories of her were cleaner now, without the layer of guilt. People said that as long as you remembered people who died, then they were never entirely gone. He wanted that to be true.

He wasn't going back to their little house on the mainland, though, not ever. One of the kids could live there if they wanted to—it was paid for. And if neither of them wanted it, he'd sell it. What he wanted was a fresh start, and it might as well be here. That was another thing that had changed. Starting over didn't seem overwhelming, and it didn't feel like failure. It felt kind of exciting.

He stretched and drew the salt air deep into his chest, and then turned around to look at the patchwork quilt of a house he'd come to love. It was a good place, and so was the island. He and the real-estate agent had already talked about him buying the property, and they were working out a plan. It would mean he had to get some kind of work to supplement what was left of Mara's life insurance and their savings plus his Social Security, but work would be welcome. It would be a good way to get to know folks too.

If buying the place worked out, as he was sure it would, he'd make some changes. The very first thing he was going to do was build a porch on the ocean side. It had to be a big one, the whole length of the house and as deep as the parlor, with enough space for a couple of rocking chairs and a porch swing. Grandkids would love a swing—all the grandkids, because he wasn't giving up on Sean.

The phone on the bench beside him rang with the newest ringtone he'd found, "Thunder Road," by Bruce Springsteen. Hannah would tease the heck out of him about his music, but it felt good to be listening to those old songs again, and this one made him smile every time it played. He thought he'd keep it for a while.

"Mr. Doyle?" piped a voice on the other end, "Constance Amberson here."

"Well, good morning to you, Miss Amberson!" he said.

"Such a bright attitude you have, Mr. Doyle. I wasn't sure when you'd be in next, and I have both some information and a question. First, I wanted to let you know that we've acquired some very interesting items you might like to see."

"Wonderful. I bought myself a bicycle a few days ago and intended to try a long ride later today." He laughed. "Let's say I need practice. Anyway, I'll drop in."

"That's good. Now, my question has to do with something you said when you were last in. You told me you'd done maintenance and some carpentry in the past.

We could put those skills to good use if you'd consider a part-time position with the museum. Would you?"

With a nod of gratitude, Jack answered, "Absolutely." He thought he could help with the dust and maybe work on organizing some of those framed pieces too.

"Excellent," she said, and he could hear her smile. "We can discuss the details when I see you."

Jack realized he didn't care much about what he'd get paid. This was more about climbing back on the proverbial horse, though having a job would probably help with getting the mortgage. It would feel good to be earning again. "I'll see you after lunch then," he told her, "and I want to talk with you about some research I'd like to do." It was about Keziah. Questions had been nibbling at the corners of his mind since he found the sketch of her at the museum. There was something about her. As Jack said good-bye and disconnected, he nodded to himself again, thinking how often problems unraveled themselves if, like Preston said, you let things play out.

He heard them before he saw them and tore open the package of hot dogs. This time they both ran right up to him, all gangly legs and lolling tongues, jostling each other as they came. "Morning, boys," he said. They didn't run at the sound of his voice anymore. The bolder of the two nosed the hand holding a hot dog, and the other one sat down in front of the bench. Progress. He'd already checked around town to see if anybody reported them lost and he even ran an ad, but it seemed they were on their own, just like him. Later he would worry about licenses and vet visits and all the other details that went with keeping dogs the right way. For now, hot dogs and pats on the head.

Jack didn't know what his future might hold, but for the first time in a long while he was eager to find out. The way things looked, his new porch needed to be big enough not just for rocking chairs and grandkids, but for two growing dogs as well, and these two were going to be big. "Names," he said out loud. "So, what do you think, Mara, something simple like Luke and Ben? Or maybe Orion and Hector?" He took out his notebook and wrote all four names. As for what else he would write, he just wasn't sure.

The End

Gail A. Webber is a retired science teacher who lives in western Maryland with the love of her life, Bill. Her published work thus far includes a number of short stories and one other novel, Time of the Cats. She loves hearing people's stories, learning new things, and finding lessons in unexpected places.

CPSIA information can be obtained
at www.ICGtesting.com
Printed in the USA
LVOW10s0543160217
524417LV00001B/2/P